Michelle Boule

Letters
in the
Snow

Turning Creek
Book 3

For my mom, Cyndie Boulé,
Because everyone needs an Iris to worry over them and love them and you
are mine. Thanks for doing all the things.

ACKNOWLEDGMENTS

I am continually amazed by the people who have blessed my life and this work I call writing. Thank you:

To my editor/word guru/encourager, Brenda Errichiello, who told me this needed to be a full length book. She was right and I am so glad I listened. To my copy editor, Stephanie Petersen, who makes sure everything is just as it should be. To Alexandre Rito for my beautiful covers. To my best friend, Yvette, because you are my biggest fan and I love you. To my family, for all your kind words and encouragement. To my boys, who make me crazier, but fill my life with laughter. To the ladies who pray with me and for me, thank you is just not enough. To Ries, who still loves me after ten years despite my faults. To God, for filling my life with blessings and making me see the world anew each day.

CHAPTER 1

Colorado Territory, 1861

Saturday was Iris's favorite day of the week, and the icy flakes falling from the sky were threatening to ruin it. The Messenger watched the falling snow from the window with a frown. It was not yet falling hard, but the gentle stream of flakes could turn into a torrent without notice. Her stomach tightened. If the flurries turned into a thick snow, it would make walking outside difficult, and that meant Henry might stay home instead of coming to the depot for dinner.

Iris could not pinpoint exactly when they had started their tradition of Saturday night dinners, but once they had started they had become expected, and it was a greatly anticipated part of her week. Henry, blacksmith of Turning Creek and Remnant of Hephaestus, was more family than friend. At first, she had invited him because she had fretted over his being alone all the time; then she had invited him because she cherished his company. Besides the harpies and their mates, there was no one Iris trusted more.

A shuffle of movement in the darkening evening caught her eye. She recognized Henry's silhouette as he reached the boardwalk in front of Vine's saloon and then turned to cross the street. Tension she had not even realized was there released itself into a smile. She should not have worried.

The door to the depot opened, signaled by the ringing of the brass bell attached to its side, and Henry, shoulders dusted with snow, came into the room.

Iris brushed snow off his shoulders. "I admit I was beginning to think the snow might keep you home."

Henry's grey eyes crinkled at the corners. It was all Iris could see of his face, the rest of him was wrapped in a scarf and hat. "This is just a dusting.

We've yet to have a full storm this year. It would take more than a few flakes to keep from coming for Saturday dinner. I'd hate to disappoint you."

Iris took his scarf as he unwound it, and hung it on a peg by the door. "I'd be alone with only Thomas for company, and these days Thomas is too busy eating to talk."

Henry took off his woolen cap and ran a hand through the matted-down dark curls that graced his head. "Growing boys have to eat."

Iris took his jacket and hung it beside the scarf. "Grown men too. Come on up."

Iris led the way to the back of the depot and up the stairs. She could feel Henry at her back, a warm comfort. Thomas was sprawled across the chair in front of the window, coltish legs dangling and a book in front of his face.

"Time for dinner," Iris announced.

Thomas's eyes flew over the page and then he closed the book. Iris caught a glimpse of the title before he tucked the book into the chair, unfolded his body, and stood up. It was one of Beadle's dime novels, a new series that Simon kept stocked at the mercantile, first for Thomas and then for others who discovered a taste for the melodramatic frontier tales. Iris did not care what he read. It simply pleased her that he did.

"Evening, young Thomas," Henry said.

"Good evening, Henry. I'm glad you're here. My bellybutton is rubbing my backbone."

Thomas plopped into a chair at the four-person table in the kitchen.

Iris chuckled. "You're in no danger of starving here." Iris turned to Henry and waved towards the table. "Sit. Everything's ready."

Iris laid the bowl of rolls on the table, and the warm yeasty smell mingled with the rich aroma of beef stew. It was a meal meant to be shared on a cold night. The pot-bellied stove in the corner gave heat to the room, and the oil lamp on the table filled the room with light. At the table sat two of her favorite people in her favorite place.

Thomas, green eyes shining, reached for the bowl the moment her hand left it.

Iris encircled his wrist with her hand. "Guests first."

Thomas frowned at the other member of their small gathering. "Henry's not a guest."

Iris gave Henry an apologetic look. "Does he live under this roof?"

Thomas crossed his arms over his chest, making him look petulant and younger than his fourteen years. "No."

"There you are, then. Even if he does come here every Saturday and is more like family, he still gets treated as a guest." Iris picked up her cloth napkin and smoothed it on her lap.

Henry's mouth twitched up and he took a roll from the bowl and handed it to Thomas, who took the offering with a grin. Both bent their heads and began the serious work of eating. Iris watched them for a few moments before blowing on a spoonful of stew and starting herself.

Henry looked up. "This is wonderful, Miss Iris."

"Thank you, as always, but I wish you would drop the 'Miss.' We've known each other long enough." It was the repetition of an old request.

"Wouldn't be proper," Henry said between bites. His grey eyes crinkled in the corners with an almost smile.

Iris turned to Thomas. "How was your day? I haven't seen you since lunch."

Thomas shoved the last of his roll into his mouth and grabbed another while he chewed. "I delivered those letters to the boarding house, then Stephen, Jonah, and I went to see if the pond by the mill was frozen yet."

From his crestfallen expression, Iris already knew the answer. "And what did you find?"

"There were still some thin bits. I thought I could run over them fast enough to make it across, but then I knew you'd skin me alive if I fell in." Thomas got up and served himself some more stew from the stove. "Anyone else want some?"

Henry handed Thomas his bowl. "I will, thank you. Don't fret over the pond. Give it a few more days. Winter hasn't done her worst yet. You'll have your fill of ice and snow soon enough."

Henry took his refilled bowl from Thomas, then asked Iris, "Did you have any disappointments in your day, like young Thomas here?"

There was a teasing note in his voice, and Iris grinned. Henry was often serious, but this was the Henry she liked most, the one who smiled with a simple tone of voice and a straight, honest face. It was a face he saved for his friends. Iris felt blessed to be one of them.

"My day was uneventful, I'm sorry to say. The mail and supply delivery isn't due for a couple days still, so it's been slow," she sighed.

Henry raised an eyebrow at her. "Idleness getting to you?"

"If I'm honest, yes. With Marina gone to Denver with Reed, things are too quiet."

"Give her a week of being home and you'll long for quiet." There was the smile in his voice again.

Iris chuckled. "Remind me of that when I am at a loss about how to keep her out of trouble." Her smile faded. The days since Marina had left had been harder than Iris had thought. A weight had settled on her shoulders that had not eased. She twisted the corner of her napkin and tried to put into words what she had been feeling.

"I know it will seem ridiculous, but having one of my harpies so far away has made me restless. I know she'll be fine. I'm more worried about the city of Denver than Marina, but I rather like having them all close."

Iris, The Messenger of her generation, was charged with watching over the harpies. It was a task she had been raised for and one that she loved. Since settling in Turning Creek, the harpies and Iris had become a family, something unheard of since the first harpies in the time of the old myths.

Henry regarded her without the air of humor he had employed moments before. His voice was steady, serious. "It's not often one of your chicks is far from the roost."

Iris chuckled over his metaphor. "I know. My mother's harpies always lived in different regions, and she traveled back and forth between them every couple years. Those trips left her morose and withdrawn." Iris forced a smile. "My harpies are different, and I'm glad they tend to stay in the valley. Marina will be back soon, as long as the weather holds. She'll be driving us loony before long."

Henry mopped up the end of his stew before speaking. "Passes aren't too bad yet. They should be able to get home."

"More?" Iris asked Henry.

"No, I think I'll leave the rest for the starving young." Henry waved a hand in Thomas's direction. The youngster was already up and getting a third bowl. Iris was accustomed to Thomas's eating habits, but she did not know where in his lanky frame the boy kept all the food he ate.

Iris smiled at Thomas's back and asked Henry, "Are you working on any special projects? I know the winter months are slow for some of your regular work."

Henry leaned back in his chair and rubbed a hand over his beard. The hair on his face was dark brown, almost black in dim lighting, and he wore it full in the winter as most men in town did. "As a matter of fact, I worked on a new project this morning for Mrs. Marina, a set of matched swords weighted for throwing. I've never made a throwing set of swords. Took me a while to settle on a design."

Iris did not miss the gleam in his grey eyes. "The challenge pleases you."

Henry's mouth tilted slightly upward. "It does. It's a special task to craft weapons for Missus Marina because she takes such pleasure in them."

Iris laughed. "That she does." Marina was unapologetic about her violent side, and, if pressed, Iris would admit that she loved the harpy all the more for it. "Would you like some tea and biscuits?"

"You know I can't say no to your molasses biscuits," Henry said as Iris stood to put the kettle on the stove.

Thomas stood and gathered the bowls from the table while polishing off the last roll. Iris ran a hand over his head when he put the bowls on the counter next to her. He was tall enough to look her in the eye now, and, with a pang, she realized he would be grown and gone before she realized it.

Thomas leaned into her and kissed her cheek. "May I be excused?"

"What are you going to do?"

"I want to finish reading that book on Achilles."

"I thought you were reading Beadle's adventures," she said.

Thomas shrugged. "I like reading more than one thing at a time."

"Variety is good. Check the mailbox downstairs first. If there's anything there, leave it behind the counter for the morning."

Thomas grabbed a biscuit from the plate on the counter and dashed down the stairs. Iris heard the bell above the door jingle and then Thomas was pounding up the stairs. He swiped one more biscuit off the plate then went into his room. Iris rose, put tea leaves in the pot of tea, and poured the hot water over the leaves.

"He'll be grown before you know it." Henry's voice rumbled in the silence of the room.

Iris suppressed a sigh as Henry said aloud what she had been thinking. "Sometimes I miss the scrawny kid who came to live here after the battle with Zeus, but I love the young man he is becoming." A general uneasiness moved through her.

Henry watched her movements as she poured their tea and placed the plate of biscuits on the table. He was silent as he took his first few sips. The quiet moments with him, although frequent, never bothered her. Iris knew Henry always spoke what was on his mind when it was worth saying, and their silence was comfortable and companionable.

He kept his eyes down when he spoke. "You're worried about the boy. Why?"

Iris was shaken again at the apparent ease with which he plucked the essence from her thoughts. "I want him to be happy. I wonder if he'll be happy here, delivering letters with me when he is grown. I am compelled by my gift to deliver letters. For him, it's just an outlet for his energy and speed." Iris sipped her tea. "He has his own path. Like any parent, I will be sad if his path carries him elsewhere, but I want him to be happy."

Henry looked into his tea. He ran a finger around the rim of the cup. "Your worry does you credit."

Iris took a sip of tea to cover her pleasure at the compliment. Most of the time, her worry made her feel helpless. With his words, Henry had made her feel useful and noble. "Enough of being morose. I'd like your opinion on something unrelated to growing boys and their appetites."

Henry straightened in his seat. "I'd be honored to give it."

"I'm thinking of putting a notice board in the depot." At Henry's questioning look, she elaborated. "Widow Finch came in today looking for extra help with the laundry and a few odds and ends. She's not the only one. People come in here all the time looking for someone or something. They leave similar requests with Daniel at the saloon and with Simon at the store. I thought it's time we start consolidating our efforts."

Henry nodded his head. "That's a sound plan. I could frame up a piece of softer wood and make you some sturdy pins or small nails to hold papers in place."

"That would be wonderful. Thank you, Henry." Iris patted his hand.

A light blush crept up his neck and he shifted in his seat. "No trouble at all."

Iris hid her smile at his reaction. Even one on one, Henry was not comfortable being the center of anyone's attention. Iris wondered if it stemmed from his personality or if it was the result of living alone for so long.

The bell announced a visitor downstairs, drawing their attention away from each other. "It's late for anyone seeking the mail and the snow would keep most people in their homes." Henry frowned. "I hope there's nothing amiss."

A sharp moment of panic threatened to grip her until Iris remembered her other plans for the evening. Excitement flooded her. Tonight, she was going flying with Dora and Petra. A light, but eager, tread on the back stairs announced Dora's arrival. Her freckled cheeks were red with the cold and her cobalt eyes shone with merriment. Dora's delicate looks hid a will of iron.

"The snow has stopped. Ready to go?" Dora asked. She stopped short when she saw Henry. "I forgot it's Saturday. I was eager to get going and it was dark, so I came early. Sorry if I interrupted anything."

Henry stood and carried his cup to the counter. "Nothing to interrupt. I think we were about done. Evening, Miss Dora. Where are you two off to?"

Iris felt her face break into a wide grin, unable to keep her glee contained. "Flying."

Henry's own face broke into a full blown smile. Its appearance made Iris's heart speed up without reason. "I can see you two ladies are wanting to be off. I'd best be on my way."

"I'll walk you down." Iris's heart still beat quickly as she followed Henry down the stairs to the front door of the depot. His broad shoulders seemed to fill the stairwell.

Henry pulled his plain woolen scarf from the peg and began winding it around his face, hiding the smile that still tugged on his mouth. Next, he grabbed his hat and pulled it over his ears. When he turned to say goodbye, only his eyes, which looked as grey as ash in the dim light, were visible.

"Thanks for dinner, Miss Iris. I'll bring the board by in a day or so."

"No rush. Thanks for the good company. Saturday is one of my favorite nights of the week." Iris wanted to step closer to him, but stayed still.

Henry's eyes crinkled further and Iris knew his scarf hid another wide smile. Twice in one night. It had to be some kind of record.

"Mine too," he replied. Henry opened the door and let in a blast of cold air. He walked out into the night and closed the door without a backward glance.

Excitement bubbled through her as she watched him until he was lost in the dark of the night. Saturday dinner and flying. Her heart might burst with the overload.

Iris bounded up the stairs. "I need to grab my coat and then I'll be ready," she said to Dora, who had helped herself to a biscuit. Dora waved her on.

Iris popped her head into Thomas's bedroom. Thomas sat on his bed with his knees up by his chin. His head was bent over a book. "I'm going flying with Dora and Petra. I'll be back in a couple hours."

Thomas looked up for a split second then looked back down at the book. "Night, Iris. Have fun."

Dora poked her head around Iris's shoulder. "Hello, Thomas."

"Hey, Dora," he said without looking up.

Dora chuckled at him and closed the door halfway. "I'd say he takes after you, but you're not related."

Iris ran a hand over the door jamb leading to Thomas's room. "I know. He's such a smart boy."

Iris went into her own room, next to Thomas's, and thought about what she would need for flying on such a cold night. She pulled a set of wool stockings out of a drawer and kicked off her boots. Unlike the harpies, whose feathers kept them reasonably warm, she only had her skin to keep her warm and it was frigid in the night mountain air. Iris unbuttoned her skirt and laid it aside. She pulled on the stockings, then took a folded shirt from her drawer. The shirt had been specially made for her by Paul Hughes, the tailor. He was not a Remnant, but his wife, Lily, was descended from Medusa. There were two long slits that ran down the back of the shirt and ended at her waist. The slits allowed her wings to emerge from her back and still covered the rest of her modestly. Iris put on a set of wool pants over the stockings and tucked in her shirt. She added wool socks to her feet and pulled her boots on over the thick socks. Finally, she took a heavy jacket from a peg on the wall, which had slits in it similar to her shirt. Since the summer nights were cool in the mountains, Paul had made her a lightweight jacket for the summer months. She only used this jacket when flying, and considered it might be time to request one with a thicker winter weight.

Dora turned and started walking downstairs the moment Iris opened the door. Dora was as eager to be off as she was. Instead of turning and going out the front door, they continued straight off the stairs and went towards the back door. The back door was seldom used, except by the harpies when they did not want to be seen coming and going in either their human form or their more monstrous one. Tonight was not a night to be seen.

Turning Creek was a rare place. A place of its ilk had not existed since the days of the old myths when the gods and their creatures mingled with mortals with a frequency that made monsters commonplace. Before the Fall of Olympus, the myths had lived among mortals, and the mortals worshipped the gods and feared the monsters. After the Fall, the myths gained freedom from Zeus, but lost the power of the protection of the gods. The passage of eons scattered the Remnants of the myths, and for generations they lived secluded, secret lives. Their powers and abilities morphed and diluted, but Remnants never forgot they were sojourners in a world that did not know them. The myths were forgotten, unknown to the mortal world, except by those who carried the magic of gods in their veins and those individuals they trusted to keep their secrets.

For the first time since the Fall, they had a safe place to live. Still, although it was safe and although Remnants from all over the world had come to live in Turning Creek in unprecedented numbers, there were still mortal residents of their town, and so their secret was held close. Mortals generally reacted badly when it was revealed that monsters walked among them. And, for mortals, badly meant witch trials, inquisitions, and innocents caught in the crossfire. Secrecy saved the lives of mortals and Remnants alike.

Iris wrapped a scarf made of vibrant blue wool around her neck. On her head she placed the matching hat, which was lined with soft, grey flannel. The scarf was uneven in places and the hat had one or two lumps. Iris smoothed them down with love. Petra, in an effort to be more domestic, had taken up knitting, and she had given Iris the first fruits of her efforts for Winter Solstice that year. Iris would have loved the winter set even if it only represented the time Petra had spent cursing over the needles and yarn. She loved it even more because it was yet another sign that her harpies were changing.

The sound of Dora tapping her foot broke through Iris's thoughts. "Don't be so impatient, my bird. I'm ready." Dora dashed out through the door.

The night was like cold black ink. Iris paused after she closed the door and took a deep breath, letting the air burn her lungs with the chill and damp of winter. The only sounds as they walked were those of the snow crunching under their feet and their breathing as they walked. The moon was obscured by clouds, and Iris wished it was a brighter night for flying. She loved watching the harpies soar through the night sky. It was one of the few times they all seemed completely at peace with the world, when they let loose and just *were*.

Caught in her own musings, Iris noticed she'd fallen behind. She increased her speed to catch up to Dora, then walked in silence. Each step marked a growing anticipation bubbling up through her veins. As far as Iris knew, she was the only Messenger since the original of her name to bear the golden wings in the flesh. Two years ago, Zeus had transformed her golden birthmark into the real thing, fulfilling a longing Iris had always felt and never been able to satisfy.

After her transformation, it had taken her time to learn how to draw her wings back into her mortal shape. It had taken even longer for her to build up the muscles in her back to bear the wings and fly for any distance. Those months had been marked by constant pain and sore muscles. Every burning muscle, every sore joint, and every night of lost sleep had been worth it to be able to join her harpies as they flew.

They reached a clearing in the trees and shrubs after walking about ten minutes west of the depot. The harpies frequently changed closer to town, but they could shift in a moment. Iris's transformation still took time, and she preferred to do it here where it was more secluded. The clearing was far enough away that even in the daylight they were hidden from mortal eyes. It would not do to alert the townspeople that all was not as it seemed in Turning Creek.

"Do you want me to wait for you?" Dora asked.

A sourness fluttered in Iris's belly. "Yes." Flying was wonderful. Pulling her power and her wings outside herself was not.

Iris took a deep breath, released it, and pushed her power out with the breath. She pictured the birthmark on her back, a pair of perfect golden wings, and imagined them emerging and growing. A burning sensation spread over her shoulders and traveled down her back. Iris bent over and placed her hands on her knees. She took another deep breath and braced herself.

A sharp pain, like a knife slicing down her back, made her shake in reaction. Iris's breath hitched as the pain increased and then receded into a sharp burning sensation. A few more breaths and the burning disappeared. In place of the pain, two enormous golden wings rose over her shoulders and brushed the snow-covered ground.

Iris straightened up and stretched them wide, giving her muscles time to adjust. Pulling them forth was the hardest part. After they were out, she only had to work out the kinks in her back and wings and she was fine. Better than fine. In the dark, the wings shone with a low, golden light. Iris brought one of them around to her front and ran a hand over the top. The feathers were soft and sensitive. She felt everything that brushed against her wings.

Iris shook them once more and looked at Dora, who had not moved. "Ready?" She could not see Dora's face well enough to read her expression.

"I know it hurts, but that is the most wonderful thing I've ever seen. I love watching you do that." Dora ran a hand down the length of Iris's wing.

It tickled, and Iris flapped her wing in response. "I'm the one in pain, and I think it's wonderful too. Not as good as flying, though. Let's go."

Dora took that as her cue and changed. Her small mortal form morphed in the span of a few blinks into a speckled bird of prey with a more angular version of Dora's human face. The harpy towered over Iris.

"Catch me if you can." Dora's voice was rough, like glass being ground into dust. She launched into the air, and Iris had to squint to see her in the dark sky.

Getting off the ground was the hardest part for Iris. She pumped her wings, feeling the muscles stretch and warm. With a boost from her legs, Iris pushed up into the night and followed Dora.

Iris never lost her sense of wonder when flying. Her heart beat painfully with awe. The cold air bit into her cheeks as she flew and inhaled deeply. Her senses were overwhelmed with the smell of evergreens in the snow and the smoke from the fires in town. She could see the lights from the windows along the two streets in town. Other lights were scattered farther out. Iris faced forward and concentrated on gaining altitude and finding Dora. A flash off Dora's lighter feathers was her beacon, and Iris pointed herself towards it.

Iris caught up with Dora and they flew northeast towards the Lloyd farm. Iris glanced over at Dora and watched the harpy for a few wingbeats. There was something different about Dora in her true form, something wilder. All the harpies were civilized enough in their mortal forms, but their nature was fierce and raw and on full display when they were monstrous birds of prey.

"I know you're looking at me," Dora said.

"I was thinking how wonderful it is to watch you fly."

"I think perhaps that isn't the total of it, but I accept it for now."

There was no warning before a black streak fell from the sky and landed square between Dora's wings before bouncing off and flying to the right. Dora screeched in anger as she flapped about and tried to regain her balance. With a curse, she made a beeline for Petra, who was cackling and quickly gaining altitude to escape.

"You're going to regret that," Dora promised.

Iris laughed from deep in her core. The dive and dash game was a favorite of her birds. They never played rough with her, but she was an appreciative audience to their wild antics.

Dora caught up to Petra and managed to pull her tail feathers before flying off. Petra circled back around and the two harpies cut through the night air together, one on each side of Iris.

"Hello, my bird," Iris said.

"I'm glad you came. I was afraid Henry would keep you or that you'd decide you'd rather be in a warm bed than out here." Petra angled away then back, searching for the right patch of air.

"We were wrapping up when Dora came. Even on a bitterly cold night,

I would rather fly with you than be tucked into my bed." Iris's face was starting to burn from the cold wind, but she would trade a windblown face for this exhilaration every time.

Dora moved so that she was flying ahead of Iris, breaking the force of the wind for her. "What are we doing tonight? Hunting? Roaming? Nothing at all?" Dora's voice floated back to them.

Petra cleared her throat. "I'd just like a nice flight tonight. I promised James I'd stay close to home. He's been a bit overbearing the last couple days. Once he settles, I want to go hunting."

Dora turned her head around to look at them. "What's got his dander up?"

Petra flapped her wings silently. A small bite of worry nibbled at Iris. "Is he all right? Is there something wrong on the farm?"

Petra drew in a deep breath. Iris could hear the amusement in Petra's voice. "No, he's fine. He's under the impression I'm a bit more delicate than I used to be. As soon as he figures out being pregnant does not make a harpy less dangerous or capable, all will be well."

Iris forgot to move her wings and dropped a few feet before righting herself. Golden joy filled her. She tried to catch back up to Petra, but Dora got there in no time. Dora collided bodily into Petra and wrapped her clawed wings around her. The two harpies plummeted towards the ground at an alarming pace. Broken laughter floated up from them as they separated. Iris shook her head and joined in their laughter. Only a harpy would appreciate that kind of hug.

"This is wonderful." Dora flew in circles around Petra, who was still laughing. "When?"

"At the end of summer, perhaps late July or August, we should have the first harpy daughter in Turning Creek." Even with her rough voice, there was no way to mistake the pride in Petra's voice.

Iris wished they were on the ground. "My precious bird. If we weren't flying I'd hug you until you couldn't breathe."

Petra looked over at her. "I know. You can owe me." Petra paused. "She'll need someone to watch over her."

The bite of worry came back with clamping teeth around her heart. Iris had no daughter to care for the next generation and no prospects on that front. It was a worry she had pushed aside for years, but with Petra and Marina settled, it was something she needed to face. It was past time for her to do some settling of her own.

They flew for another hour before parting ways. The worry over her situation and the joy over Petra's news stayed with Iris throughout the flight. By the time she lay in her bed, her shoulders ached and her heart was conflicted. A new generation was coming, and it was her duty to make sure they were well cared for by continuing her own line and providing them with their own Messenger. For the first time in a long time, the burden of being The Messenger was heavy on her heart.

CHAPTER 2

It was a sunny day. Even in winter, the good weather meant more people would be out to take advantage of the day. The snow had melted in most places, and the comings and goings into and out of the depot filled Iris's day with a peace and purpose. Some people thrived on finding quiet solitude. Iris found energy and focus in being a constant presence in the life of her town and her harpies.

Iris was the proprietor of the only mail service in the region. She was the Remnant of the original Iris, Messenger of the Greek gods, and she possessed an inborn need to deliver the missives of others. The mail depot and the saloon were the unofficial hubs of the town—albeit for very different reasons.

Iris went out to collect the letters that had been left in the mailbox. The air bit at her, but the sun was already at work, banishing the worst of the cold from the winter air. Next to the door of the depot stood a large wooden box with a hinged lid. It was big enough for packages, but today it only held three letters, two small and one thick. Iris gathered them and went back inside the warmth of the depot.

A large pot-bellied stove with a crackling fire kept the room comfortable from its post in the back corner of the depot. Against the back wall, two round tables, large enough for four if you sat close, waited for occupants. One table was covered with a half-finished game of checkers. L.A. and Johnny would be along sometime today to finish their game. Iris knew better than to touch their board. They always knew when the pieces had been touched.

Iris walked around the counter and laid the letters down. She poured herself a cup of tea from the pot she had set on the edge of the wooden surface. The counter was made from a tree that had been struck by lightning shortly after she had first come to Turning Creek. Henry had helped her sand down and shape half the trunk into the gleaming flat surface of a counter. Iris ran her hand over the surface of the wood. It still gleamed, though now it had the marks of age and a patina of its own from being well loved by many elbows and hands.

Iris smiled at the memories held in the wood and turned to her letters. The two thinner ones were for town residents. The thicker one was for Pearl Nasso, who lived to the southwest on Shaker's Way. It was time for the harpies to check in with her. Iris resolved to send the letter with Dora or Petra when they next came to town. Marina, who had spent most of her time in town since marrying Reed, was still in Denver with Reed to represent Turning Creek in the bid to become an official state in the United States of America.

A proprietary feeling of pride filled Iris as she thought of the harpies and the role they had taken in Turning Creek. They had chosen to live together, and they had claimed the valley and its people as their own, to defend and to care for. The choices made by her harpies were changing their nature on a level she did not understand. The changes had brought more peace and happiness to their lives, and hers by extension, but she was concerned about the long-term consequences of the shifts. It was part of her legacy to guide and watch over the harpies, and she took her responsibility seriously. Even with her gift of foresight, she could not see where these alterations in their character would take them.

Besides a certain softening of their character, Iris thought choosing a mate would cut Petra and Marina's lifespan. They would still live half of their three hundred years and might still outlive their mortal mates. The magic that wove a Messenger's life together with her harpies tied her own lifespan to that of her charges. She wondered if the same would be true of the harpies and their mates. If it was similar, once found, the harpies' rate of aging would shift to match the men they had chosen. Iris thought her lifespan would also adjust to theirs. It was right that they were all tied together. This was new ground, for all of them, and Iris had not found the answers she sought in her books.

In need of counsel, Iris had written to her mother with the news of Turning Creek, her harpies, and her concerns. She had also penned a letter to her grand-mere and great-grand-mere, who lived together in Tuscany, within a hundred miles of the remaining two of her great-grand-mere's harpies. She had sent the letters almost a year ago, after Petra had settled with James, but before Marina had chosen Reed as her own. The events of the past few months had done nothing besides confirm Iris's suspicions. More than ever, she wanted the council of the Messengers older than herself. She did not often miss her mother and grand-meres – the harpies filled that void – but when she needed advice, they were the ones she longed for most.

Iris picked up the letter for Pearl and put it in one of the bottom left slots. The other two letters went into slots near the middle of the shelves. Iris picked up her tea cup and ran her fingers of the bird-hole slots, which took up the wall behind the counter. Her filing system made little sense to everyone else, but she could file letters with her eyes closed. Iris could feel each letter tugging on her consciousness.

She closed her eyes and a map of the valley and beyond overlaid the slots in her mind. Every parcel of land claimed shone brightly in her mind's eye and every parcel claimed had names attached to it. The Nasso farm was southwest. Thomas Neal lived in the northeast on a ranch with his wife and three sons. Heinrich and Prudence Gerlich lived on a farm to the south. The names and faces and locations ran through her memory.

The bell over her door rang, and a middle-aged woman with a brown braid over her shoulder came into the depot. She had a smile on her face and was followed by her middle daughter, Natalie, whose brown hair was covered by a knitted cap.

"Good morning, Mrs. Stewart. Natalie. What brings you all the way into town today?" The Stewarts lived on a farm at the base of Silvercliff. Iris knew Mrs. Stewart was a Remnant, but not the details of her lineage.

Deborah Stewart took off her gloves. "I was hoping the supply train would've come already this week."

The supply train was not a train at all, but a string of mules led by Spuds over the mountain passes to the towns he passed. No one had any notion of what name Spuds had actually been given at birth. He was just Spuds to everyone that knew him. In the winter, he came every other month, and he was late.

"The snow must have held him up somewhere," Iris said.

"That's what Simon said when we went for supplies. I was hoping to get stocked up before the storm comes." Mrs. Stewart sat down on one of the stools at the counter.

Iris held out the plate of biscuits from her tea tray. "Would you like a ginger biscuit?"

Natalie looked to her mother first, who nodded her approval, before taking one. "Thank you, Miss Iris."

Iris glanced at the dust floating in the rays of sunshine pouring in through the front window. "It doesn't look like a storm is coming."

A smile played around Mrs. Stewart's face. "It'll be here before you know it. I know these things. Is there any mail for us? It might be some time before we're back this way."

Iris made a mental list of Remnants who could sense the weather while she turned and pulled two envelopes from the Stewart's slot. The list was very short. Dryads and nymphs had an affinity with nature, which often resulted in abilities ranging from communing with nature to sensing weather. Iris opened her senses to Mrs. Stewart, searching for the leak of power that marked her as something other than mortal. Mrs. Stewart's power was too strong for a nymph or a dryad, but it was contained, and Iris could not get a sense of it beyond that.

Mrs. Stewart laughed, not offended in the least by Iris's snooping. Iris blushed. Her curiosity had gotten the better of her manners. "I'm sorry. That was uncivilized of me."

Mrs. Stewart laughed her easy laugh again. "You can trust me, Messenger. The snow is coming, but it is naught but a winter storm. Stay warm tonight."

Iris returned her smile, though she still felt the prick of guilt. "I will. Thank you for the warning."

Deborah and Natalie Stewart left, and Iris nibbled on a biscuit while she thought. There were very few Remnants who could not hide their nature. The power and nature of a harpy, created to steal and torment souls, always betrayed their presence. The Messenger of each generation was another. The responsibility of The Messenger to keep records of history and deliver letters meant they were sought by Remnants for the knowledge they held, and thus known to all.

Iris knew from which line most of the Remnants of Turning Creek descended. Most readily told her that information when they first came to the depot. Most, but not all. Some kept their identity close, and they were given this leeway, though they came to the depot like the rest, to request entrance into the valley and ask for leave to stay. Few were denied entry even now, though all learned, sometimes the hard way, that the harpies kept a strict peace.

Even mortals, when they happened to settle in Turning Creek, eventually found their way to the depot. Iris had fostered the welcoming aura here. While Vine's saloon had more room, and Widow Finch's boardinghouse had food, Iris offered nothing more than a friendly smile and a service everyone desired. The joy of a well-written letter penned with a specific person and purpose in mind was a rare and blessed gift. It was one Iris thought few people on earth would pass up.

Iris pulled a dull red leather journal from under the counter. The volume held part of the writings of Elpis, the fourth Messenger and first of her name. Iris read until her teapot was empty and her biscuits gone. Elpis had not been as happy in her calling as Iris. One passage stuck out.

I have returned from visiting Hagne. Nothing ever prepares me for the growing cloud of anger and bitterness that seems to grip the harpies after they leave their mothers. My own mother warned me of this, but I believed the fate of mine would be different. That something would be different. I prayed to the gods that enough time had passed that the rage of loss over Podarge would have passed into the Underworld. Instead it seems to have

Iris tucked a ribbon in the book and rose from her stool. She arched her
arms high over her head and stood on her toes. Her joints cracked and she
shook her arms. Her brain was as full as her body was stiff.

Her mother had counseled her to wait until she had settled into some
kind of routine with her harpies to read the account of the fourth
Messenger. Now, Iris knew why. It was as unlike the account of Iris, the
first Messenger, as night is to day. The first Iris's tales were characterized by
humor and bravery as she recounted the harpies as they led the revolt
against Zeus. Their story took a turn with the loss of Podarge. It would take
generations for the Messengers to fully realize the depth of what they had
lost when Olympus fell.

Podarge, the lost fourth harpy, had fallen in the battle that had
destroyed the rule of Zeus and the other gods. She had been entombed
with the fallen from both sides of the war in what remained of Mount
Olympus. Her line had died, and the remaining three harpies and their
daughters to come would never be the same.

Iris tapped the cover of the journal. She needed to get some air and clear
her head. Like the emotions contained within letters, the past held a weight
to it. Iris was ever conscious of the mantle of her calling. Most days, she
welcomed it and its purpose. On rare, other days, she felt every pound of its
burden.

Her harpies, while still occasionally ruled by violence, were not
overcome with the bitterness of previous generations. A part of her knew it
was not her doing alone. Iris suspected it was something they were all doing
together, moving into a different era, one different from the times devoid
of hope that Elpis had described and one that was also different than the
bitterness of her mother and grand-mere's harpies.

Iris tucked away the cobwebs of her thoughts and pulled a bag made of
oiled leather from a peg on the side of the shelves. If Deborah Stewart was
correct and snow was coming, Iris might as well deliver some letters around

town before the snow came. She considered the slots. Not all letters called to her to be delivered right away. Some wanted to wait for their time, and she let those be. She opened her power to the letters and pulled the ones calling loudest to her. She placed them in neat bundles in her bag. She put on her coat, wrapped up in her scarf, and went out into the sun to deliver letters and a little bit of hope.

Turning Creek contained two streets, spaced quite far apart, Main Street and Second Street. Like the depot, the buildings on Main Street tended to have shops on the first floor and living areas on the second. Second Street was the opposite, consisting of mostly family residences. One exception to this was Grant Korman, who had a cobbler and leather shop on Second Street. She would head there first.

Iris crossed Main Street and angled left to walk around the saloon and through the empty lot between the boarding house and Vine's. There was smoke curling into the sky from Henry's forge. Iris wondered if he was working on Marina's swords in an effort to get them done before the harpy returned. She waved to Widow Finch, who was sitting in a chair next to her empty vegetable garden.

The Korman house was on the far side of Second Street, across from the empty lot. The other houses around it were the natural color of the wood used to build the structure. Grant Korman had painted his house a jaunty blue. It was the kind of blue that made you long for the warmth of summer and a night under the stars. A wooden sign with a pair of shoes on it swung from the front eave of the house. Iris opened the door and went inside.

"Good afternoon to you, Miss Iris. Are you bringing the mail today?" The musical voice of Molly, Grant's wife, greeted her. Molly's blue eyes, almost the exact color of the house, sparkled.

Iris flipped open her bag and pulled out an envelope. Iris could feel the words. They were heavy with the love between friends and laughter. "I have a letter from Prudence Gerlich for you."

Mrs. Korman's eyes shone even brighter. "That's the best news I've had all week. It's been a spell since I've seen my friend." Prudence and her husband had suffered from burns after running into a Lernaean Hydra last fall. They tended to avoid town. "It's such a shame that she keeps herself hidden after being burned in that house fire. As if her friends care a whit for what her face looks like."

Mrs. Korman was a mortal, and she had no notion about what had really happened to the Gerlichs or how bad the burns had been. Iris responded, "I'm glad she still writes to you often. She takes great pleasure in your letters. Thomas retrieved this one from her just a few days ago."

Iris passed the letter to Mrs. Korman, and the emotions of the words, thankfulness and longing, left her hands.

Mrs. Korman took the envelope with a wide smile. "Would you like to stay for tea or coffee?"

Iris shook her head. "I have other deliveries to make, but thank you for the offer. Do you have anything you would like me to take?"

"Not today. Is there anything else? My Grant is expecting a package from back east."

"That's all for you, I'm afraid. Spuds and the supply train are late."

"I hope the pass is clear enough," Mrs. Korman frowned.

Iris ignored her own anxiety. "Spuds always seems to find his way. He'll be here soon enough. I'll keep an eye out for that package."

"Thank you, Miss Iris."

Iris breathed in the smell of leather and smiled. "It's my pleasure."

Iris left the Kormans' and went to the boarding house. Widow Finch was still sitting in the chair. Iris waved towards the garden beds, covered in snow. "Anything growing?"

The crow's feet at the corners of Widow Finch's eyes compressed as she smiled. "Nothing but the passage of time. I came out here to get some air and rest before I started dinner."

Iris sat in the chair next to Widow Finch. "How's your day going?"

"It's moving along. Got some letters for me?"

"Not for you so much as for some of your occupants." Iris started opening her bag, but Widow Finch put a hand on her arm.

"You can leave them on the front desk. Rest here awhile with me. Anything new around town?"

Iris leaned back and relaxed into the chair. "It's been a quiet winter so far, and with Marina gone these past weeks, it's quieter than normal."

The widow frowned.

Iris felt an old irritation rise. "You should give her some leeway. Marina fights hard for this town, for you."

"She causes a ruckus wherever she goes." Widow Finch was a woman who liked order.

Iris wanted to know what kind of Remnant the widow was but was too polite to ask. It was something without much power, as she was unable to enforce her disapproval on others. Iris sat up straight and turned her full glare onto Widow Finch. "She does get into trouble, but she has a heart of gold and she would give her life to defend you. She'd never admit it, but it hurts her that you mistrust her. You need to lay your disapproval aside and be thankful that you have her watching over the town."

The longer she spoke, the more of her power leaked from her. Her irritation rose with each word. Iris did not have the power the harpies possessed to persuade others or to cause fear. Her power was different, and yet could result in the same outcome. Authority could be bestowed through trust and force of will.

Widow Finch's shoulders slumped. "I didn't know that my feelings caused Mrs. Marina distress. Please forgive my harshness, Messenger. I will not be so careless in the future."

Iris pulled her power back into herself. She laid a hand over the widow's. "I don't want your apology. I want you to treat her better with your deeds."

Widow Finch nodded. "I am grateful to her. I just wish she was less brash in her choice of entertainments."

Iris laughed. "Then she wouldn't be my Marina."

A chuckle escaped Widow Finch's lips. "She does keep you on your toes, doesn't she?"

Iris sighed in long suffering. "You have no idea how much." The two women laughed, and Iris was glad she had spoken up. Messengers had always trailed behind the harpies to smooth over the results of their less-endearing personality flaws, and Iris was no different.

Widow Finch stood. "I'll take the letters. I've got to get back inside. I've work to do, and my toes are starting to feel the bite."

Iris opened her bag and handed her the letters. "Thank you for reconsidering, about Marina."

The widow took the letters. "Thank you for your honest counsel. You're a credit to your line."

Iris ducked her head with the praise. The question of what line the widow was from was on the tip of Iris's tongue. "Thank you," was all she said.

Iris walked back to the depot. She turned before going inside. The smoke was still curling up from Henry's smithy. Simon was stacking wood under the window of his store. From there her gaze slid north and west, where the sun was disappearing behind the peaks of the mountains. The snow on the opposite peaks was red and orange in the darkening sky. It was a perfect view, and Iris felt the beauty of it swell inside her.

A couple strolled north towards the outskirts of town. They were too far away for Iris to see who they were. They walked close, their arms linked as he turned his ear towards her shorter head. The woman's head flew back as she laughed and elbowed her partner. Iris watched the couple, and the beauty of the sunset was replaced by a nibbling envy. She turned and went inside, closing the depot's door on all of it.

<h1 style="text-align:center">CHAPTER 3</h1>

Clouds covered the sun and the light from the windows was thin. Iris sat at the counter, angled to catch as much light as she could on the pages of her book. Her lunch sat beside her, half eaten. Her tea cup was empty, and Iris made no move to refill it. Iris turned the page and continued reading Elpis's chronicles.

I have had two items of news which disturb and disrupt my soul. The last of my harpies has passed on to Charon's boat. Hagne lived beyond her three hundred years, though I do not think she felt blessed by the extra time. Now that she is gone, I know my own time approaches. I do not grieve the closure of my own life.

My own family brought me joy, and I have left the next generation of harpies in the capable hands of my daughter and my daughter's daughter. Their task will be no easier than mine. The bitterness of their mothers has filtered into their daughters. It tangles with their violence, and I see nothing but darkness in their future. This is the failing of our line: that we could not save our harpies from themselves. I pray to the gods it will not always be so, but my life has taught me that optimism is not often rewarded.

There was a commotion outside. Irritation laced through her as the noise pulled Iris from the words on the page. Thomas was sprawled on a chair in the back. His chin rested in his palm and his eyes were half closed.

"Thomas." The boy jerked awake. "Go see what's going on outside, please."

Iris looked back down at her book. She only had half a page left.

Stories have begun to reach my ears. Stories of Remnants who are not staying hidden. Some do great harm to their neighbors, pillaging and murdering like in the days of old. Some are careless with their true nature, and their mortal neighbors lash out in fear. If the Remnants are to survive in this new world, where we live in the mortal world, we must learn to stay hidden or lose all. We must act justly and blend in, or our mortal brothers will do to us what the harpies did to the gods of Olympus.

This is the true account of my time in service as The Messenger to the fourth generation of harpies.

Iris closed the book with a heavy heart. It was little wonder that her mother had told her not to read this for many years. The picture Elpis painted was not a pleasant one. With the benefit of historical knowledge, Iris knew that many of Elpis's predictions had come true. The harpies did sink into ever increasing bitterness and violence. She had also been right about the reaction of mortals to the Remnants among them. Remnants who showed themselves or acted cruelly were dealt with swiftly and violently by the mortals around them.

Thomas pressed his nose to the glass. "Spuds is here." The noise had grown in volume.

The uneasiness of Elpis's account ebbed away. Her harpies were not the same as the ones Elpis had shepherded. Hope in her time was a meaningless endeavor. Turning Creek was a different place.

Iris placed the journal of Elpis under the counter with a scowl. "Great. Let's go see what he has brought us."

Thomas grabbed the door handle to open it. Iris stopped him with one hand and shoved his coat in his direction with the other. He put it on in record time and was out of the door before Iris had fastened her own coat. She left the depot with a smile, her amusement over the eagerness of youth taking the place of the harsh words she had read.

Despite the grey of the day, half the town was clustered around a string of ten mules. The piles of goods and bundles were piled high enough to defy gravity. It was a wonder the mules did not topple over from the height and weight of their burdens. Though it looked like the stacks were haphazard and dangerous, Spuds took care when loading his girls, as he called the mules. Iris could not see Spuds in the crowd. He was a short and stout man with the voice of a giant. His booming laugh rolled out of the front of the crowd, and Iris was drawn to the sound.

The crowd parted enough that Spuds got eyes on her. "Miss Iris. I have two bags for you."

Iris moved into the center of the crowd and bent over to give Spuds a hug. He smelled like a man long on the trail, and she did not breathe deep. "I was beginning to fear you had finally been consumed by the mountains."

Spuds clutched his heart. "You wound me, fair lady. I'm the master of these mountains. Besides, if I did die, my mules know the way. They would drag my cold, dead body here without my assistance to be sure."

Iris laughed. "Let's hope it never comes to that."

The rest of the crowd laughed with them, drawn in by Spuds. As always,

Spuds attracted people to him with a kindness and air of joviality. The mortals thought he was simply a friendly mountain man. He was, in actuality, a Remnant who could infuse those around him with feelings of good cheer. He did not offer information to his lineage, and Iris never asked.

Spuds turned and started ordering men to unload the mules. The conscripted men were eager to help. The sooner everything was unloaded, the sooner all the new items and news could be shared. Soon the mules were unloaded. Bags and packages were piled high on the boardwalk in front of the mercantile.

Spuds walked around the piles and pulled two medium-sized, bulging bags from the assortment. "Miss Iris, angel of the mountains, here are your letters and things. You've quite an assortment this round."

Iris smiled at the endearment. Spuds was as crusty as the mountains he traveled, but he always had sweet words for the women of Turning Creek. "Thank you. Come to the depot before you leave." Iris took one bag and handed the other to Thomas. "How long before you head back over the pass?"

Spuds patted the closest mule. "A few days. Got to let the mules rest, and I want to fill my belly with Widow Finch's fine fair. Won't be too hard to sleep in a bed for a span of some nights either." His packages for Iris delivered, he turned away and was enveloped by other townspeople, clamoring for news. There would be a large crowd at Vine's tonight to hear the stories and mull over their meaning.

Iris stepped back out of the crowd. On the edges of her sight, she saw movement. Henry stood outside his shop, wiping his hands with a towel. Despite the cold, he had his shirtsleeves rolled up and was without a jacket. His stiff work apron was tied around his waist. Something shifted at the sight of him, standing there apart from the others.

Iris tuned to Thomas. "Can you handle both bags? I want to talk to Henry."

The boy nodded, eager to please. "Of course. Want me to sort them?"

Iris thought of all the letters in the bags, filled with news. "No, I won't be long." Thomas's face fell. Iris smiled and touched his cheek. "Don't fear. You can help. I want to speak with Henry, then we can get started." Thomas grinned and turned towards the depot with the bags.

Iris crossed the street. She kept her gaze focused on Henry as she walked and dodged people milling towards the mercantile. When she finally stood next to him, she looked up into his face and smiled. She could feel heat rolling off him through the cold of the day. Iris stepped closer. It was cold outside.

"Spuds has arrived," she said.

Henry's mouth twitched up. "I see that. Looks like he brought you quite a bit of mail."

"I'm sure most of the town will be through the depot in the next couple of days. It'll make for some good conversations."

Henry shifted his weight off his bad foot. "I know that makes you happy."

"What're you working on today?"

"Mrs. Marina's swords. Would you like to see them?"

Iris did not miss the eagerness in his voice. He wanted to show them off, and she wanted to see them. "Of course I do."

Henry led her inside. Though he walked with a slight limp, he radiated strength. Hours wielding a hammer had honed him into a force stronger than the metal he bent to his will. Iris enjoyed the view as they walked into the heat of the shop. She had never taken enough time to appreciate Henry as much as he deserved.

Two sword blades, unpolished and without pommels, lay on the workbench. They were shorter than a traditional sword and longer than a knife. Next to the blades, a sheet of paper with an intricate design sketched on it was held down with an ingot of copper-colored metal. The scrollwork looked old, like the markings found in temples and hidden away places in Greece, places that had long since given up their secrets to time.

Henry waved a hand over the paper. "I've been working out some designs for the blades themselves. It's been a while since I made metal in the old way. What do you think?"

Henry did not often speak of his other talents. The fire from his forge contained a spark from the forge of Hephaestus in Olympus. With it, he could give metal properties that no mortal blacksmith could bestow. He had never told Iris how that spark had been preserved through the generations.

Iris leaned down to get a better view of the drawings. The movement brought her closer to Henry. She ran a finger over the sketches of the scrollwork. Square spirals gave way to lines of flowers interspersed by other geometric designs. Hidden in the pattern was a harpy in flight, easy to miss at first glance. "It's beautiful."

"You don't think it's too fancy for swords? Mrs. Marina is not one for frills, but I thought she'd make an exception for something pointy. The scrolls aren't just for show. Cuts made with these knives will not heal fast. The lethal intent of the wielder will make the wound worse depending on the rage behind the swing."

Iris threw back her head and laughed. "You have her pegged. Rage she can do. They'll be perfect."

Something flashed in Henry's eyes as he watched her, and Iris thought he was pleased with her praise. "Your calling suits you."

He cleared his throat. "As does yours." He shifted his weight again.

A flare of awareness at how close she was to Henry pressed itself upon her. Her left arm and shoulder rested against his as they stood side by side at the bench. Iris felt her face flush and took a step back, as annoyed at her embarrassment as she was baffled by it.

Iris clasped her hands in front of herself. "I'd better go sort those letters before the depot is overrun." Iris laid a hand on Henry's arm and felt him tense under her touch. "Thank you for showing me the swords. I can't wait to see them finished." She turned to leave, but was stopped by his voice.

"Have a good day, Miss Iris."

Iris turned back to him and smiled. "Come have tea with me soon, Henry." She left him rooted in the spot by the bench.

All the way back to the depot she puzzled over her reaction to Henry. Outside of the harpies, he was her closest friend. It was ridiculous of her to be uneasy with him. Iris mulled it over until she crossed the threshold into the depot, and then she forgot everything but the letters.

Spuds had been right. There was quite an assortment. She could feel the pulsing of the emotions left on the paper even without touching the bags. Thomas hopped from foot to foot behind the bench. Iris did nothing to tamp down her own excitement. Since the first Messenger, those of her line had shared an affinity for the written word, and letters in particular. The day Spuds arrived with the mail from outside the valley was a day Iris loved above all else. Her hands tingled in anticipation.

"Shall we get started?" she asked. Thomas nodded. "You take that bag, and I'll work on this one. Make two piles, in town and out of town. I'll sort this bag into slots then sort your piles."

Thomas pulled the string of the smaller of the two bags and pulled out some envelopes. Iris ruffled his hair and opened her own bag.

As soon as she reached her hand in, sorrow and grief assaulted her. Her heart stuttered and her hand went numb. Her knees threatened to buckle, so she gripped the edge of the counter and took a deep breath. The sorrow in the bag was meant for her.

Thomas was at her side in a blink. "What's wrong?" He slipped an arm around her waist.

Iris gripped the edge of the counter and willed her voice to be steady. "There's a letter in the bag for me. It's overflowing with grief. It caught me by surprise."

Iris closed down the wall of her senses, and the feeling of sorrow was muted from a wail to a sniffle. She reached into the bag again and ran her hand around in the letters. Normally, a bag of letters held so many different emotions, they were like echoes of the real thing. This one held its own power, which could only mean one thing. Her mother had written her and the news was sure to break her heart.

Iris's fingers jerked when she connected with the letter; the feeling jolted all the way to her shoulder and lodged in her chest. She pulled it out with shaking hands. The envelope was not as worn as the letters from her mother and grandmothers usually were, and it was thicker. Either this one had not traveled as far or it had not traveled by the usual means. Her mother's firm handwriting was on the front. Her heart twisted, and she knew that one of her grandmothers was dead. This letter contained great sadness, but also the barest hint of hope.

"Who's it from?" Thomas asked.

"My mother. I didn't expect a reply to my letter for months yet." Iris broke the blue wax seal. A leather journal, worn soft with age, was wrapped around the paper. Iris set it aside and read the letter.

My dearest daughter,

By the time you get this, it will be winter in your valley. I am sending this missive most of the way with a Remnant who can travel swiftly, as my news cannot wait.

It is with a heavy heart that I reply to your most recent letter. The last of your great-grand-mere's harpies died a week ago, and she went to join them this morning in the Underworld.

Naomi was slain by some villagers who had grown bold with indignation at the treatment they'd received from the harpy for many years. Your great-grand-mere always said Naomi would come to a violent end and reap the sorrow she had sown. Your letter, so filled with hope over your own charges, gave her hope in her last days. Hope, something which is hard to come by in this place still lost to the old ways.

Your grand-mere has taken her mother's death hard. Her own harpies have sunk into their own bitterness, resorting to extreme violence to rule those unfortunate enough to reside near them. Grand-mere and I fear that none of them will live to reach their full three hundred years. She believes she has failed them. For the time, I have convinced her to join me in Tuscany, where I can watch over her.

Despite all this, things go well with me. My two charges have made themselves scarce, but they are not dead. I would feel it if they departed this world, so I know they live still. I am certain they are causing trouble in some corner of the globe, but they have never taken my counsel to live in peace.

Now to get to the heart of the matter and your question. I am fascinated by the behavior of the Turning Creek harpies. I have gone over the accounts of our line again and there have been no generations of harpies who have worked in tandem since the first and second generations.

That one of your harpies has chosen a permanent mate is unique as far as I can find. You wrote that you feel it has changed her, blunted her bitterness and anger and calmed all of them. I can tell from your stories that they are still violent, especially when defending their territory. The story of them working together and with the mortals to keep the valley safe is nothing short of astonishing.

You asked about the grey hair Petra is exhibiting. I think your theories on a shorted life is likely correct. Time will reveal the answer to this riddle. I think, like you suggest, that this is but an outward sign of an inward change. I think their loyalty to each other, their choosing of mates, and their defense of their territory and its people are all connected.

In some of the early writings of Iris, the first of her name, she discusses agapeo. Agapeo is sacrificial love. It means to give yourself completely into the hands of another. It bestows not only love, but trust and sacrifice. Agapeo has its own power. It was why the ancients rarely swore agapeo love. It gives power when it is given.

If your harpies have moved so far beyond their nature that they feel this love for another, it may account for the changes you see in them. Though they have not used the word, I suspect this type of agapeo love is what your harpies feel for each other, for their mates, and for you. I know now that I was right to name you after the first of our line. Not since the first four has there been such a love between The Messenger and her harpies. You are blessed by the gods to have won this boon.

Love has long been a force of change in the world. It could have brought Petra's mate back from the dead, as you suggest. There is no other power in the world able to wipe out bitterness and loneliness like sacrificial love. Please keep a chronicle of the happenings in your valley. I have a strong feeling that things in your small corner of the world are more important than you know. There are tides moving that I have not seen, but that flow on the corners of my dreams. Changes are coming, and you may hold the answers.

You mentioned Petra is settled. What news of Marina and Dora? You know Dora holds a special place in my heart because of the loss of her mother.

Your harpies are settling and will soon have daughters of their own. At the risk of being a predictable nagging mother, they will need their own Messenger. It is time for you to settle yourself. Is there no one in Turning Creek that has struck you?

How does your flying progress? Above all things, I wish I could see your wings. I wept over the feather you sent. It is the most beautiful thing I have ever seen. Grand-mere and I have been discussing the probability of you passing the wings down your line. We possess differing opinions on the matter, but I am hopeful it will be so.

I am sending a copy of the journal of the second Messenger. I hope you find it useful in your studies. Please write soon. I know the winter will delay a reply, and there is talk, even here, of strife and war brewing in your land. Your letters have brought hope into our corner of the world. I am sorry that I had to bring grief into yours.

Be safe, my daughter. You and your harpies are a credit to your lines, and I am exceedingly proud of all four of you.

Love and Charis,
Your mother

Iris laid the letter on the counter. Thomas, who had been sorting letters while giving her sidelong glances out of the corner of his eyes, ceased his work and came alongside her.

He wrapped his arms around her. "Bad news from your mom?"

Iris squeezed him tight. "My great-grand-mere has passed from this world, as have her harpies."

Thomas patted her back. The bell on the door sounded and cold air invaded the moment. Iris gave Thomas one last squeeze. She wiped her eyes as she turned to face their visitor.

Jacob Wells, lean and strong with warm brown eyes, stood watching them as the door closed off the flow of cold air.

"I'm interrupting. I'll come back later." He turned and put his hand on the door.

"No, you're welcome to stay." Iris sniffed one last time, folded her mother's letter, and put it under the counter. Mr. Wells was a mortal, and there were things in her letter she did not want him to see.

He walked over to the counter. "Anything I can do to help?" Concern crinkled the space between his eyes.

Iris sighed. "There's nothing anyone can do. My mother wrote me to tell me…" her voice caught and she had to clear her throat, "my grand-mere died." It was in actuality her great-grand-mere, but how would she explain that her great-grand-mere had lived for two hundred and seventy-six years?

Mr. Wells reached across the counter and placed a calloused hand over hers. Its warmth filled Iris with connection and comfort. This was what it meant to live when sadness touched you. It was about finding connections with others and finding strength to breathe another moment, then another, and another.

He squeezed her hand. "My condolences. I lost both my parents to pneumonia one spring. I had two younger sisters, and I was the only one left to care for them. They're both married now and living in the town where we grew up in South Carolina. You never get over missing someone, whether they're dead or just really far away."

Iris covered his hand with her left hand. "Thank you." She removed her hands from his and smoothed them over her skirt. "What can I do for you today?

"I heard Spuds finally got over the pass. I came to see if I had any letters from my sisters. I'm sorry if I rushed over. It looks like you're still sorting things out. Nettie is expecting her first baby, and I'm anxious for news."

Iris waved at the two sacks of letters. Thomas had made some headway on his bag, but the bag in front of her was still brimming over. "I've not yet sorted through these. Do you want to wait or come back later?"

Iris was pleased when Mr. Wells pulled out a stool from under the counter and sat down. She went back to work. Iris stuck her hand into the bag, keeping her walls up. She did not want to be bombarded with the emotions circling around the stack when her own were barely in check, and with an audience no less.

"Can I get you some tea or biscuits?" she asked.

Mr. Wells scratched his angular jaw. "Biscuits?"

Iris smiled. "Cookies."

"Can't say no to cookies."

Iris looked at Thomas. "Will you go bring the tea tray down and put some water on down here?"

Thomas kissed her on the cheek and pounded up the stairs. It sounded more like a herd of satyrs than one boy. Iris shook her head. "Teenage boys are never quiet." She grabbed a handful of letters and turned towards to slots to sort them, giving Mr. Wells her back. "We haven't had much of a chance to talk since you came to town. You've been busy getting the mill ready. How's it coming?"

Jacob Wells had arrived in Turning Creek in the fall with just enough time to build a small house and the frame of a mill. The would-be mill stood on the east side of town by the river that gave the town its name.

"It'll be ready come spring. All it needs is some elbow grease and time."

"You said your sisters live in South Carolina. People come to the mountains for many different reasons. Why are you here? If I may ask such a personal question." Iris turned to look at his face as she spoke to judge whether he had taken offense. It was not only Remnants who liked to keep their secrets.

Mr. Wells's face remained open and he shrugged. "Nothing important. I liked the idea of the west and the mountains. I wanted to see something different than the hills of the Carolinas. I left my sisters and their husbands the mill back home, which made everyone happy."

Jacob Wells did not seem like a man with secrets. Iris went back to her sorting. "It's a shame, all the talk about succession from the Union by some of the states."

Mr. Wells's voice acquired a slight edge. "The southern states have a right to make their own decisions regarding slavery. Folks there rely on that way of life. Taking that away would be hard on people."

Iris thought of the accounts of the war against Olympus and its aftermath. "There's talk of war. War is hard on people too."

Thomas came back down the stairs, quieter since he carried a tray. He set it on the edge of the counter and put a plate of sugar cookies in front of Mr. Wells.

"Thank you, Thomas." To Iris, he said, "Turning Creek seems fairly isolated. Even if there's a war, it will take a long time to impact our lives here."

"War has a way of touching us all."

Mr. Wells chewed a bite of cookie. "We'll see. I'd be worried for my sisters and their families, but I don't like to borrow trouble. I have hope things will be worked out before it comes to such dire straits."

"Perhaps," Iris said. She picked up another handful of letters and found one addressed to Jacob Wells. Iris opened her senses enough to feel the joy radiating from it. Iris walked around to the front of the counter and held out the letter. "I think this is the letter you wanted."

Mr. Wells took the letter and ripped open the seal. He scanned the letter quickly, a wide grin blooming on his face. He jumped up from the stool and swept Iris into an embrace. He twirled her around and whooped. His joy was contagious, and Iris felt a laugh escaping her. She never would have guessed she would laugh so soon after hearing news of her great-grand-mere. Iris blushed.

"It's a boy." Mr. Wells put her down and gave her a sheepish grin. "Sorry, my enthusiasm got the better of me, and I forgot you can't go around twirling pretty ladies whenever the mood strikes you."

Iris blushed in earnest.

Mr. Wells said, "They named him Nathanael Jacob after his daddy and me. They're all doing great."

"No apologies needed. New life is always worth celebrating well. Congratulations on your nephew."

Mr. Wells couldn't stop the grin from taking over his face. Iris felt herself returning his smile. His brown eyes twinkled with delight. "Thank you, Miss Iris, for your felicitations."

Iris tucked a loose strand of blonde hair from her eyes. "Please, my friends call me Iris."

"I would be honored to be counted as your friend, just as long as you'll call me Jacob." He took a step closer to her.

Iris smiled again and said, "Thank you, Jacob."

Jacob stayed while Iris sorted the rest of the letters.

CHAPTER 4

The clink of checkers was the only sound in the room. L.A. and Johnny were deep in their fifth game, the tie-breaker for the round. To intrude upon them at this critical moment meant certain death—or a tongue lashing at the very least. Iris wished to avoid both. The two older men spent a part of almost every day when the weather was nice in the back of the depot playing checkers. They said it was to escape their wives, but Iris knew it was their way of getting into town for some gossip, and the saloon was not their style. She was glad they had both braved the snow today. Their presence, even though it came with some loud arguments over their games, kept the loneliness pecking at her at bay. Iris looked back down at the book she was reading without seeing its bright colors.

It was the loneliness that caught her off-guard. Iris had known her great-grand-mere's passing would make her sad, but the concurrent loneliness was making her grief nearly unbearable. She missed her harpies and felt adrift, anchorless.

Her earliest memory of her great-grand-mere was sitting on her lap in the garden while she read the accounts of the first Iris. If she closed her eyes, she could see the burst of spring flowers sheltering the gazebo in the middle of the garden. She could feel her great-grand-mere's voice wash over her as she leaned her small back against the older woman's chest. Her favorite book had been this illustrated volume of the original myths.

The relationship between the goddess Iris and the original four harpies had been one defined by loyalty. Iris flipped the pages of the book she had loved as a child. When she left Tuscany to follow her harpies, her great-grand-mere had given her the book as part of the library she would take with her. Iris ran her fingers over a picture of the harpies on the Isle of Strophades. History had not been kind to the actors in this myth. She flipped another page. The goddess Iris was on her knees before Zeus. Her long golden hair and wings streamed behind her as she wept and begged for him to have mercy on her sisters.

Iris's heart constricted in empathy. The hearts of the Messengers had been breaking over their harpies since the beginning. All except her. Her harpies were different, though they had started out as violent and bitter as the rest. There was merit to her mother's theory, but she did not yet know what the full effects of the changes in her harpies would be.

The bell rang over the door and Iris looked up. The checker game continued unabated. Lily Hughes, the tailor's wife and a fine master of the needle herself, came into the depot. She took her scarf off from around her head and neck, sending tiny bits of snow to the floor. There were new lines around Lily's eyes, but the tightness and the way she had tucked into herself after being kidnapped had relaxed over the last couple of months. Marina had told Iris enough about what had happened in the Nasso's basement prison for Iris to know the extent of the family's evil. Experiences like that left their own kind of scars and pain behind, but Lily's strength and love for her family shone in her will to overcome.

"Good morning, Lily. I see it has started snowing again. Mrs. Stewart was in here at the beginning of the week and said that it would start up soon."

Lily's eyes crinkled at the corners when she smiled. "Hello, Iris. The snow is just a dusting, but the sky looks like there is more to come. It may be our first big snow of the year."

Iris tucked her mother's letter inside the illustrated book and closed it gently. "How are Agnes and Amy?" The Hughes had twin daughters who kept their parents busy with their escapades.

Lily ran a hand over her hair, smoothing it back to her already tidy bun. "If anything was going to drive me to drink, it would be those two. I caught them shooting arrows at scraps of cloth in the back garden yesterday. I don't even know where they got the bow and arrows."

Iris coughed. Marina gave a set of bows and arrows to Stephen and Jonah last month. Iris had little doubt the boys had shared their bounty with the girls. "I hope no one got hurt."

"After some negotiation, we allowed them to keep the weapons, but they had to swear to only practice in the direction of the woods." Iris made a note to give the trees behind the tailor shop a wide berth when going to the clearing to fly. Lily sat with a sigh on one of the stools.

Iris put her back to Lily to hide her smile and made a show of straightening some already perfectly aligned envelopes. "What can I do for you today?"

"I ordered some books for the girls, and I was hoping they had been in the bags Spuds dropped off here yesterday."

Iris pulled the brown-wrapped parcel from the set of larger slots near the bottom of the wall. She laid it on the counter. "I believe this is what you are looking for."

Iris shifted her eyes to the door as the bell rang again. Jacob came in. His head was bare and his face full of smiles. "Hello, ladies." He tipped an invisible hat to them.

"I didn't expect to see you so soon," Iris said.

Jacob's grin widened and he waved a letter in the air. "I wanted to write to my sister straightaway to make sure it went back out of the valley with Spuds when he leaves." He handed the letter to Iris. "How are you, Mrs. Hughes?"

Lily stood up and bowed her head to Jacob. "I'm fine, thank you. I have to be going. The girls said they were going to go see if the creek was frozen over yet. I want to make sure they're still alive."

"If you see Thomas, send him my way."

"I will. Thank you for the books."

After Lily left, Iris faced Jacob. "Do you have other business on this side of town today?"

Jacob put his hands in his pockets and rocked back on his heels. "As a matter of fact, I do. I was hoping you'd make an introduction for me."

"An introduction?"

"Yes. To the blacksmith, Henry Foster. I haven't met him yet, and I need some custom work done for some fastenings for the mill. I would've gone earlier, but I was more concerned with getting a roof over my head before the snows than meeting everyone. I want to build what mechanical parts of the mill I can during the winter, then be ready to assemble it all come spring."

Iris nodded. Many had been surprised at Jacob's arrival so late in the fall, but no one had grumbled. Having a large working mill in town benefited everyone.

Iris rested against the counter. "This is a small town, Jacob. We aren't so formal around here. You can just go introduce yourself to Henry, you know."

Jacob grinned. "Oh, I know that. I just wanted an excuse to walk down the road with you."

Iris felt her face heat. She cleared her throat. "I can't say no to that."

She walked around the counter and back to the table where the game was nearly over. L.A. was desperately trying to keep Johnny from his last man. "After this game, you two go home before it snows in earnest."

L.A. looked up from the game. "Snow?"

Johnny picked up a black checker and jumped the last red checker. He howled in triumph. "Superior intellect wins every time."

"Snow," Iris repeated over L.A.'s groan. "I sent Thomas down to Simon's. If he gets back before you leave, tell him I took Mr. Wells to see

Henry.”

Johnny nodded. “Yes, ma’am. We’re leaving, so we’ll stop by Simon’s for a bit of a chat before heading home.”

L.A. squinted at Jacob. “What kind of man takes a lady out in the snow?”

Jacob rocked back on his heels. “I suppose the foolhardy kind who likes the company of smart, beautiful women.”

L.A. hooted with laughter. He bussed Iris on the cheek. “He’s a saucy one. Watch out for him now, Miss Iris.”

Johnny’s face was without a smile. “You’re welcome to take Miss Iris on a walk, but just because she ain’t got no man in her house doesn’t mean she’s not watched after.”

Jacob’s smile never faltered. “Warning noted. I promise I’m a gentleman.”

“Good, then. Miss Iris, see you after the snow passes over.” Johnny said as he and L.A. left.

Iris put on her scarf and cap and smiled at Jacob, though now her face was probably too covered up for him to see it. He held open the door for her and they stepped out together.

The sky was light grey, not the color of iron that usually marked a large snowfall. Gentle flakes fell in the air and the smell of wood fires filled her nose. Jacob held out his arm. Iris hesitated, then took it, ducking her head to hide her grin and the blush she felt flooding her face. The heady feeling Jacob’s compliments gave her was provocative.

Jacob led her across busy Main Street. They wove around wagons and horses. It seemed word of Spuds’s arrival had spread, and everyone was in town. There was a determined, but jolly, bustle in the air. Since supplies and mail arrived less frequently in the winter, the week after Spuds came over the pass with his packs held a holiday atmosphere. Some people might be disappointed if they arrived at the depot only to find it empty. Iris belatedly thought she should have asked Jacob to wait until Thomas returned. *It is too late now*, she thought.

Iris heard the bellows before they came to the opening of Henry’s shop. The clank of the hammer rang in the air. Iris let go of Jacob and walked towards Henry, who was turned slightly away from them. The air in the forge was heavy with warmth and the smell of fire and metal. Iris walked around so Henry would see them out of the corner of his eye.

His hammer paused and his grey eyes met hers. His lips turned up in a quiet smile. “This is an unexpected pleasure.”

“Good morning, Henry.” Iris motioned to Jacob. “I bought the miller, Jacob Wells, to meet you. He wants to ask you about some fittings. Jacob Wells, this is Henry Foster, the best blacksmith you’ll ever meet.”

Henry put the metal he had been pounding in a vat of water. It hissed and popped while he wiped his hand on his thick apron. "Miss Iris is free with her praise, though I thank her for it. Pleased to meet you, Mr. Wells." The two men shook hands.

"I can't believe anyone as pretty as Iris would ever lie. If she says you're the best, then the best you must be." Jacob watched Iris as he spoke, an easy grin on his face.

Iris felt her face color. A bit of unease ran through her, and then Jacob's smile widened into the boyish grin he showed off so often. Iris could not help but smile back. Henry's grey eyes flicked between Iris and Jacob, watching the spoken and unspoken conversation. He turned his back to them and wrapped his hand around the handle of his hammer. His fist tightened then released, clutch and release. Henry carried the hammer to his work bench.

He turned to face them again. His face was wary. "What can I do for you?"

Jacob pulled a piece of paper from his jacket pocket and handed it to Henry. "I've made some drawings with measurements with what I need. I know we've no wheelwright in town, but I need some metal bands to fashion some wheels and cogs for the mill. I thought you'd be the next best thing."

Henry ran a hand along his jawline and put the paper on his bench, smoothing it out. "This looks fairly straightforward. I can have this to you in a couple weeks."

"No rush. I don't need 'em for about a month or so. I'll need some other fittings and pins, but I need these first. I wanted to see your work before I commissioned you for all of it."

If possible, Henry stood straighter. Jacob and Henry were close in height, but Henry had a size and strength advantage. "I can guarantee my work. I can make anything made of metal that you might need and a few things you'd never think to ask for." Iris blinked at the sudden tension. It was the closest thing to anger she had ever seen from Henry.

Jacob held his hands out in surrender. "No insult intended. I had to make sure. It's business, you know."

Henry relaxed. "No insult taken. We don't know each other, and it is sometimes best to be cautious when getting metalwork done. A wrong bend here or there could cost you years of work and the mill itself."

The tension eased and the two men started negotiating price. Iris wandered away and sat on the bench by the wall of the shop. She watched them, one lean and one broad, but both strong. Jacob kept glancing at her and smiling. Once he winked, and Iris looked away, but not before she caught sight Henry's mouth turning down when he too noticed.

The business was concluded and the men shook hands. Jacob walked over to where she sat with a confident stride. "Can I walk you home?"

Iris hated to quell the eagerness she saw in his eyes. "I'm going to stay and chat with Henry for a bit, if you don't mind. Thank you for the wonderful company. Will I see you again soon?"

Jacob smiled and bowed to her. "I think you shouldn't worry about that. Thank you for providing me with an introduction. You'll see me soon. Good bye, Mistress of Letters."

Iris laughed. "Flatterer. Stay warm."

Jacob whistled as he left the smithy. Iris watched him go, chuckling to herself. He certainly was charming.

Henry shifted his weight and looked down at her with an unreadable expression. Something pinched in her chest. Iris patted the bench beside her. Henry hesitated and the pinch in her chest increased. When he moved to join her, her breath came easier. Jacob was a shameless flirt, to be sure, but she did not want Henry to think ill of her for enjoying the attention. The thought of Henry ever thinking badly of her hurt.

Iris turned her body so she could face Henry. He shifted to face her, his eyes closed down to her. For once, Iris wished her friend was easier to read. "I hope I'm not keeping you from work."

"Your interruptions are always welcome."

"I have some news and no one to share it with. I had a letter from my mother. My great-grand-mere has joined her harpies in the afterlife." Against her wishes, her eyes filled up and spilled over. She thought she had cried enough yesterday and today over the news, but there were still tears to be shed.

Henry reached up and wiped the tears away with the calloused pad of his thumb. His touch was feather light and gone in an instant, but Iris felt branded. "I'm sorry for your heartache, Miss Iris."

Iris sniffed. "Thank you, though I am sorry for crying. I hadn't intended to do that."

"We should never be ashamed to mourn for those we love when they are gone from us," Henry said.

Iris reached out and laid her hand over Henry's. "Thank you. What I intended to talk to you about is something else my mother told me." Iris patted Henry's hand then put hers back in her lap, where they twitched with the need to scoop up his hand again. "When I wrote to her last fall, I told her about my harpies: the grey hair, how their natures are changing to something more. More loving. More caring. More loyal to others. I've gone through all my books, but I only had some vague theories."

"I take it your mother had something less vague to share," he said.

Iris took a deep breath to continue, and her senses were filled with the smells of the forge and Henry. She paused for a moment, dizzy. She took a deep breath, then continued, "Have you heard of the word agapeo?"

Henry cleared his throat and said, "It's an old and binding vow, from the first myths. My parents pledged it to each other when they married."

"That's beautiful. I don't think I've read any accounts of it being used that way."

"It is an old practice and not commonly done anymore." Henry looked away from her.

Iris continued, "My mother said she thinks my harpies are unique since the first four. She thinks them working as a family unit to defend a territory and taking permanent mates is changing their nature. My harpies are becoming better, stronger than their predecessors because they are allowing themselves to love completely."

"Love has a way of changing people, moving them to action towards better things." Henry's eyes came to rest on her face.

"So you think the theory has merit?" Iris asked.

"What's your gut telling you?"

"I think she's right. We already know love and sorrow had a hand in bringing James back from Zeus. Only time will tell us what the true repercussions will be of the changes." Iris poked at a tangle of threads in her scarf.

"You worry for them," Henry said.

Iris nodded. "I do, but," she smiled, "I also feel blessed to be their Messenger. There were many nights as a child, I remember waking up and hearing my mother and grand-meres weeping over their charges. I may spend nights in worry over them, especially Marina, but I've rarely wept over them in despair." Except for those months after the defeat of Zeus on Atlas's Peak, when Petra had left, broken in mind and heart.

"You're thinking of when James almost died." Henry's voice brought her out of the bite of that memory. "She came back and all is well."

Iris wiped away the memory and smiled at Henry. "You know me too well."

Henry turned to look at the snow falling with greater frequency outside. "You'd best be getting back before it starts to snow in earnest."

Iris rose and smoothed out her skirts. Henry followed her movements, and Iris had to crane her neck to look up at him. "Thank you, Henry. You're the one person I feel I can tell all these things to."

"I'm honored to be your confidant, and I'll hold that office for you as long as you need it."

Iris cocked her head. "I hope that's forever. I can't imagine not needing you for a friend." She never wanted to know what it would be like to not be able to come here and sit and talk with Henry. The silence stretched, and Iris became more aware of the warmth radiating from Henry, spilling heat like the forge that stood behind him.

Henry paused and looked out at the snow again. "Thank you. Go home now, Miss Iris. We both have work to do."

CHAPTER 5

A delicate snow fell overnight. The fresh layer blanketed the older snow from the previous day, returning the world to a crisp whiteness. Iris, cup of tea in hand, opened the door of the mail depot and walked onto the wooden boardwalk that ran the length of Main Street. Steam from her cup curled into the air and her breath created little clouds in front of her face. Turning Creek was quiet in the morning air, and Iris was alone.

She turned to watch the sun finish cresting over Silvercliff, the mountain on the east side of the valley. The gold and red washed over the range in a blinding display of majesty. Iris held her tea to her nose and sniffed the tang of the steam before taking a sip. There was no finer way to begin a morning than this, but if she lingered much longer, her tea would turn as cold as the February air. Iris turned to go back inside and get ready for the day. Even with the snow, she was sure to have at least a handful of people stop by. There was still plenty of the mail Spuds had brought in that needed to be delivered.

Something cream colored caught Iris's eye as she turned towards the door. The corner of a letter peeked out from under the lid of the mailbox. Iris remembered checking the box after supper. It had been empty. She looked around the boardwalk. No footprints led to the mailbox, which meant the letter had been dropped off after dinner and before the snow in the middle of the night.

Iris opened the hinged lid and the letter fluttered to the bottom of the box. The corner of the letter had been wedged deliberately under the lid so it would be plainly visible. Every letter was a world of new possibilities for someone, and her fingers tingled. Iris reached in and picked up the tri-folded piece of paper. It was sealed with ordinary candle wax and a plain round press. Iris flipped it over and was astonished to see it was addressed to her.

She stood there with the sun over her shoulder and her tea growing cold, staring at the letters written in a bold hand. The air around her stilled and the chill of prophecy danced up her spine. Iris held her breath, but no sense of doom followed. No words formed inside her head to steer her in the right direction, only a sense that once the seal was broken, everything would be different. Of all her gifts, Iris liked the one that granted her prophecy the least. Nothing good came of knowing the future.

Iris ran her fingers over the paper, tracing the letters that had been strung together to form her name. She did not recognize the handwriting. Iris reached for the sense of the letter, the fingerprints of emotion left by the writer. A jumble of fear, longing, and hope filled her senses. Her chest tightened with their strength, and she had to force air to move through her lungs. She opened her eyes and the feeling faded though her fingertips, which were numb. Whatever the letter contained, it would not give her the sorrow her mother's letter had, but no letter that strong would leave things as they were.

Iris carried the letter and a growing curiosity inside. She walked around to the backside of the counter, placed the letter addressed to her flat on the gleaming wooden surface, and stared at it. She sat and took a sip of her lukewarm tea. Iris flipped over the letter and examined the seal. The plain seal and common wax told her nothing.

Iris tapped her fingers on the counter to try to restore some feeling to them. The hope and fear of the letter had curled inside her. She pulled up her walls to separate herself from the feelings the letter bled into the air. It continued to tug at her like an insistent child. Like the letter from her mother, the emotions from this letter were strong because it was addressed to her.

Iris took a breath. A pressure was building underneath her ribs, making it hard to breathe. She slid a finger under the seal. The sound of it breaking was loud in the empty room. Iris unfolded the paper and smoothed it flat. The same slanted, masculine writing on the front of the paper filled the sheet. There was no salutation.

I have composed this letter many times and with so many variations that I am no longer sure of the proper words to use. I wonder if I will wake tomorrow and think that I have dreamed writing this. Being near you is a waking dream I cherish, and mourn when the time is over.

When one sets out to court a woman of letters, a correspondence on paper seems both the logical and practical way to begin. I have not practiced the fine art of letter writing, but writing you is a task I would face every day if it meant I might one day receive a missive in your own hand. Touching paper you lingered over as you wrote, thinking of just the phrase to use, would be the sun in my day.

You have brought light into my life and I hope these words have brought you even a

Please forgive the anonymity of this letter. I seek your favor as an ordinary man seeks the favor of a woman he admires. You have a heart as beautiful as the smile which greets all who enter your domain. If you would permit me the liberty of continuing to correspond with you this way, I ask that you tie a ribbon on the mailbox outside of the depot.

I am, always, your humble servant.

Iris read it through twice, finished her cup of tea, and then went upstairs to her apartment to brew another pot. She took the letter with her, letting the tangle of its emotions wind itself around the ones twisting in her. Fear, longing, and hope had been poured into the letter and now they ran through her, and she let them. She had never been pursued in this way.

I've never been pursued seriously at all, she amended to herself. At a time when she needed to begin to consider the future of her own line, she suddenly had a letter from an admirer and Jacob Wells being attentive. She needed to consider the possibilities of who had written the letter, but Iris wanted to enjoy the moment. She would have to consider the source of the letter, but for now, simply having it and feeling the intent behind it was more than enough. She laid it on the smooth plank table in her kitchen and ran her fingers over the folded page, then went to fill the kettle with water.

The tinkle of brass bells broke through the sound of the hissing kettle on the stove. Iris poured the hot water over the tea leaves and filled the ceramic pot to the top. She put an extra cup on a tray. It was not often she wanted to be alone, but this would have been a nice morning to have a few more moments of quiet.

She turned her head towards the stairs. "I'll be right down."

"It's just me," Dora's voice floated up to her.

"Come on up," Iris replied. If she was to be interrupted, she was glad it was one of her harpies.

Dora's footsteps on the stairs preceded her freckled face. Iris walked over to the harpy and wrapped her in a hug. Even in her human form, Dora returned the embrace with enough of her harpy strength that Iris thought her ribs might crack. Iris did not complain. She never did when the harpies chose to show affection. It was yet another indication that they were different than their predecessors.

"Good morning, my bird. Would you like some tea? I just made a new pot."

Dora smiled. "I'd love some."

Iris took the basket of leaves out of the pot, poured two cups of tea, and placed one of them in front of Dora. She nudged the jar of honey towards the harpy. Iris watched her while she spooned the gold liquid into her cup. Dora's pale skin showed every freckle and blemish. This morning there were lines around her eyes and faint smudges beneath them.

"Is everything all right? If Marina were in town, I would've guessed you were out all night flying in the snow. Then I might have also been sad you hadn't asked me to join you."

Dora sat heavily into a chair. "Margaret Meyers was delivered of a healthy baby girl a couple hours ago. It was a long labor. I was up helping Dr. Williams all night." Lee Williams was the Remnant of Asclepius, a powerful physician during the time of the old myths.

Iris put a plate of biscuits on the table. "Here, I made these yesterday. Why did you come back to town instead of going home?" Dora lived high up Silvercliff in a small cabin surrounded by herb gardens.

Dora took one of the molasses rounds off the plate. "Dr. Williams needed some things from his cabinet and the mercantile. He said no rush, but I can fly faster over the snow than he can travel on horseback. The list he gave me is mostly foodstuffs and some tea to help with the bleeding that comes after a birth. I think he wanted to make sure the Meyers had what they needed for a while so Margaret did not have to do much for a few days."

Iris sipped her tea. "You've been helping Doc out often."

A creep of red traveled up Dora's neck. A quiet joy stole through Iris at its appearance, followed swiftly by a longing of her own. Her gaze rested on her letter still laying on the table. If she was stealthy, maybe she could move it before Dora saw it.

Dora's face continued to flame as she looked everywhere but at Iris. "Where's Thomas?"

"He's still asleep. Don't change the subject."

Dora spied the letter and snatched it up before Iris could grab it. Iris felt her own face heat. She took a sip of tea to cover her embarrassment. Dora raised an eyebrow at her and began to read it. Her eyes widened and flicked back to Iris more than once before she finished it.

Dora waved the letter in the air. "When did you get this, and why was it not the first thing you told me about when I came up?"

Iris willed her voice to be steady. She could not keep herself from returning Dora's grin. "It was in the box this morning."

"Any idea who sent it?" Dora waved the paper again and Iris snatched it from her.

Iris tucked the letter into the pocket of her skirt. "None. There were no footprints or anything leading to the boardwalk, and the handwriting is unfamiliar to me, which is odd. I thought I knew everyone's handwriting."

Iris took a bite of a biscuit. Molasses and sugar filled her mouth. Its sweetness matched the burgeoning delight she felt. Her affinity for letters lent itself to the ability to recognize handwriting once she had seen it. Turning Creek and the surrounding region had grown considerably in the past two years, but it was still small enough that Iris knew every soul permanently residing in the valley.

"You are going to leave the ribbon out for him." Dora stated it as fact.

Iris had already decided to leave one out. Sheer curiosity alone compelled her to try to find the author of the most wonderful letter she had ever received. "I was considering it."

Dora's lips thinned. She pointed her finger at Iris. "That is a beautiful letter. He deserves a response. You can't refuse if you do not even know who it is." There was an undertone of anger to the harpy's words.

Iris eyed Dora before speaking. "Is something bothering you?"

Dora crossed her arms, and Iris saw a flash of belligerence in her eyes that briefly held the menace of a predator. It was gone when she blinked. Dora kept an iron reign on her harpy at all times. Iris knew something more than this letter was rubbing Dora's feathers the wrong way. The other two harpies would have let their instincts and emotions rule the conversation, but that was not Dora's way.

Dora relaxed. "It's nothing. I'm sorry."

Iris left it for now. Dora would come clean eventually. "I do intend to leave a ribbon," she took a sip of tea, "and a letter of my own." Iris let her feelings show in her smile.

Dora's grin was back. "It's too bad Marina isn't here. She'd love this."

Iris snorted. "She would be positively gleeful for the entertainment this offered and would enjoy tormenting me. Marriage has not dulled her drive to get the last and most clever word in every conversation."

"Poor Reed. Unfortunately for him, I think he is the only man alive smart enough to get the better of her." Dora reached across the table and grabbed Iris's hand. "As The Messenger, you're not restricted in your mate. You can have a normal family and a normal husband."

With Dora's words the source of Dora's hostility became clear, and her heart constricted. She turned her hand in Dora's and squeezed. "Petra and Marina found love against all odds. My bird, there's hope for you too. You and your sisters are not like the generations before you. You've chosen a different path, a path together. You are making a new way."

Dora shook her head. "It was an anomaly the first time with Petra, and a miracle the second with Marina. I don't think there's enough good fate in the world to extend to me too. The gods were never that generous. I'm content enough to see my sisters happy. I know my daughter will have a family, something none of us have ever had, and a hope that she may be able to choose her own fate. Those things alone make me happy." Dora smiled and Iris knew there was truth in her words.

Iris put her other hand over Dora's. "I think there are miracles enough left in the world for you."

Dora's lips quirked up. "Is that an official prophecy?"

"Just old-fashioned optimism," Iris winked. "I would like to see all of you settled before doing any settling of my own."

"I can't be settled if there's no one to settle with," Dora said.

Iris had her own ideas for Dora, but she kept them to herself. Iris was about to offer Dora breakfast when foreboding crept up her spine. The air around them moved though they were inside. Iris's mouth went dry and the fear that accompanied prophecies of ill news filled her. Her hand tightened and Dora's blue eyes hardened.

The harpy looked out from Dora's eyes, alert to the magic in the air. "What's wrong?"

Iris closed her eyes. It was not the kind of prophecy that took over, but that did not make it less menacing. Iris hated the prophecies that invaded her mind and spoke through her. She preferred the ones that came and allowed her to see and yet did not seek to control her.

The words of the prophecy strung through her mind like the beads of a broken necklace. She took a deep breath and gathered them together until the words made sense. The direction was clear, but the purpose of the words was not.

When she spoke, it was with her own voice. "We need to go to Doc's. Now. Someone has need of you." The air around them stilled, opened up, and the oppression of the prophecy was gone.

Iris opened her eyes. Dora's power, raw and violent, rippled from the woman across from her. The prophecy had stirred the harpy. "The words do not sound menacing, yet they came with power."

Fatigue replaced the energy that had run through Iris moments before. "Prophecy rarely offers details. Even the true moments of seeing are full of riddles and holes. We should go and see who or what waits for you."

Dora stood and grabbed their coats from the pegs. Iris swayed as she stood. She gripped the table. The solidity of the wood and the smoothness of it gave her strength.

Dora gripped her elbow. "You should stay."

Iris straightened. "No, bird. I'll go with you. I think I can walk down Main Street and back."

Dora raised an eyebrow to her but remained silent as they walked downstairs. Iris put on the coat she was offered and was relieved the harpy did not argue. In truth, she did not have the energy for an argument. Dora offered Iris her arm when they went outside.

Iris linked her arm with Dora's. "Thank you, my bird."

They walked briskly, marring the unbroken, ankle-deep snow, past the mercantile, the dark sheriff's office, and the tailor shop. A wooden sign with a caduceus and snake hung above the door of Doctor Williams's office, marking him as a physician to all and a follower of Asclepius to those who knew that name. Dora released her arm and passed under the sign and through the door without hesitation.

Deborah Stewart stood in the middle of the office. Her brown hair was half falling from her bun and her dress was wrinkled, as if she had been wearing and sleeping in it for days. When she saw them, she burst into tears.

"I need help. My girls are all sick. They have fevers and a rash. Nancy stopped eating yesterday. I don't know what to do."

Iris led her to a chair, and the woman collapsed on it and covered her face with her hands. Iris patted Mrs. Stewart's shoulder.

Dora knelt in front of Mrs. Stewart, who took a deep breath and looked up. "I know where Dr. Williams is. I can go get him and we can be at your house in a couple hours. What are you doing for the girls?"

Mrs. Stewart seemed to gather the pieces of herself together. "I've been laying cool rags on their bodies and trying to make them drink broth whenever I can."

Dora patted the woman's clenched hands in her lap. "That's a great start. I have some tea and some things I want to send home with you until Dr. Williams and I get there."

Mrs. Stewart nodded. "Thank you."

Dora stood and looked at Iris. The lines of tiredness had deepened in the corners of her eyes, but there was determination shining in their blue depths now. Iris worried that Dora would not stop to rest or eat for the remainder of the day.

All thoughts of her own fatigue left her. Iris said, "You should both take some food with you. You can't take care of anyone else if you collapse yourselves, and I know you won't have much time to cook. Does Doc keep any food upstairs?"

Dora shook her head and continued to rub Mrs. Stewart's hand. "Not much. He usually just drinks coffee and eats bread and cheese until the boarding house opens."

"I'll go get some food from the depot to send with you."

Dora opened her mouth to protest. Iris saw the moment she changed her mind. "I'll give Deborah what she needs and go get Doc. She can wait for you here and you can send the food with her."

Iris went to Dora and wrapped her in a hug. The prophecy had not included a warning for Dora's safety, but Iris worried nonetheless. "Check in when you can."

Dora returned the hug. "I will."

Iris rushed back to the depot, following the trail through the snow they had made. From her shelves in the kitchen, she pulled down a large piece of cloth and laid it flat on the table. She put cheese, scones, some dried apples, and what was left of the molasses biscuits in the center of the cloth and tied it closed. Iris cradled the bundle in her arms and prayed blessings of health and safety over it while she walked. The cold air burned her lungs and her body protested the pace she set, but Iris did not slow down.

Mrs. Stewart sat in the same chair where Iris and Dora had left her, curled into herself. She looked up with haunted eyes when Iris entered Doc's office. Iris set the bundle down next to a satchel on the chair beside Mrs. Stewart. Iris pulled the woman to her feet.

"How did you get into town?" Iris asked.

"I rode one of the mares." Mrs. Stewart's voice was flat.

"Good. I'll help you secure these and get you on your way." Iris put her hands on Mrs. Stewart's shoulders. She was taller than Iris by a few inches and Iris looked up into the woman's face. "Your family needs your strength. Gather it to you as you ride and be ready to do what must be done when you get there."

Mrs. Stewart nodded. The haunted look faded and was replaced by determination. "Thank you, Messenger."

"Come." Iris pulled her outside to the horse that was waiting. Iris helped her into the saddle and secured the bundle then the satchel. "Travel safe. May the gods protect you and your family."

Iris watched Mrs. Stewart travel north up Main Street then turn east towards the rising peak of Silvercliff. Doc and Dora would do all they could for the Stewarts. Iris's heart still went with the woman as she traveled towards the troubles of her family. The sky was the color of lead. It would be snowing again by the end of the day. The lack of sun bled worry into Iris's bones. She shook herself to rid her heart of the weight and went back to the depot.

Iris tried to make herself busy to still her mind. There was a heap of blankets on one side of the reclining couch by the window and a pile of books perched precariously in the corner. Iris clucked her tongue. Thomas had left the books out again. Clutter Iris could abide, but books and papers had proper places. She was pleased that he loved reading as much as he did. She was displeased by the disarray he left in his wake.

She scanned the titles and returned the books to their places on the shelves. Thomas was reading through the histories of the first Fall of Olympus. He was fascinated with the war that had scattered the Remnants into the world. He loved the stories of the first four harpies almost as much as he loved the penny westerns he ordered through the mail.

Even with her hands occupied, her mind wandered and worried. It seemed that even though she lived in harmony with her own harpies, she was destined to use her anxiety for them in other ways. Marina was far beyond the valley, and Iris felt her absence in the lack of laughter in her days. Dora was off fighting sickness, which could not be slain by violence and which could be contagious. Petra was carrying a new generation for which Iris had yet to provide a Messenger and protector.

Iris sighed to herself and carried a blue quilt patterned with red poppies, her favorite, from the chair by the window to her room. She rummaged in the basket by the bed and found a length of long blue ribbon, which she put in the pocket of her skirt. Her hands brushed the letter and she felt again its hope and fear. Its writer deserved her answer.

Iris made tea and took a cup downstairs. With precise movements of habit, she laid out paper, a quill, and ink on the counter. Iris sat on her stool, finished her tea, and composed the letter in her head. She could not tell from the letter if the writer was a Remnant, and she must choose what to reveal carefully. When she was sure of her words, she dipped her quill and began to write.

Thank you for the wonderful letter. Since you spent precious time composing it, I felt it only fair that I should send a letter of my own in reply. I hope it does indeed brighten your day.

I have never been asked to be courted before, and I can hardly refuse when you employ the method to which I am most susceptible. I am flattered by your attentions and by your lovely words. Please consider this letter my consent. As a boon for giving my consent, I request a piece of information in return. Please tell me something about yourself.

I respect your desire to remain anonymous, for now, but I would like to know how I should address my letters to you. I look forward to continuing this correspondence. I will sign it with an old blessing my mother taught me that means "grace to you."

Charis,

Iris

Charis was the Greek word that was used as a salutation of welcome and leave-taking. It was an old-fashioned way to end a letter, but it felt right. Iris waited for the ink to dry, then rolled the parchment and tied it with the blue ribbon. She tucked the letter underneath the counter. She would put it out in the early evening when it was least likely to be disturbed but when there was till daylight enough for it to be seen.

The front door to the mail depot opened and the brass bell rang merrily, announcing the entrance of L.A. and Johnny.

"Good morning, Miss Iris. How are you this fine day?" L.A. stopped at the counter as Johnny went back to set up the checkerboard.

"I'm well, though I'm not sure I'd call a grey day like today fine. How are you?"

"Well, enough, I guess. I found a few late apples on one of my trees and brought you some." He laid a burlap sack on the counter. His blue eyes twinkled. "A gentleman should always bring gifts for a lady."

Iris took the sack and placed it on the end of the counter. "You better watch yourself. If your wife hears about all the flirting you do, you'll be in trouble."

L.A. shrugged. "How do you think I roped that little beauty in the first place? She couldn't resist my charms." He sighed dramatically. "She's a wonderful woman."

Iris laughed. "Go play checkers. I have some soup we can all have for lunch before I send you home."

Iris pulled another piece of paper from beneath the counter and made a list of families that needed a visit. In the fall, Reed and Marina visited every family in the valley and a few beyond. They made a note of which families might need extra food or other assistance once the snows set in and food was scarce. The harpies hunted extra game in the fall when the animals were fat for the winter and smoked the extra meat. It hung now in Dora's smokehouse, waiting to be distributed.

It had been a good year in Turning Creek, and Iris's list was short. Most of the families on the list had moved into the area too late to store what they needed for the winter. She noted how many people were in each family and what supplies they might need. Simon always donated oats and flour to the effort and James gave wheels of cheese to whomever needed it. The people of Turning Creek took care of each other in good times and bad.

If the weather was not too bad, the harpies could make deliveries next week. Delivering to the Remnant families was easy. The harpies flew to the homesteads and carried the supplies in their talons. Mortal families posed more of a problem. Reed and Marina made the deliveries to those families in a sleigh pulled by very ordinary horses. Those deliveries would have to wait until the weather cleared and Reed and Marina returned from Denver.

Iris ran her fingers over the list and what it represented: a change. Harpies who gave instead of took and who helped instead of burdened. No matter what else she accomplished in her life, she had this to be proud of. The surge of pride was accompanied by a desire to have all her birds under one roof where they could laugh together.

The spare room upstairs was empty often now. Petra stayed on the farm with James. Marina lived in the small apartment above the sheriff's office with Reed. Dora kept to herself when she was not helping Doc. Iris chuckled at herself for the happiness and sorrow she felt at the passing of time. This must be like what a mother feels when she looks at her toddler and realizes her child has grown into a woman. Her harpies were no longer fledglings in need of her constant care. The sharp pain of loss shook her anew. She missed her mother and her grand-meres. She missed her harpies. In a place surrounded by people who loved her, Iris felt very much alone.

CHAPTER 6

The following morning, there was no letter in the box to replace her own. The cold damp of the snow sunk into her woolen socks as she stared into the empty box. Iris swallowed her disappointment and told herself not to be a ninny. Letters had their own time. Time to be written. Time to be delivered. She knew this and yet the disappointment was still there, a heavy weight on her heart.

Iris went inside, leaving the snow and cold for the warmth of her rooms. Then, she remembered today was Saturday, and that meant Henry would be coming for dinner. A quiet happiness replaced her desire for a new letter. She scanned through her shelves. She had enough meat for stew. Iris went through the motions of her morning, making her bed, brewing tea, and picking up the new stack of books Thomas had left out. When the upstairs was as tidy as it could be, she went downstairs.

From under the counter, she pulled her own leather journal and opened it to a blank page. It had been a month since she had updated the history of her own harpies, and she had Petra's news to record. The writing consumed her and she lost track of time.

A prickling on her neck made her look up from the paper. Someone was coming. The bell above the door rang and a familiar form came through the door. Henry's wide shoulders blocked the weak winter light from the outside until he closed the door and shut it out completely. A woolen cap and scarf covered most of his face. Only his serious grey eyes were visible. The corners of his eyes were crinkled with a smile she could not see.

"Good morning, Henry. I had not thought to see you until tonight."

Henry's large hands unwound the plain brown scarf, revealing his face by inches. His face, like most of the men in the winter, was covered with a short, dark beard. He bestowed a rare wide smile on her. "Good morning, Miss Iris. How are you today?"

"Enjoying the day."

Henry took off his woolen cap and ran a hand through his dark, curly hair. "It's always best to enjoy the day we are given, no matter what it brings."

"Well said. What can I do for you?" she asked.

"I'm shoveling the snow off the boardwalk and I was wondering if young Thomas was available to help."

Iris looked out the window. Steady snow floated past the window. She looked at Henry again. "It's still snowing." She cocked an eyebrow at him. "Have you been shoveling snow all morning?"

"Only this side of Main Street, and I thought it best to get some of the snow out of the way before more came."

"I'm not sure if that is smart or idiotically futile. By yourself?"

Those wide shoulders went up and down. "It's not that different from wielding the hammer."

"I let Thomas sleep in. He's still in bed, but it's long past time for him to get up. I'll go wake him." Iris came around the counter and motioned to the pot-bellied stove in the back of the room. "Go warm yourself up."

Iris laid a hand on Henry's arm. She felt him stiffen at her touch and then slowly relax by degrees. "Thank you for shoveling the boardwalk. It's very kind of you to think of it. I'll be right back."

Iris went upstairs and thought about Henry, who lived alone. He held himself rigidly when he was touched and seemed uncomfortable when she touched him. Iris had seen Marina hug the blacksmith before, but could not recall anyone else doing so. She wondered how often people who lived alone were touched by others. She had lived alone above the depot before she had adopted Thomas, but there was always a harpy or someone underfoot. As churlish as the harpies were, they were very affectionate with each other and with her.

Iris knocked before going into Thomas's room. His clothes were hung neatly on the pegs and folded on a shelf below the wall pegs, but everything else in the room embodied various stages of chaos. Books, papers, a map of the region, and his gun lay in a pile on the nightstand. Iris had resisted the gun, but Marina had been firm that Thomas should be armed when out on his own rounds. He did not have claws to defend himself. Only his wits, the harpy had said.

Iris stepped over a plate and a cup to stand beside the bed. Blond, tousled hair was the only part of him visible. Unexpected tenderness made her reach out and smooth down the tuft of hair. Iris shook the lump under the covers. "Thomas, rise and shine." The lump groaned. "You've slept in long enough. Henry wants you to help him shovel the boardwalk."

The covers moved up and down with a sigh. "All right."

"Get dressed and come down for some food. Don't dally too long.

Henry will be waiting on you."

Thomas sat up and rubbed his eyes. "Morning. I'll be down soon."

Iris ruffled his hair. "Good morning to you too, though it's nearly noon."

She fingered the letter in her pocket while she went back down the stairs. Henry had never been anything but friendly and polite to her, but she wondered if the letter could be from him. Iris walked over to the stove. Henry stood directly in the front of the fire, but shifted to make room for her.

Iris felt the heat from his presence like another fire. He held himself a few inches away from touching her. "Have you eaten anything?"

"Not since early this morning."

"Thomas will be down soon, but you have time for a scone and some tea if you want."

Henry shifted his weight from his right foot to his left. Iris wondered if his foot was bothering him. "I don't want to impose," he said.

Iris looked at the blacksmith and the way his talented hands twisted his stocking cap. She made up her mind to get him out and around people more often. Saturday nights alone with her and Thomas were not enough. Marina and Petra often visited Henry, but Iris was certain he did not entertain other visitors besides the people who came for his services.

Iris dismissed his protest with a wave. "Your presence is never an imposition. I have some fresh molasses rounds for you. You can have some instead of scones if you'd like."

The smile on Henry's face transformed his face into something Iris would almost call boyish. "Well, now. Wouldn't do to say no to biscuits. Though if you feed me biscuits every time I come in here, I'll be too round to fit in the door."

Iris returned his smile and laughed. "I promise not to bribe you to stay with biscuits too often or you'll stay away, and I do enjoy your company."

"The company is worth whatever hazard too many biscuits might cause." Henry's hands were back to twisting his cap.

Iris was unsure if his comment was Henry being polite or Henry flirting. Either way, she was happy he agreed to stay. She enjoyed Henry's quiet company.

Henry shifted again. "I finished the board you wanted for posting messages. I'll bring it tonight when I come for dinner." He looked unsure for a moment. "That is, unless you've had enough of me for one day."

Iris elbowed him in the side. "If you were anyone else, I'd say you were fishing for a compliment. I like having you here on Saturdays. If you don't come, I'll march down Main Street and drag you here myself."

The idea of a woman half his size dragging him bodily through town must have amused him. He laughed and Iris felt the sound of it crackle over her skin. Iris stepped back, seeking distance. She led him over to the counter and gave him the promised tea and biscuits.

"I do have one request, though," he said.

"What would that be?"

The smile faded from his mouth but his eyes still shone. "I would like to be the first to post something. The valley is growing by leaps and bounds. I need an assistant, someone to do some of the easier tasks, like shoeing and simple repairs, so I can spend more time doing delicate work. One day, I hope to have a son or daughter who will take over and become my true apprentice, but for now, I just need an extra set of hands." His eyes stayed on his food while he made the statement.

Clomping footsteps on the stairs heralded Thomas's appearance. Iris turned to the young man when he entered the room.

"There are scones and tea here. Come join us," she said.

Thomas flopped onto a stool next to Henry and pulled the rest of the plate of scones towards himself. "Are there deliveries today?" he asked around bites.

"Just some around town. The weather looks too bad for that, though. I'll do them tomorrow once the snow settles. We need to do some longer range deliveries outside of town soon, including a supply run for those that need it."

Iris wanted to go flying. If the snow was still heavy on the ground, she could at least make some deliveries to Remnant families. The mortal families would have to wait.

Thomas took the remains of lunch and the dishes upstairs. Iris ran her hands over the slots behind her desk, moving letters around. She could feel the warm pressure of Henry's eyes on her back while she performed the task. When she turned around, he colored and looked at his hands.

Iris had the sudden urge to walk around the counter and touch him. Instead, she grabbed a small bundle of molasses biscuits she had wrapped up for him and walked over to where he stood.

"Here. Take these." Iris's fingers brushed his palm as she laid the bundle in Henry's large hand. His fingers twitched before closing over the worn, blue rag. "Thank you for clearing the boardwalk and for getting Thomas out of the house. He has the impatience and energy of the young. Being cooped up inside is hard on him. And me."

Henry tucked the biscuits into one of the pockets of his jacket. "Someone's got to do the job, and I've got the time. Thank you for the biscuits, Miss Iris."

Iris laid a hand on his arm and was pleased that he did not stiffen at her touch this time. "Henry, you know you can call me Iris."

Warm grey eyes twinkled at her. "I do know that."

"But you won't, will you?"

"No, ma'am."

Iris sighed and handed him his woolen scarf from the peg. "Get out of here then. Go shovel some snow."

Iris looked out the window at the steel grey clouds and the white puffs falling from them. "It looks like the snow won't stop anytime soon," she said. "You'll have to do all the shoveling again tomorrow."

"There's no end to any work. Doesn't change the fact that it has to be done." His deep voice was muffled through the layers of fabric.

"Tomorrow, come get Thomas before you get too far down the boardwalk. It was nice to have you stop by. I'll see you later for dinner."

Henry inclined his head. "Thank you, Miss Iris."

She scowled at him for the polite use of her name and, though she could not see his mouth, the corners of his eyes crinkled with a smile. Iris took a step closer to him, though she was not sure what pulled her forward.

Thomas, bundled up and ready for work, breezed between them and the moment snapped away. "I bet I can shovel snow as fast as I deliver letters," he boasted as he went out.

Iris laughed. "Good luck keeping up with him, I'm glad he can exhaust you for a change instead of me."

"I promise to return him properly tired after a day's hard work." Henry walked through the door.

Iris watched him as he picked up the shovel leaning against the outside wall of the depot and followed Thomas. She stayed there, in the open door, letting in the frigid February air as Henry crossed to the other side of Main Street. His stride was confident, despite his limp, and Iris could not look away from the grace of his movements. When he reached the other side of the street, he glanced back at her where she remained, staring. He paused when he saw her, tipped his hat to her, and bent to his work.

CHAPTER 7

The snow continued unabated through the rest of the afternoon. Mrs. Stewart had been right about the snow, though it had come days later than Iris had anticipated. Iris busied herself by writing a reply to her mother's letter.

Iris thanked her mother for sending a speedy reply. She wrote that while she agreed with her mother's assessment of the cause of the changes in her harpies, there were still unanswered questions. Why them? Why now? What would be the lasting effects of Petra and Marina's choice to take a mate, to live beside him and commit to him heart and soul? Would the generations that came after follow this pattern or revert back to a life of solitude and violence?

Iris rubbed the end of the quill over her lips and frowned over the letter. She had filled an entire page with questions and worry. Her mother and grand-mere would think she spent her days wringing her hands and fretting over every trifle.

Iris laughed at herself. *It isn't that far from the truth,* she thought. To prove to herself that she did more than fret, Iris concluded her letter with news of her harpies.

You will be pleased to know that Petra and James are expecting a daughter in the summer. A new generation is beginning even as we lose the oldest and wisest among us. How I wish great-grand-mere would have lived long enough to share my joy in this. By the time you receive this letter, another will have found its way to you regarding Marina settling down with Reed Brant. She has met her match in her choice of mates and he balances her in the same way James tempers Petra. I do not think it will be too many months before Marina has a daughter of her own on the way as well. I believe in time Dora will also be settled. I think she wants the same path her sisters have chosen. She does not know how to get there, but she is more patient than the other two and will take her time.

I know your next concern will be for me, given Petra's news. With Petra and Marina settled and content, it is time for me to see about the continuation of my own line. I have long had my own wings over my eyes, so focused was I on my harpies, as was right. I have felt a pressing loneliness more often of late and I think it is my own desire to expand my family beyond the harpies and Thomas.

You will be happy to know that I am currently being courted by an anonymous letter writer. As you can guess, his plot of using my own affinity against me has met with great results. There is also a miller, new to the area, who has become friendly recently. I believe my letter writer and Jacob Wells, the miller, are one and the same.

He seems kind, and I look forward to getting to know him more. The only drawback to his suit is that he is a mortal and does not yet know of our existence. I know you were very happy with Father, though I remember how hard it was when he died. He was a gentle man in a house dominated by women. I am not yet sure if Jacob Wells is as forbearing a man as Father.

There is one other, but I am, as yet, unsure about my feelings and his. Just rest easy, knowing it is unlikely I will die as an old maid. Whomever I settle on, I will have a house that is always full of loud harpies and Thomas, who is now easily taller than me. I blink and the boy grows a foot. It makes me happy to see him flourishing and yet makes my heart ache at how quickly it happens.

But I am getting ahead of myself and must enjoy each day as it comes. I wish you could be here to see the mountains. I wish with all my heart you could fly over them with me. Know that I think of you often and love you dearly.

Charis,
Your Loving Daughter, Iris

Iris dried the ink and folded the parchment. Spuds would leave as soon as he was able, and Iris wanted her mother's letter to go with him.

A gust of wind rattled the windows, and Iris looked up from her task. The sunlight was obscured by a murky grey sky. A glance around the room made Iris realize how dark it had gotten while she'd worked on her letter. She lit the lamp on the corner of the counter and the warm light filled the space. She pulled her shawl tighter around her shoulders and went to stand by the window.

The snow fell steady and thick. Iris could see the saloon across the street, but barely. There was stomping outside the door, then it opened to admit Thomas and a swirl of snow into the warmth of the depot.

Thomas shook himself, sending ice and snow flying. "We had to stop shoveling. Henry sent me home. The snow's coming down faster than we could shovel it."

Iris took his jacket and scarf from him. "Go warm yourself by the fire. There's warm cider on the stove." She had put enough for three in the pot, hoping Henry might stop at the depot when the work was finished.

Iris shook out Thomas's jacket and hung it on a peg. She looked out the window, but she could see nothing but white. Iris went to join Thomas by the stove, which radiated heat into the room. She poured herself a cup of cider and sat in a chair.

Heavy snow always carried dangers. People got lost in the snow all the time. A man could set out to check on the animals in the barn during a storm and be found ten feet from his destination when the snow stopped. Buildings collapsed under the weight of wet snow. Any number of things could happen.

"You're worried over something," Thomas remarked.

Iris gave him a weak smile. "I seem to spend a great deal of my time in worry."

"Worrying over a thing doesn't make it easier. It just makes the time leading up to it worse." Thomas's green eyes were wiser than his years.

Iris eyed him shrewdly. "Henry's rubbing off on you." It was not a bad thing.

Thomas shrugged and mumbled into his cup. "My mother wasted a lot of time worrying, and it never put food in my belly or saved her from Zeus."

Acute pain for the losses he had endured pierced Iris. She put her cup down and kneeled in front of the boy and held his hands. "I'm sorry, Thomas. Part of my nature is to look after the harpies, and a certain amount of worry naturally comes with that. I'm sorry if it upsets you. I feel the futility of it and yet I find myself doing it regardless."

Thomas squeezed her hand. "My mother was a good woman, but weak. You have a backbone she never possessed."

Iris smiled. "Keeping up with Marina requires a certain amount of gumption."

Thomas smiled, the wise sage gone and the youth back in place. "I'm thankful to be here with you. I feel at home here and I care about you. It makes me sad to see you worry, is all."

It was more talk than she usually got out of him. Iris hugged Thomas. "I love you too. I'll try harder to worry less, for you."

Thomas nodded and finished his cider. "Can I read until dinner?"

"Of course. We'll eat when Henry gets here." *If he gets here*, she thought as a gust of wind rattled the windows in the front of the depot.

Iris tried her best to keep her new promise to Thomas, but the howl of the wind and the snow that piled up over the next couple of hours made it difficult. After she was done prepping dinner and it sat warming on the stove, Iris tried reading the journal her mother had sent. It did little to distract her. If anything, it made the waiting worse. With a sound of disgust, Iris snapped the book closed and went down the stairs.

The fire in the stove downstairs had been allowed to burn down low.

Iris took a small stick from the box by the stove, pulled the handle on the door, and lit the end of the twig in the flames. She carried it with care to the lamp on the edge of the counter and lit the lamp. Once the wick was well lit, she turned up the lamp and placed it the large front window of the depot. If Henry was struggling through the snow, she wanted him to have some beacon to follow, a lighthouse in the snow.

That task accomplished, Iris paced around the room at a loss. Every time she walked close to the window, the band around her chest tightened. She took a deep breath, willing the worry down. On her twentieth circuit of the room she pressed her nose to the cold glass, but she could see nothing but inky blackness. She continued pacing.

She had lost count when the door swung open and slammed against the wall. The bell was drowned in the sound of the wind as a wide-shouldered bundle turned and wrestled the door closed. The door latched and Henry stood, back to the door and chest heaving. Her relief at seeing him was acute. The bands of worry were replaced by a sweet relief.

Iris stalked over to him and placed her hands on his forearms. She felt him shivering with cold. This close, she had to crane her neck to see his face. "You should not have come in this storm. I would never have forgiven myself if something had happened to you."

"I'm sorry. I didn't bring your new bulletin board. I was afraid the wind would rip it away." His usual smooth voice was ragged.

Iris tried to shake him, but it was like trying to move a tree. "Idiot man. I could care less about the board. You could have lost your way and been frozen like ice. You're shaking like a leaf."

Henry's breathing returned to normal and he straightened. "Nothing but a bit of snow. It's a straight shot down the boardwalk. The worst part was crossing the street without the buildings to guide me. Your light in the window helped. I nearly overshot the door until I could make out the light through the snow. I told you I would be here, and so here I am."

Iris realized she still held on to him. She released his arm and muttered, "Foolish." She smiled at him. "I'm glad you did not freeze to death. Take off your scarf and coat. You can have some of Marina's whiskey to warm up. She keeps a bottle upstairs."

Henry took off his scarf, hat, and coat. "Whiskey would be welcome."

Iris settled Henry in front of the stove upstairs and gave him some warmed cider braced with whiskey. His fingers were blue and his nose was red. He closed his eyes and sipped the cider. Iris watched him. Henry safe and warming by her fire gave her peace and put her worry to rest. She worried over those she cared for.

Iris opened the pot on the stove. The smell of rosemary and chicken curled around her nose. She ladled soup into bowls and called Thomas to the table. They ate the first part of the meal in silence.

When Henry was halfway through his serving, he said, "This reminds me of soup my mother used to make on nights like this. She tried to teach me to cook, but it was hard to drag me from the forge."

"It was my great-grand-mere's recipe. My sister, Katina, was always a better cook than me and spent whatever time she was allowed cooking with great-grand-mere." Iris had not thought of her sisters or brother for months, and sadness touched her at their memory.

Henry eyed her. "You do not often speak of your siblings. Are they still alive?"

Iris stirred her soup. "No, they had mortal life spans like my father. Their children live in a village not far from where my mother and grand-mere live. I believe they visit occasionally."

Thomas finished his soup and rose to get more. "Do you miss your family?"

Iris knew he was thinking of his mother, whose loss was still new. "I do sometimes think of them, but I do not miss them the way you mean. As soon as I was born, The Messenger's mark was plain on my back. I was set aside from that moment. I lived separate from the rest of my family, with my grand-mere and great-grand-mere. I never had a chance to form a strong bond with my sisters and brother. I cared for them, but I did not love them the way I love the harpies." Iris smiled at Thomas as he sat back down with a steaming bowl. "Or you. My true family is here. The longer I live, the more I learn that family encompasses many more than those with whom you share blood ties."

Henry used a piece of bread to sop up the last of his soup. "I was an only child, but I was set apart at a young age too. My mother lost three other children soon after birth, and so she spoiled me. My father didn't always approve, but he indulged her as long as it didn't interfere with my work."

"I don't remember my father. He died before I was born. My mom said she knew the moment I was born that I would be of the line of Achilles like him," Thomas said.

"She would be very proud of you." Iris stood to put her bowl on the counter and squeezed Thomas's shoulder.

Henry joined her at the counter. "Let me help with the dishes."

Iris pointed to a bucket of water. "I had Thomas bring in water before the storm got bad. Pour some of that in the basin."

Henry washed and Iris dried the bowls and placed them back on the shelf. A gust of wind rattled the window.

Iris put the last spoon away. "Thomas, will you run downstairs and see how bad the snow is?"

Thomas went clomping down the stairs. Henry wrung out the rag and took the towel from Iris to dry his hands.

"I know what you're thinking," he said.

Iris thinned her lips into a line. "You do seem to have a knack for reading my mind."

"I got here. I can get home."

The familiar bands of worry tightened. "It's darker now, and there will be no lamp in a window to guide you."

Thomas came back up the stairs. "The front and back door are half-covered. The snow is still coming down thick."

Iris put her hands on her hips and used her tone of voice she used on the harpies when they were being particularly stubborn. She hoped it worked on blacksmiths the same way. "Henry Foster, there is no way in any circle of hell I am letting you leave the depot tonight. I have an empty room with three empty beds. You can stay here until the morning. Hopefully, by then, the snow will be done and you can make your way home in the daylight."

Henry hesitated. Iris thought she would have to try again, but he cut off her protest. "I can see you'll blister my ear off if I argue and I know you'd worry yourself sick if I left. I'll stay if it means that much to you. Even Marina obeys when you use that tone. I'd be a fool not to listen."

The tension in her shoulders relaxed. "Thank you." Iris grinned. "Since you are going to stay, would you like to share some spiced wine?"

"I think that's an excellent way to spend a night like this," he said.

Thomas gave Iris a hopeful look and she laughed. "Don't even think about. If Marina was here, she might slip you some, but I won't."

Thomas looked crestfallen. "I'm going to read in my room. Can I take the lamp?"

Iris ruffled his hair. "Yes, the light from the fire will be enough for us. Not too long, though. I don't want you straining your eyes."

Thomas took the lamp, and Iris turned to Henry. Grey eyes watched her. An awareness of his presence washed over her and heat crept up her neck and face. She hoped the room was dark enough to hide her flaming cheeks. This was an inconvenient time for her to remember Henry was not only her friend, but a man. She squashed down the realization.

Iris cleared her throat. "If you put another log in the stove, I will go and make up one of the beds for you in the extra room."

Iris left to perform her task. The motions of pulling the sheets from the cedar chest in the harpies' room and putting them over the mattress gave her time to put her wayward thoughts to rights. She folded an extra blanket on top of the bed. The stove would keep the upstairs of the depot warm, but it would still be a cold night. Iris wanted Henry to be cozy and comfortable.

Unbidden, Iris thought of another way for Henry to stay warm on a long, cold night. Iris slapped a pillow into place on the bed as if she could beat her mind into submission. Henry had never given her any indication that he desired anything from her other than friendship. She was letting her own concerns over continuing her line see things that were not there.

When she returned to the main room, Henry was sitting in front of the stove with his elbows on his knees. He did not know she was there, and she watched the firelight on his face. Iris admired his strong jaw and cheekbones. It was difficult for her to stay on the side of the line she had drawn herself when he looked like that. Whatever he was thinking about made him smile, and Iris felt her own face echo the movement.

She moved into his line of sight. "What are you smiling about?"

Henry straightened and his smile slipped. "I was thinking about you fussing over me and how you are happier when you have a reason to fuss."

Iris got the wine and spices out and dumped them in the kettle. "You have me all figured out."

Henry sat back in his chair. "I wouldn't say that, but I do notice things."

She rather hoped he noticed less than usual tonight or she was in danger of scaring her friend away. It had taken her long enough to get Henry this at ease in her company.

Iris sat in the chair opposite Henry. The chairs were closer to the fire than each other. His eyes were dark in this light and they shone with the smile his lips did not make. Iris pulled her own gaze away and looked into the fire, but she tracked his movements out of the corner of her eyes.

Henry rubbed a hand over his beard. "You said you were separated from the rest of your family early for training. Did you ever miss them growing up?"

Iris considered the question. It was not one she had been asked by anyone, even her mother. "I'm not sure missing them would be entirely accurate. I lived apart from them, but I saw them often. They were more like cousins or distant relatives to me than siblings in some ways, especially when I watched them get older and live out their mortal lives."

Henry leaned his elbows onto his knees. "I missed running through the fields and woods with the other kids in the village. I would see them running down the street with their hair matted by a day in the woods, and I envied them their freedom."

Something long buried surfaced in Iris, and Henry's words touched the heart of it. "I never regret my calling, but when I was young I longed to spend a day without the burden of it."

"Sometimes the largest burdens come with the greatest blessings." Henry's voice was lower than the cry of the wind and Iris had to lean towards him to hear it. These were the words of the sage she knew so well.

"You always say the wisest things at the right time." Iris turned her head to smile at him, but his gaze remained focused on the fire. "Do you ever regret your calling, especially since it comes with certain physical challenges?"

Iris had never mentioned Henry's club foot before, though she knew it pained him. Her heart was loud in her ears as she worried that she had crossed a line with him. The lump in her throat grew with the silence and Iris started composing an apology in her head.

Henry rubbed his leg absently. "No would be a simple answer, though few things are simple. I have a special padding in my shoe, which eases the pain of standing for so long, but it never goes away. It's a reminder of my burden. Not unlike the pain of your wing birthmark before Zeus made them real and you fulfilled your need to fly. My foot doesn't keep me from the calling I love or from being content."

Iris got up and opened the lid of the kettle to check the wine. The smell of mulling spices added a sweet tang to the dryness of the wine. She pulled two mugs off the shelf and filled them with the warm liquid.

Iris handed Henry a cup. "Careful. It'll be hot."

"Thank you."

Iris blew on her wine. The bite of the spices made her mouth twinge as she took her first tentative sip. "Some afternoons, after a long history lesson from grand-mere, I would long to do normal chores, but I knew that having a calling was a blessing. There was never any doubt in my mind that I was made by the gods to be The Messenger. There's a peace to knowing you are doing the right thing at the right time. It made up for all the time spent away from my siblings and father. I wish all choices were as easy to know and follow."

"Idleness and lack of direction send people down the wrong path. We're fortunate, I think, to have always known what we would be." Henry sipped his wine. "This is good. Thank you."

This was the most open conversation she had had in a long time. Iris usually listened. This conversation felt more like a give and take.

"And yet we were not given a choice," she said.

Henry drank his wine and frowned into it. "No, though I can't think of another place where I'd be happy except in the mountains with the people here. It's a good life and I know I'm needed."

Iris looked at his profile as he stared into the fire, resolutely watching its dance while she watched him. He was needed, she realized, by her. He was as important to her as one of the harpies or Thomas. Something liquid uncurled within her as her eyes traveled over his strong nose, high cheekbones, and long lashes. His presence became a radiation of heat stronger than the fire.

Iris looked away and chastised herself. This was Henry, of all people, and he had never shown her any interest in that way. He treated her the way he treated Marina and Petra. She blushed at the place her thoughts had led her, to a place she had not been invited.

There was a whisper of cloth as Henry shifted in his chair. "I do wish sometimes that I held more answers about some things than I do, but I never wish for more choice."

The truthfulness of the answer reverberated in her soul. Answers, books, and writing were the things that drove her. Iris turned back to him and started to see that he had turned his body towards hers. "I have spent so much of my life reading and looking for answers to questions about all manner of things. Half the time, I feel like I'm still floundering around, a fish who accidentally hopped up onto the bank of the river."

Henry drained his cup. "That's an apt description, though I'd never describe you as floundering."

Iris gestured with her almost empty one. "Would you like more?"

"I've nowhere else to go and it's been a long time since I had the opportunity for a late night chat."

Iris suppressed her smile and took his cup. "A long time?"

Henry spread his hands. "Honestly, I've never sat up late to talk by a fire with anyone."

His words were melancholy and renewed Iris's conviction that asking him to stay had been right. "I admit I've had more opportunities than I'd prefer to stay up late. Marina and Petra can be long winded, especially when they're working their way through a bottle of whiskey."

Henry chuckled low, and Iris's hands paused in their work as she listened to the sound. She took a deep breath and finished pouring the last of the wine into the two cups. When she passed Henry his cup, her fingers met his and she ignored the tingling the contact left in them.

Iris cradled her cup. "I've been wondering about something, and I think we're good enough friends that I can ask, but I don't want you to tell me more than you want to."

Henry leaned back in his chair. "You did say you liked searching for answers. You can ask me anything you'd like and I'll answer if I'm able."

Remnants did not often share their secrets, and Iris would never ask another Remnant such a personal question about their line, but this was Henry. She trusted Henry and there was something she wanted to know. The words rushed out before she could reconsider. "Last year, you told Petra the fire in your forge on the mountain was part of the fire from the forge of Hephaestus on Mount Olympus. I've noticed that there are days you do not light the forge in your shop, so where do you keep the original flame? How has it been maintained and passed down all these years?"

Henry stilled, and Iris was sure she had faltered and damaged something between them. Her lungs contracted. Her chest cracked as she watched him, silent and unmoving, certain her questions had crossed a line.

When Henry finally moved, Iris jumped. He placed his cup down on the table without a sound. Iris steeled herself for the sight of him leaving.

Instead, he turned to face her.

"That was more than one question."

Iris's breath was shaky with relief. "I'm so sorry. I never should've…"

Henry held up a hand to stop her. "I trust you and I know you. Curiosity is part of your calling, and you mean no malice by it. I know you write things down, but I'd ask you not to commit this to paper."

Iris licked her lips and leaned forward. "I won't write it down."

"Before the last battle during the uprising, Hephaestus took an ember from his forge and melded it to his soul. He knew part of his magic came from that fire. That essence became the filament of power that is passed down from each generation. My forge does not always have to be kept burning because I carry the fire within me. I am the forge."

The last four words landed with power and the fire in her stove blazed. Iris's blood raced as it did when she discovered something new in a book she was reading. It bubbled over into a wide grin. "That's amazing." He was amazing. The words fell woefully short. She squeezed her hands around her mug. "Thank you for trusting me."

Henry looked away from her and into the fire, which had resumed its normal height. "It's nice to tell someone a secret sometimes. You can forget what a burden they are after so long keeping them hidden."

Iris wanted desperately to ask what else Henry was hiding. "Every Remnant becomes good at keeping secrets at an early age. I've kept my fair share as well, most of them not my own."

"I know you hold many secrets close, as you'll hold the one I've given. You never know, maybe it will come in handy to you one day."

Iris gripped her nearly empty cup harder to keep her hands still. "If I ever get tired of starting my own fires, I know who to call."

Henry turned his cup in his hands. "I think I'd best get to bed. It will be a long day of shoveling tomorrow, and I've kept you up late enough."

The disappointment was swift. Iris swallowed it down. She was not ready for this time to be over. She finished her wine and took his cup. Iris looped a finger through both handles and carried them to the counter.

The sound of Henry standing turned her around, and then she did what she had been wanting to do for some time. Iris laid a hand on Henry's arm. It was solid and warm and she squeezed her fingers. She felt him go rigid, as he often did when touched. Her fingers burned with the contact.

"Thank you for indulging me and staying the night. I would have worried over you." She dropped her hand and stood looking at him. Waiting.

He broke the moment by taking a step back, away from her and towards the extra room. "It's nice to be worried over now and then. Good night, Miss Iris."

"Good night, Henry. Leave the door open to let the warm air in. I'm going to bank the fire and then turn in myself."

Iris was unable to rid herself easily of the disappointment and frustration she felt at the evening's ending. She turned around so he would not see the look on her face, and busied her hands removing the kettle from the top of the stove and rinsing it out with water. Iris tried to ignore the sound of Henry walking into his room and the rustle of the mattress as he sat on the bed. She heard his boots hit the floor and she clenched the edge of the counter.

By degrees, she let go and knelt in front of the stove to add logs to the fire. Her face reflected the heat of the fire until her cheeks burned with it. Iris closed the door to the belly of the stove, yet remained on her knees. She had to get her feelings, or whatever it was that had pulled her towards Henry tonight, under control. There had been many opportunities for him to indicate he was even the least bit interested, and each had passed as they always did. They were friends and nothing more. She was lucky to count him as that. *No sense in being greedy*, she thought.

To get to her room, she had to walk past the extra room with the open door where Henry sat. She moved briskly to her room, but she chanced a glance into the dim light of Henry's room. He sat with his elbows on his knees and his head in his hands. Iris's feet stumbled. She found her footing and continued on into her room without stopping. She closed the door behind her and slumped into it.

She should have stopped and asked him what burdened him, but she had already pushed and prodded him tonight into places he had never shared before. She did not want to push too far. Iris pictured Henry again, bent over with his hands over his face, and she wanted to go to him, run her hands through the curls on his head, and kiss his brow. Her hands twitched with the need and her heart ached.

With heavy determination, Iris changed into her winter sleeping gown and opened the door. She crawled into her own bed and lay still, listening. She strained for a long time for sounds from Henry's room. She fell asleep, hearing nothing except the occasional crack of the fire and the whining of the wind outside.

CHAPTER 8

Iris opened her eyes. It was dark and quiet. There was no howl of the wind or creaking of timbers. Iris pulled the covers down and the cold air in the room tickled her nose. The wood had burned down in the fire, leaving the rooms cold. There was no sound from the other two rooms.

She considered staying in bed. Iris moved her legs back and forth under the covers, feeling the coldest corners of the bed, and wondered if it was worth it to get up. Her bladder made the decision for her. With a deep breath for fortitude, she threw off the covers and swung her legs out of bed. After using the chamber pot under the bed, she padded from her room and into the kitchen.

The coals in the stove were still red, and Iris coaxed them back into life with some small sticks. The flames licked over the wood and grew. Iris fed it and watched as it crackled and popped in the silence. She turned to look out the window to look for evidence of the sunrise. The black of night was broken in the east by grey, a herald of the day to come. Iris went back to her room and pulled her favorite quilt off the foot of her bed. The red flowers looked black in the darkness. She wrapped the familiar weight around her shoulders and settled herself onto the couch to watch the sun rise over the mountains.

The tempered grey spread into the dark blue of the sky and became streaked with orange and red. The faces of the mountains Iris could see were cast in shadow by the approaching sun. She sat, in her warm cocoon, until the rim of the burning yellow crested the peaks and the day washed over piles of shining snow. It was an ordinary sunrise in the Rockies, but Iris never tired of seeing it.

There was shuffling and movement behind her that held more weight than Thomas. Iris held herself still and waited to see what Henry would do. It was too late for her to go get dressed and appear more decent for him.

Iris fiddled with the end of her braid and waited.

Iris could feel him as he came closer and she turned her face from the window. His curls were a little wild, though it looked like he had tried to tame them, and his shirt was neatly tucked in. Henry looked as he always did, solid. He hesitated on the backside of the couch, looking down on her with an expression she could not name.

"Good morning. I was just watching the sunrise. Will you join me for a few minutes?" Iris scooted her feet closer to her body to make room and patted the open space.

Henry walked around and sat as far away from her on the small couch as he could. He looked out the window at the bright orange painting the sky and said nothing. Iris kept her eyes on him. The early light played over his face and Iris caught her breath.

She must have made a sound because Henry turned to her. "Sunrise is a beautiful time of day."

He was only a couple of feet away from her. His eyes, which she had always thought to be a lovely grey, were shot with shards of blue. They were looking at her as if he expected her to say something. With a jolt, she realized she had been staring.

Iris pulled her blanket tighter around herself as if she could keep her thoughts in that way. "Would you like coffee or tea this morning?"

Henry eased back on the couch. "I can take either. At home, I switch back and forth depending on the day, but there's no need to rush. You were enjoying the sunrise and I can make tea."

"You're my guest, Henry. You shouldn't have to serve yourself while I lounge and do nothing," she replied.

"But I'm your friend who has been here enough to know you keep the tea on the second shelf to the left and the coffee right next to that." Henry leaned closer to her as he spoke, the blue in his eyes dancing.

This easygoing version of Henry was all the jolt she needed in the morning to start any day off right. "Have it your way. Make tea. However, I will not sit here like a lump. I'll make eggs. There's bread for toast and jam. I need to put on clothes first. I can't spend all day in my night rail and a quilt."

Henry did not smile at her words as she had intended. He leaned back into the couch as if he had just noticed she was tousled from sleep and not in her clothes, though he had been sitting by her for a handful of minutes. Iris swung her stockinged feet out from under her blanket and stood up. Henry continued to watch her but said nothing.

A prick of irritation burst the lightness of the moments before. "I'll be out in a few minutes," she said. "Feel free to start the water for tea."

Iris went into her room, closed the door, and threw the quilt on the bed. She yanked the sheets up on the bed, tucking them up under her pillows.

The blankets and quilts followed, all receiving similarly harsh yanks and pulls. She folded the poppy quilt, laid it on the end of the bed, and sat down.

She was frustrated with Henry, but she was more frustrated at herself. First last night, and then again this morning, she had wanted Henry to act differently with her. Henry was predictable. Like the mountains she had watched this morning, he was rugged, solid, and unmoved by the fluttering of awareness he had recently inspired in her. This was the last time she was going to indulge in a tantrum or make a fool of herself. He was her friend, nothing more.

That settled, Iris got dressed. She chose a set of warm stockings and pulled pants over them. Today would be a day of work in the snow, and she did not want to drag around the weight of wet skirts. She tucked a blouse into the pants and pulled a soft, blue-grey sweater over her head. Iris pulled her pale hair out of its braid and pulled a brush through it before re-braiding it.

Henry did not turn around when she walked out of her room. He was busy at the stove. The soft crackle and smell of cooking eggs filled the small kitchen. Iris stopped so that she was just close enough to almost touch Henry's broad back. She peered around his side. The kettle was on one burner and the pan of eggs on another.

"I thought I was supposed to make the eggs," she said.

Henry paused then flipped the eggs over. "My hands were idle, and I can cook eggs."

"I think I have some pancakes from yesterday, unless Thomas ate them." Iris flipped over a towel covering a basket on the shelf. "We're in luck. There are about," she counted the stack, "seven left. Just enough to go with the eggs." She pulled out the pancakes and placed them on the back of the stove to warm.

Iris set aside some of the eggs and reserved two of the pancakes for Thomas before placing the rest of the food on the table. Henry took cups from the shelf and poured them tea. Moving around her kitchen doing the mundane tasks of the morning with Henry settled her.

"What're your plans for today?" he asked her after taking a few bites.

"I was thinking of flying out to the Nasso farm. Pearl's pretty isolated up there in the winter, and she might need some supplies. I have a letter for her."

Henry took a sip of coffee. "Did she tell you she was thinking of farming lavender?"

"Yes, at Winter Solstice. I told her fields of lavender sounded lovely."

"I made a small copper and tin still for her to distill the lavender. It's not too heavy. She wanted it as soon as possible, but with the snow, I'll be hard pressed to get it there. Would you be able to carry it?"

She had never carried much weight at all when flying, mostly just letters and small packages. "I was going to take her some flour and oats, but I can reduce my load by taking less and sending Marina once she gets back."

Henry's lips quirked up in his almost smile. "Marina has taken a shine to that girl, and Pearl needs a bit of tending."

Iris's mouth curved up to finish the smile Henry started. "After what happened last fall, I'm glad Marina took her under her wing of her own accord. I would have encouraged her that way if she hadn't. Marina has a heart for the lost, though she'd never admit it, and Pearl needed support from someone she respected."

"It might take a bit for me to get back to my cabin through the snow and get back here. Can you delay your trip until then?"

"I'm not in a hurry," she replied. "There's plenty to do around here, and I plan on helping with some of the shoveling."

"Good." Henry finished his food and then sat at the table and waited for her to finish.

"Leave the dishes," she said, waving her hand. "Thomas does them in the morning as payment for sleeping later than I do and having breakfast made for him. I'll wake him up when you leave and send him out to help once he eats."

"I'd best get going then."

"I'll walk you out."

Henry followed her down the stairs, a solid presence at her back. She went behind the counter and pulled Pearl's letter out of its slot. She grabbed her leather satchel from under the counter and placed the letter in it.

Henry had put on his jacket and was in the process of winding his scarf around his neck when he cocked his head slightly to the side. "How do you know where the letters go? Your slots are not labeled as far as I can tell."

Iris walked around the counter to stand in front of him. She did not want the counter between them. "I can feel them." She closed her eyes and reached her awareness out to the letters. She could hear their whispers and pulls. "They speak to me, and I know where they go and who they are for. The feeling is strongest when the letter is from a Remnant, but it works on all letters. I keep them in a kind of map of the area since I don't need them to be alphabetical."

Iris pushed the awareness of the letters into a peripheral place in her mind and opened her eyes. Henry had taken a step closer to her and her senses were filled with the pulling of his presence instead of the letters. He blocked out everything. His eyes looked right into her heart, and she pushed her awareness of him away as she had the letters. She reminded herself she was supposed to be reining herself in.

Iris shifted her weight and smiled. "I've never told anyone else that, so don't give away all my secrets."

Henry found his voice. "I wouldn't dream of it. Besides, you know some of mine now too. Next time you come to the forge I'll explain how I put magic into the metal." His face disappeared behind his scarf.

Iris smiled. "Then I'll know more secrets about you than you'll know about me."

"You'll just have to figure out something else to divulge."

"Deal. I'll see you soon. No rush. If the snow is as bad as it looks, I might delay a day."

"I'll be back soon enough," he said.

Iris held the door open when he left, and looked down Main Street. There were drifts as high as her waist in some places. It was going to be a long day for everyone. Iris went upstairs and woke up Thomas, then prepared to go outside. Iris took her own outwear off the hooks by the front door and bundled up. The town would come to life today, everyone pitching in to clear the boardwalk and streets. She wanted to get the front of the depot done early.

Iris took the snow shovel from where it leaned against the side of the building and got to work. The roof of the porch in front of the depot had kept the snow from piling up too high in front of her door. In no time, she was warm from exertion as she moved the snow. Her hands were busy, which left her mind idle.

Her mother was right. Now was the time for her to start her own family and continue her line.

She had put off that particular responsibility long enough. With Petra pregnant and the next generation of harpies on the horizon, Iris knew it was past time. Iris felt herself break into a grin at the thought of Petra and James having a girl.

Turning Creek was a growing place, and there were options here for Iris, men who were kind and responsible. Jacob seemed interested in her and Iris enjoyed his easy company. She wondered again about her hunch that Jacob and her letter writer were one in the same. It would be like him to fight the battle on two fronts. Iris did not add Henry to her list of possibilities. It was obvious he did not think of her that way.

Daniel Vine finished shoveling the area in front of the saloon and waved to Iris. "I'll have flip, cider, and mulled wine after the snow is cleared," he yelled across the street.

Iris returned his greeting and said, "I'll pass it along."

Daniel went back to work, moving down the boardwalk towards Widow Finch's. Iris paused in her own work to watch him. He had betrayed them all to keep himself safe, but since then he had tried harder to make inroads with the Remnants in town. Iris thought he deserved a second chance, though she still did not trust him completely. He was making an effort and that was a start.

The door to the depot burst open and Thomas ran outside. Iris opened her mouth to yell at him to slow down but it was too late. His foot caught a patch of ice and his feet slipped from underneath him and he landed with a whack on his back.

Iris dropped the shovel and ran as fast as the snow and ice allowed. She knelt beside him. "Are you all right?"

Thomas, the air completely knocked from his lungs, was having trouble breathing. Iris's chest hurt in sympathy and she brushed hair from his eyes. He had forgotten to put on a hat. It took Thomas a few tries to get air into his lungs, then he burst out laughing.

Iris shoved his shoulder. "You know better than to run about like that. You scared me."

Thomas sat up, still laughing. "I'm fine. Got the wind knocked out of me is all."

Iris stood and pulled him up, wrapping him in a hug. "Silly boy."

Thomas returned her embrace. She could feel him shaking with silent laughter. "Hand me the shovel you dropped, and I'll start moving towards the mercantile."

A man was shoveling a path around the saloon and moving determinedly towards her. Jacob looked up and waved. Iris waved back and watched his progress. It did not take long before he was stomping his feet on her porch.

"Good morning, Iris. Nice day to enjoy the sunshine." His jacket collar was up and he did not have a scarf on to cover his mouth. He was smiling wide enough to show his white teeth.

"Good morning, Jacob. You must have started the day early to already be this far into town from the mill."

Jacob planted the shovel in the snow and leaned an elbow on the handle. "I was watching the sunrise and thinking about getting into town. I knew everyone would be shoveling snow today and I didn't want to miss any of the fun. I came by to see if you needed some help, but your porch is already cleared."

Iris smiled. "I was awake watching the sunrise too. I'm glad I'm not the only one who enjoys the early morning scenery. There'll be warm drinks for everyone later at Vine's. Will you be there?" If she meant to see if there could be something between her and Jacob, there was no time like the present.

Jacob's grin widened. "Only if you can promise me the company of the most enchanting woman in town."

Iris felt her face heat instantly. "I'll have to look around and find one for you then."

Jacob laughed. "You hunt her down while I shovel snow."

Iris smiled. "Deal. If I can't find anyone suitable, I hope I'll do."

Jacob tipped his hat and said, "I think I can manage with you." Iris laughed.

Over Jacob's shoulder, Iris saw Henry coming back towards the depot, following the trail in the snow he had made earlier. He had a shovel slung over one shoulder and his head was down, watching his footing. He looked up when he heard her laughter. His steps faltered, but he continued until he stood beside them.

Jacob turned towards Henry. "Good day to you, Mr. Foster. How are you this fine morning?"

Henry's face was stoic as Jacob's was jovial. "Fine." He held out his lumpy package to Iris. "This is the bundle for Miss Pearl."

Iris took it then asked, "Would you like to write a note for it?"

Henry shifted his weight before answering. "Yes."

Iris waved him towards the depot. "I've got paper and ink inside." Henry started walking to the depot without looking back.

Jacob picked up his shovel. "I'm headed back to Second Street then. Glad I got to see a bit more sunshine today. Don't forget about finding me some company now, or I'll be crying in my cider all alone."

Iris returned his easy grin. "I wouldn't dream of it."

She turned around to help Henry. He was standing on her porch, watching them. The contrast between the two men could not have been starker. Iris sighed and walked into the depot. She did not need to turn to make sure Henry followed her. She could feel his presence.

Iris got out the paper, ink, and pen for Henry. Instead of staying behind the counter, she walked around and sat on the stool next to the space where she had laid out the writing things. Henry put the bundle down, took off his gloves, and hesitated. His lips compressed into a line before he picked up the pen with his left hand.

Iris held her breath as he started to scratch out the words. It had been enough time since she'd seen his writing that her memory of his exact penmanship was blurred. His handwriting was deliberate, broad, and neat. When he had completed the first line, Iris looked away with the weight of disappointment settling over her. The handwriting was not a match for the one in her letter. Even though she had known better, a part of her had hoped that Henry had been the one who had written to her. While it was possible he was disguising his writing in some way, Iris doubted it. It had been a foolish wish, and Iris was tired of being a fool.

The sound of writing stopped and Iris turned back to Henry. His face looked grim as he handed her the paper. Iris took it with her senses wide open. Determination and resolve were the only things radiating from the letter. She folded it, took it and the bundle, and put them in a large slot near the floor.

"I may not go until tomorrow morning. Is that all right?"

Henry stood. "It is."

"Will you be at Vine's later?" She did not know why she asked.

"Most of the town will be there. It'll be nice after a long day."

Iris walked around the counter again, stopping next to him. "I'll walk out with you. Thomas took our larger snow shovel, but I have a smaller one I can use to clear the boardwalk." They went outside and parted ways to work.

It was not long before it seemed the entire town was outside in the snow. Children ran around, throwing snowballs and building tunnels in the snow being piled on the edges of the road. The shrieking of the young and the laughter of the adults was the music that filled the winter air. One stray snowball hit Widow Finch as she was helping Beth Kramer in from of the mercantile. She picked up some snow in return and then the war was on.

Snow flew all over the street, back and forth between factions until everyone, young and old, were wet, tired, and happy. The snow warriors headed to the saloon, laughing and talking in small groups. Thomas came up beside Iris and slipped his hand in hers.

"You got me good with that last one to the face," he said. His nose and cheeks were red.

"Yes, sorry for that. You should've ducked faster." She squeezed his hand.

Henry joined them from somewhere in the crowd. He was bareheaded and his curls were wet. "I learned one thing today. Never challenge the ladies in a snowball fight."

Iris laughed. Beth, Lily, and she made an unbeatable team. Lily had terrible aim, but made the perfect snowballs. She had provided plenty of ammunition for both Beth and Iris. They had holed up behind a drift, and it had taken a full on assault to overtake them.

"I'll make it up to you by fetching you a drink. Do you want, cider, flip, or wine?" Iris stopped just inside the doorway and looked up at Henry.

His face was adorned in a half-smile. "Cider will be fine."

Iris shifted her gaze to Thomas. "You worked hard today. A bit of cider for you too?" He nodded. "Good. Go sit with Henry and save me a seat."

Iris chatted with Beth while she waited at the bar. Daniel and his sisters worked with efficient speed, filling pints and mugs. Iris got three mugs of cider and turned around to look for Henry and Thomas. She turned smack into Jacob. He had a mug in his hand and a teeth flashing grin on his face.

The chattering and laughter was loud and echoed through the room. He leaned down and spoke loudly into her ear. "This is quite a gathering."

Jacob turned his head, allowing Iris to speak loudly into his ear. "The first snow day is always more of a festival than a workday."

"Do you have a place to sit?" he asked.

"Somewhere." Iris craned her neck around Jacob. Everyone around them had inches on her and Iris could not see through the crowd. "Can you see Henry and Thomas anywhere?"

Jacob turned and scanned the room. "They're in the back corner. Let me carry one of those mugs." He took one of the mugs in her hand.

"Thanks. Lead the way. I think you'll be able to get through this crush faster than I could. I'm so short no one would ever notice me trying to weave through."

Jacob's breath tickled her ear. "I can't imagine anyone not noticing you." He spun around and started walking before she had a chance to blush.

Iris smiled all the way to the table. Henry and Thomas had succeeded in holding one of the small four-person tables by the fireplace, which was filled with a roaring fire. Jacob put the mugs he carried on the table and held out the chair for Iris. She thanked him and he winked at her. Her quiet laugh was lost in the noise. She placed mugs of cider in front of Henry and Thomas.

Iris sipped the cider and let the warmth travel through her. The sweet tang of the cider was tempered by the burn of the whiskey.

"I hear I missed a street-wide snowball war," Jacob said.

"You did. I can't remember the last time I had more fun." Iris laughed.

Jacob's eyes twinkled at her. "I was shoveling one of the houses down from the mill. I'm sorry I missed the fun."

"Folks around here know the winters are harsh. They seldom pass the chance to enjoy the first big snow because they know in a couple months they'll be sick of it." Henry's deep voice carried under the sound in the room.

Jacob smiled. "I think I spent half my childhood slinging snowballs in the winter and fishing in the summer."

"Sounds like you had an easy childhood." Iris thought of all the books she had read and the languages she had learned in the winter months when the snow had been piled around the eaves. There had been little time for snowball fights.

"I worked a fair bit, but there was always time to play. What did you do as a child?" he asked.

Iris glanced at Henry before answering. "I spent a lot of time reading. My mother was a scholar, and I had more aptitude for languages than the rest of my siblings." It was not a complete lie, but Iris felt a twinge of guilt at telling it.

"I've never met a woman who was a scholar before. Your mother must be an interesting lady. No wonder you're so singular. Pretty and smart." Jacob looked at her as though he was seeing her in a new light.

Henry took a sip of his cider. "Miss Iris is the smartest person I've ever met."

Iris looked at Henry. His lips were compressed into a thin line. She looked back at Jacob. "You're both flattering me unnecessarily. My grandmere was smarter than my mother and I combined. She taught me to read when I was very small."

Jacob laughed. "I had to be dragged to school at first, then I realized it wasn't so bad. I even liked reading after I got a handle on it." His smile was hard to ignore, and Iris could not help but return it.

Henry put his cup down on the table and stood. Iris shifted her gaze. "You're not leaving already, are you?"

Henry walked around the table to stand next to her. She felt his presence like a draw. "I've work to do. Thank you for the company." Iris watched him as he left. Even with the fire, she felt chilled without him there. She put a smile on her face and turned back to Thomas and Jacob.

They were good company. Jacob was attentive, and Thomas told both of them about the new penny serial he was reading. Iris pulled Henry's mug to her side of the table when hers was empty. She wished he would have stayed longer. The hairs on her neck went up and she twisted in her chair. Dora was approaching their table.

Dora sat down with a heavy sigh that Iris saw but did not hear over the noise in the room, which had only gotten worse as people drank and warmed up. There were circles under her eyes and lines of fatigue graced her mouth. Iris put a hand across the table and Dora grabbed onto it. Dora squeezed hard enough to hurt, but Iris did not complain.

Iris pushed Henry's half empty-cup in Dora's direction. "You need this more than me." Iris nodded at Jacob. "You know Jacob Wells?" Dora and Jacob nodded. "You do not have good news."

Dora cradled her mug and took a sip. "No. The middle Stewart daughter, Natalie, died overnight. There was nothing Dr. Williams could do, and this morning Mr. Stewart took to his bed."

"There was nothing that could be done?" Iris asked. Doc, like the original Asclepius, could sometimes bring people back from the other side, but the soul had to be willing and it did not always work.

Dora shook her head and closed her eyes.

"I haven't met the Stewarts. Where do they live?" Jacob asked.

"East of here, on the base of my..." Dora corrected herself, "on the base of Silvercliff."

"How's the family doing? I lost a brother young. I thought my mother would never stop crying." For the first time since Iris had known him, Jacob's mouth was in a flat line.

Dora took a deep breath. "I'm sorry about your brother. I'm going to go back and check on the Stewarts tomorrow. Mrs. Stewart is wrecked. Mr. Stewart is holding what is left of his family together, even though he is sick. Dr. Williams seems to think the others will likely pull through, though he is concerned that the illness may spread."

"That poor woman," Iris said. Life in the mountains was hard, and death was never far from the door. It was still painful when it came calling.

"That's what helped my mother. She had the rest of us to take care of and it was enough until the grief had abated some." Jacob finished his own cider. "Ladies, it was a pleasure sharing your company. Iris, I hope to see you soon. Thomas, thank you for the thrilling recaps of your serials." He tipped his hat and left them.

Thomas stood. "Can I go see Jonah and Stephen?"

"Be back before dark," Iris said and bussed him on the cheek when he leaned down.

Dora waited until Jacob and Thomas were out of the door. "That man is sweet on you."

"Perhaps. He's very charming, for sure. I'm going to visit Pearl tomorrow. Do you want to come?"

Dora twirled her mug. "No, I promised Dr. Williams I would go back to the Stewarts'. He's spent a lot of time there and needs a break to check on the Myers baby and some others. I'm not sure how long that visit will take. You changed the subject. Do you think Mr. Wells wrote the letter?"

"I don't know. It seems likely. Who else would have written it?"

Dora shrugged, but a small smile tugged at her mouth, the first one Iris had seen on her today. "He can't be the only man in Turning Creek who's noticed you."

"He seems to be," Iris muttered. Irritation at Henry flared.

Dora snorted. "If you say so."

Iris narrowed her eyes at Dora. "What's that mean?"

Dora took a large swallow of cider. "Doesn't mean a thing."

"Mmm, sure." Iris placed her hand on Dora's arm. Dora's freckles stood out on her pale skin. "You need to get some good sleep in your own bed, my bird."

Dora nodded. "I know. I promise to fly straight home and sleep until morning."

Iris gathered all the empty cups to take them to the bar. "Come by when you can and let me know how things are at the Stewarts' place. I want to help if I can."

After leaving the cups on the end of the bar for Daniel, Dora linked arms with Iris and they walked outside. The sky was a leaden grey and small flakes of snow fell from the sky in a slow trickle.

"So much for all the shoveling today," Dora said.

Iris breathed in the cold air. The jovial air of the day was gone, replaced by the cold reality of winter in the mountains.

CHAPTER 9

Iris lay in bed that night, thinking about letters and men, and wondering why they were both taking up so much of her mind when she should be sleeping. She rose from her bed as soon as the sky began to lighten, and padded out of her room to stand at the large window in the main room on the second floor. From there, she could see up and down Main Street in the weak dawn light. The snow fell, as steady and slow as the night before. The footprints of the day before were covered, but the drifts were not high and the road was passable. All the work had not been entirely in vain.

Iris grabbed her shawl off the chair where she had flung it before crawling into bed the night before, and slipped some leather slippers on her feet. She checked on Thomas, who was snoring quietly, then went downstairs. It was frigid on the first floor. She stopped to put some new logs on the coals in the stove to get the fire going. When that task was completed, she took a breath and turned towards the door.

With a twist of trepidation, she stepped out into the cold air. Her breath made tiny clouds around her head. It was doubtful this morning would be any different from the other mornings. It had been days now since she had received the first letter. The box by the door had contained letters almost every day, but none of them had been for her. Just to be sure, Iris lifted the lid of the mailbox.

Sitting, dry and alone, at the bottom of the box, was a rectangular sheet of paper with a familiar scrawl on it bearing her name. With a shaking hand, Iris reached in for the letter. The strength of the emotions captured in the paper caused her to suck in a breath. Gone was the fear from the previous letter. A flood of hope and determination rose over her from the letter. There was strength in these words. She felt herself smile in response to the emotion and looked around. Main Street was deserted. There were no traces in the snow for a clue to who had left the letter. She took her treasure inside.

Iris went upstairs and laid the letter on the table. She put on water for tea and glanced often at the folded sheet of paper. With deliberate movements, she made tea and tried to ignore the presence of the letter. When the tea was done, she poured a cup and walked back to the window. She wrapped her hands around the warm cup and breathed in the citrus scent of bergamot and black tea. Anticipation was a clanging in her heart.

Iris placed her cup on the table and picked up the letter. The sound of the wax seal snapping loose was loud in the quiet room. She spread the single sheet flat on the table.

Dearest Iris,

I pray it is acceptable for me to address you thusly. Thank you for allowing me to continue to write to you. I was humbled to receive a reply in your own hand. I have it now, folded close to my heart, and I tremble to think of your hands upon its surface. Even if I never receive another letter from another soul during the course of my life, I shall treasure it always and be content.

You asked me two questions in your reply. Let me answer the easiest one first. You may address me in any way you choose, but for now, you can call me friend.

As for the second request, it required some time for me to pinpoint what I wanted to share with you. I was raised in a loving family by parents who doted on me. I have seen with my own eyes the joy that can come from having a partner who loves and respects you. I decided at an early age that I wanted the kind of house I grew up in, one with a lot of love, when I was old enough to make a choice for myself.

I hope this confession fulfills your request admirably. I have found during the course of this correspondence that writing a letter holds different joys than a spoken conversation. Among its chief benefits is the ability to reread the words of your reply more than once and imagine you writing them.

You are an amazing treasure. The moment I saw you, I knew what it was to long for you and that feeling burns through all my days, even when you are not around.

I hope to have a reply to carry beside the last one soon.

Charis,

Your Friend

Iris read the letter again, then walked over the window and reread it. She resisted the urge to skip back to the table where her tea was growing cold. She finished the tea and reheated the water to make more. While the water heated, she dashed to her room and put on a faded blue skirt, cream colored blouse, and a sweater. She took the first letter from her nightstand and put it into the pocket of her skirt.

The water was ready when she returned to the kitchen. Before pouring the water over the leaves, she slipped the new letter into her pocket. While she did this, she resisted the urge to think about who could have sent the letters. She decided, for a few hours at least, she would put her curiosity aside and just enjoy having them. It was a heady thing, to be wanted in this manner.

Iris delayed leaving for Pearl's farm, hoping all morning that the snow would stop. It did not, but instead continued, slow and steady, until lunch. Resigned to flying through the icy precipitation, Iris packed her leather satchel with Henry's package, a letter, a magazine wrapped in brown paper, some oats, tea, and cheese. She was uncertain what Pearl might need, and she could only carry so much. Iris would ask Pearl to make a list and send Marina once the harpy got back in town. Iris looked out the window of the depot. *If Marina ever gets back to town*, Iris amended.

Spuds had settled in for the foreseeable future. The passes around the valley were filled with snow and ice after the storm two days ago. Marina and Reed had to travel from Denver. Marina could carry large deer for miles in her harpy form, so, in theory at least, she could manage herself and Reed. However, Iris was not sure Reed would succumb to being transported this way, plus they would have luggage from traveling.

Iris changed into her shirt and jacket with the slits in the back. She then pulled her blue hat over her head and wrapped her scarf securely around her face and neck. It would be a cold flight, but not a long one. Iris went out the back door of the depot and walked into the woods to the clearing. She took a deep breath and began the process of pulling her wings out. It never got easier.

Iris flapped her wings to work out the stiffness in her back. No matter the pain, flying was always worth it. Iris bunched her muscles and launched into the air. She gained altitude and flew west, away from town, then banked south towards Shaker's Way. The rings of mountains on the southern end of the valley were covered in white. The joy of soaring swept through her as she drank in the sight of her valley.

Viewing the mountains from this height never got old, and she rarely flew in the light of day. Her golden wings made her conspicuous. Iris had decided it was a cold enough day that people would remain inside. If they did venture out, they would likely walk quickly with their heads down. That, the weather, and the altitude would shield her from prying eyes. If any mortals saw a flash of her wings, they would assume it was the sun glinting off the snow.

The snow was closer to ice at this height and pelted the unprotected areas of her face. She would have to wrap up her scarf better for the return trip. She had lost feeling in the skin around her eyes and cheeks when she saw the smoke rising from the main house on the Nasso farm. Relief and the desire to be warm drove her speed. Iris started circling down, keeping the house in the middle of her circuit. She landed lightly on stiff legs in the yard in front of the large ranch house.

The house had once been the home of Tyler and Edna Nasso, their five sons, and their one daughter. Now, it was home only to Pearl, the youngest and only surviving member of the Nasso family. The harpies had allowed her to live because she had sworn fealty to them. Marina checked in on her from time to time, and Iris took up the slack when she could not.

Iris shook the aching chill from her limbs and stepped up the steps of the porch, treading with care while balancing her wings. She was too cold to hold them very far off the ground, and the tips trailed in the snow. Iris knocked on the door, then leaned against the doorpost and pulled in her wings. Pulling them in hurt, but it was a dull ache. Nothing like the sharp sting of setting them free.

Iris was still leaning against the doorframe, catching her breath, when the door opened. A pair of overlarge brown eyes met hers. Even if Iris had not already known Pearl was the Remnant of the Sphinx, the girl's posture and form screamed feline.

"I wasn't expecting you, Miss Iris." It was neither a greeting nor a reproach.

"I have something for you from Henry, and I wanted to check on you since the storm came. I know you're alone out here."

The girl, for she was only sixteen, relaxed visibly as Iris spoke. "Is it the distilling device?" Iris nodded. Pearl opened the door all the way and waved her in. "I'm sorry, please come in."

Iris followed her into the warmth of the house. "Did you think I was here for a different purpose? You seemed worried."

Pearl took Iris's coat and scarf and motioned to a seat by the fireplace. The front room of the house was large and open. It served as sitting room, kitchen, and eating area. Two doors were closed off to the left and a third was open to allow heat to filter in from the main room. Pearl indicated for Iris to sit by the fire.

"Would you like tea? I drink coffee when Miss Marina comes, but I usually make tea," Pearl said.

Iris loosened her scarf but did not take it off. "Tea is fine, thank you, but you did not answer my question. Were you worried when you saw me?"

Pearl's hand trembled and the kettle clattered down on the stove top. She turned to face Iris with hands clenched by her side. "Sometimes, I think the harpies will change their minds and decide I'm more trouble than I'm worth, that I can't be trusted. I worry each time they come that they have come to kill me. I would not want to hurt them."

Pearl raised her eyes and Iris could see the predator inside looking out at her. Iris had enough experience with the harpies not to be truly threatened by the look in those eyes alone. She was also not foolish enough to dismiss it altogether. Pearl wanted to let her know that while she was cooperating, she was not helpless. Iris estimated the distance to the door and the time it would take her to change and escape.

Pearl continued, "I would not want to hurt them, but I wouldn't go down without a fight. I don't want to die. I'm not my family." Her voice cracked on the last word and Iris took pity on the girl.

Iris stood up and walked slowly towards Pearl. "You're not your parents or your brothers. You are just you. The harpies let you live because they each know what it is to regret family and choose a different way. They know how determined you are."

Iris reached out tentative arms and wrapped Pearl in a hug. The girl stood stiffly for a moment, then relaxed into her. Iris thought of Henry and how he always stiffened when touched before relaxing in the same way. People who lived alone were not touched by others often. It made for a hard and lonely existence.

Iris squeezed the girl. "They don't check on you because they fear the worst in you. They check on you because they care for you and want you to succeed here in starting over. Don't tell her I told you, but Marina has a soft spot for you the size of the moon."

Pearl wrapped her arms around Iris and squeezed until Iris was sure her ribs would crack. She ran her hands down Pearl's back. She blinked rapidly to relieve the burning in her eyes. Pearl released her and Iris tucked stray strands of hair from the girl's face.

A smile brightened Pearl's face. "Thank you. I needed to hear that more than you know."

Iris could not help but smile in return. "Now, would you like to see what Henry has sent?"

Pearl nodded eagerly. Iris opened her satchel and handed Pearl the note first. Disappointment still tumbled through her at the sight of the handwriting. She swallowed it down and handed Pearl the brown paper-wrapped bundle. Pearl tore at the paper eagerly.

She squealed. "This is perfect. Mr. Foster is amazing."

"It looks like a scaled down version of the distilling vats Daniel has at the saloon," Iris said.

Pearl turned and laid the device on the table. "That's exactly what it is. You put the plant juice or tea here and heat the still. It distills plant juice down the same way you make alcohol. I'm going to use it to make lavender oil. If it works well, Mr. Foster is going to make Miss Dora one to make medicinals for Dr. Williams."

"What made you choose lavender?"

Pearl measured tea into the teapot, and cradled her new still up. "I wanted to grow something different. I'll maintain the vegetable garden for the house, but the other fields will be fallow or lavender. I want to start out small and grow as I'm able. Lavender doesn't just smell good, it can be used for many things. I want to make something that is useful, something that helps people. It doesn't hurt that it's pretty and smells wonderful."

Iris had to bite her tongue. Pearl and her harpies were not that different at the core. "I think you'll do beautifully."

Pearl poured the hot water over the leaves and closed up the teapot to let it brew. "I've been thinking."

"About what," Iris prompted.

"I think I can manage the planting. I want to stagger the fields, but I'm worried about some general field maintenance and harvesting. I'll need some extra hands." Pearl chewed on her lower lip.

"There seem to be a steady stream of newcomers into town. You should be able to find someone to help."

"I don't want to hire just anyone. I want it to be someone I can trust. A Remnant."

Iris sat back in her chair. "Would they have to be a Remnant?"

Pearl stood and gathered the tea things. She poured tea into two cups and offered one to Iris. "I'd rather not hide what I am. Having a mortal around might complicate things. I don't want to lie and keep secrets."

Iris took a sip of the tea. "Could it be a mortal who already knows the truth?"

"Maybe. I've never spent much time around mortals. My family kept me close to home." Pearl sipped her tea. "Yes, I think maybe I could accept a mortal, as long as they were accepting of what I am and weren't too nosey."

Pearl's words gave Iris pause. She had been there when Reed and Adam had been told about the harpies. Marina had insisted on telling Reed, and Adam had to be told after all the events that had happened on the Lloyd's dairy farm. Robert, Adam's brother, had been captured by Zeus and thus his entry into their world had been rocky. They had each taken the news as well as could be expected under the circumstances, but they had each already come to trust people they learned were Remnants.

All it would take for things to go wrong in Turning Creek was one person with more fear than sense. Perhaps Pearl's caution was justified.

"What about Adam or Robert Mullins? They already know the truth and are hardworking and trustworthy." Iris asked.

"They work for Mr. Lloyd and Mrs. Petra," Pearl said.

Iris cradled her teacup in her hands, letting the heat fill her fingers. Her toes were still considerably less warm than the rest of her. If only she could warm them as easily as her fingers. "James has been hiring extra hands for their expanding herds. He may be willing to spare one of the brothers to help you. You could hire one of them and a couple other men during harvest. They could help you hire temporary help when needed."

Pearl straightened in her seat. "That might work. I've a couple months to think it over. I'll mention it to Mrs. Petra next time she comes and see what she thinks. I wouldn't want to ask either of the Mr. Mullins until I spoke to her.”

Iris sipped her tea. “I almost forgot.” She pulled the other things from her bag. “I brought you some oats and tea. Is there anything else you might need? Unless the snow gets too bad, I expect Marina home in a few days. She can bring whatever you need from town then.”

Pearl smiled. “Company is all I need. I’ve plenty of smoked meat thanks to Miss Dora, and plenty other things stored by. My mom had already done the bulk of the canning before…”

Pearl trailed off and Iris reached across the table to take her hand. “I’m sorry, Pearl.”

The girl sniffed. “For what? The bad choices of my family?” Pearl threw her shoulders back and looked Iris dead on. “I’ll have to live with my part in what happened every day, but I don’t regret that I’m free now, free to make my own decisions about my life. If that makes me a monster, then so be it.”

Iris had seen this emotion so many times in the harpies, the need to be monstrous instead of having a heart. Iris reached out to Pearl and took her hand. “I’m sorry that you have had to face this at all. They are empty words after all that happened, but well meant. Remember that, whatever their actions, your family made you who you are up until now, but what you decide from this point is all you. Choose well.”

Pearl blinked slowly and a smile that did not reach her eyes tugged at her lips. “Thank you. Marina told me to take heed if you ever gave advice.”

Something between love and thankfulness flipped within her. Iris snorted. “She’d do well to take her own advice. I think she only listens to the counsel of others a quarter of the time.”

Pearl finished her tea and rose from her seat. She knelt in front of Iris. “Messenger, I am thankful for what you’ve given me. The harpies gave me mercy, but you’ve shown me friendship and treated me as fledgling of your own. I’m more grateful than you could ever know.”

Iris placed a hand on Pearl’s bowed head. The girl’s submission made her feel ancient in both knowledge and experience. Iris cupped Pearl’s face and lifted her eyes.

“By the gods, you are a precious gift. Never forget that you can be anything you choose, but choose well. There are people who care for you now. I, for one, want to be able to write a chronicle about the Sphinx who changed the course of not only her line but of her family’s.” Iris leaned down and kissed Pearl’s cheek. “I tell my birds all the time: they choose their own paths. Find your own way, Pearl.”

It was good advice. Iris wondered why she could not take her advice for herself. For her it was not so much a question of which direction but with whom that concerned her the most. The man she was most affected by seemed indifferent to her. She had two other, or possibly one, if her letter friend and Jacob were one in the same, suitors who sought her out. She enjoyed Jacob, but he was not the one she noticed first when she went into a room.

Iris left Pearl and prepared to fly home. There was nothing out of the ordinary about the flight. The snow fell in a steady stream and hit her face as she cut through the air. Uneasiness stole over her the longer she flew. Iris looked around, but she could see no reason to be unsettled. There was no wind, and the flying was straightforward even though the snow continued to fall.

The feeling of wrongness followed her home. It was dusk when Iris touched down in the clearing outside of town. The snow on the peaks was orange in the east and the snow at her feet was grey in the gathering gloom. She pulled in her wings and sought the comfort of the depot. The creeping feeling did not ease until she had closed the door behind her and sought refuge under her own roof.

CHAPTER 10

Iris sucked on the end of her pen and reread her last letter from her friend. There was a blank piece of paper sitting on the counter, mocking her. She did not know what to write. Iris jiggled one of her feet in a random rhythm and watched the snow continue to fall. It had been three days since the big storm, and the snow had not stopped falling.

The sound of the back door opening interrupted her thoughts. Dora's voice entered the room moments before she did.

"Good morning. Are you up yet?"

Musing over her letter would have to wait. "Yes, I've been up for a while." She turned the letter over on the counter and walked over to the stove to pour another cup of tea. She handed it to Dora and they both sat at the counter.

"Have you had breakfast yet?" Iris asked.

"No."

"Good. Stay and eat before you leave." Iris shoved a plate of scones at Dora. "Eat these while I make some eggs. The sky looks like more snow. I'd like you to be snug in your cabin before it hits."

Iris went upstairs to get a pan and some eggs. She brought them downstairs and began cooking eggs on the stove in the back of the depot.

Dora polished off a scone in silence, then asked. "Did you write a reply to that letter?"

Iris's face felt hot. She kept her back to Dora, stirring the eggs. "Yes."

"And?" she prodded. "What did it say?"

Iris continued to stir the eggs, though they were done. "That's personal."

Dora snorted. "What did it say?"

Iris took the pan to the counter and scooped a generous portion of eggs on Dora's plate and then her own. "I thanked him for the letter."

"For Hera's sake, Iris. What did the letter say?"

"I gave my permission to be courted." Iris ate her eggs and ignored the gleeful harpy at her table.

"Good."

"It may not be the right time for me yet. I still have responsibilities." Iris gave Dora a pointed look.

Dora's face sobered. "When you find it, don't hesitate overlong or you will find yourself in a place where it's too late."

Iris wanted to ask her exactly who it was causing the lines of grief on her face. She put eggs in her mouth instead, knowing now was not the time to question Dora when she was tired and prickly. Harpies had short tempers; even Dora, who was the most level headed of the three.

Dora shook herself. "All I'm saying is that you've cared for us for so long, it's time for you to look after yourself."

"I was born to be you and your sisters' protector. I don't regret my role or my place in things. You bring me nothing but joy. You are my family." Iris said the words and their truth rang in her soul. She reached across the counter and put her hand on Dora's arm. "Is something bothering you?"

"I'm sorry about being so down in the mouth. I stopped in at the Stewart's place before coming into town. Mr. Stewart died. He went very suddenly. The other two girls are still sick. I have to go by the doctor's and let him know. It's made me thankful for you and mindful of my regrets, but also very tired." Dora put her fork down and covered Iris's hand with her own.

"My bird. You need some rest. You worry so for others. You're so different from Marina and Petra in that way. Your worry spurns you to practical action, like learning medicine."

Dora smiled. "And they solve their worry with violence. I know. And I need them to remind me sometimes what we are." Dora pushed her plate away. "I wonder what the fourth harpy was like in the time of the old myths. Would she have been more like me or more like my sisters?"

Iris had often wondered the same thing about Podarge, the harpy who had been lost in the battle against Olympus.

"I hope she would have been more like you. I'm not sure the world could have withstood another harpy like Marina or Petra."

Dora laughed and Iris was glad to hear it. "Gods, the two of them are quite enough." Dora rose from the counter and walked around to Iris. She wrapped her arms around Iris and squeezed her tight. "Thank you for reminding me of the blessings I do have. I'm glad you're our Iris."

Thomas's door opened and his voice came down the stairs. "Is there still breakfast?"

"I can make you some eggs," Iris said. "Bring down however many you want and some bread."

The door closed and they could hear him rummaging about overhead.

Thomas stomped down the stairs and went directly to the stove. He cracked the eggs into the still warm pan and began stirring them around.

Iris stood behind him. "I didn't know you could cook eggs." She crossed her arms over her chest.

Thomas shrugged and a sly smile spread across his face. "If I told you I could make them, you wouldn't do it for me."

Dora laughed loudly. It had been too long since Iris had heard that sound from her. Iris ruffled Thomas's hair. "You're sneaky."

Thomas kissed her on the cheek. "Your eggs do taste better than mine."

"Now you're just buttering me up," she said.

"Well, sure. I don't want to make them next time." He laughed and scooped the eggs onto a plate and carried them to the counter. "I told Mr. Foster I'd help with the shoveling if there was some to be done." Thomas spoke around a mouthful of eggs.

Iris brought a new cup of tea to the counter and sat. "If we keep getting this much snow every day, things could get dangerous."

"How so?" Thomas asked. He had grown up in a warmer climate where the snow only lasted a handful of days, not a handful of months.

Dora answered as she watched Thomas reduce the pile of eggs on his plate. "Some buildings can't take the weight on the roofs and they collapse. People get snowed in and run out of food. Animals in pastures die. People go out in the storm and get lost or buried. The worse the snow, the greater the chance of it building up and causing problems." Dora moved a scone from her plate to Thomas's. "Here, I think you need this more than me. You're too skinny."

"I feed him constantly. He eats everything in sight," Iris said defensively.

Thomas smiled at Iris. "I always have enough. Running makes me hungry. As long as I can run, I doubt I'll ever get soft around the edges." Thomas stacked the empty plates and the egg pan together and carried them upstairs. He came back down and kissed both Iris and Dora on the cheek. "I'll be home later, and if you leave the dishes, I'll do them."

"Tell Henry he's welcome to come by for lunch, and take your hat and scarf," Iris reminded his retreating form. He grabbed his hat and scarf from the peg and put them on as he opened the door.

Dora regarded Iris with eyes that had lost some of their sadness. "What did the latest letter say?"

Iris felt her blush rising. She reached across the counter and flipped over the letter she had been reading and rereading.

Dora scanned the letter, then smiled wickedly as she folded it and gave it back to Iris. "That man is in a bad way."

Iris grinned. "I know." Both women laughed.

"Are you going to write back?" Dora asked.

"I want to. How could I not respond? I've just been struggling with what to say." Iris felt her smile widen further. "All I really want to write is, 'Who are you?'"

The depot door swung open. A swirl of snow and Henry came through the door. In his hands he held a three foot by four foot framed board. Iris shoved the letter in her pocket and her face flamed up. She looked down, unable to meet Henry's eyes.

He hesitated and looked from Iris to Dora. "Morning, ladies. Did I interrupt something?"

Iris laid a hand over the letters in her pocket and, though she had not thought it possible, felt her blush deepen. "No, not at all."

She made the mistake of looking at Dora, who burst out laughing. "I didn't think you could turn that deep a color of red."

Dora laughed again. Iris glared at her until she cut her laugh off with a cough. Henry said nothing but looked at them with a calm expression. Nothing ever seemed to ruffle him.

"I was just leaving." Dora gave Iris a hug and whispered in her ear, "If you get another, let me know. I want to read it."

Iris hugged her back and said, "Nosey."

"Bye, Henry."

"Bye, Miss Dora." Henry turned to Iris. "I ran into Thomas on the way over. I know you invited me for lunch later, and I could've brought this then, but I have a request."

Iris waved him in. "Come out of the cold. I'm intrigued."

Henry lifted the board. "Where do you want me to put this?"

Iris motioned to the wall to the left of the door. "I think I want to hang it there, so you can lean it against the wall. Do you want to warm up by the fire?" The coals in the stove had eaten up the new wood and the fire was now burning brightly.

Henry put down the board and unwound his scarf to reveal his face. "No, I'm not going to stay. There's too much snow to shovel, and I've some smithing to do later on. I'll hang this later for you today, if you'd like."

"Later today would be fine. You have a request?" Iris prompted.

"I know you have a large collection of books here. I've read the few I have many times. I was wondering if you had one you'd be willing to lend me for a time. I promise to take exceptional care of it. I thought if I asked you now, you'd have time to think about it before I came back."

Iris did not hesitate. "Of course you can borrow a book. I don't generally lend them out, but Reed has been borrowing some, trying to learn more about Remnants. I wouldn't mind lending you something. Do you have a preference? History? Fiction? Something else?"

"I'll read anything, but I think the history ones would be my preference." Henry shifted his weight.

Iris laid a hand on his arm. Even through all his layers of clothing, Iris could feel the strength in him. "I will look and find the perfect book for you by lunch." She squeezed his arm and dropped her hand back to her side. It tingled with awareness, and she flexed her fingers.

Henry did not notice her discomfort. He wound his scarf back around his neck and face. "Thank you, Miss Iris."

"One of these days, you'll decide we're good enough friends to drop the miss." Iris opened the door for him.

"Perhaps, but not today."

Iris could see the smile in his eyes. "Go on then. I'll have a book and some lunch ready for you later."

Henry had been right. Iris had shelves and shelves of books. Over the years, her mother had sent her journals from previous Messengers, books, and scrolls. All had been passed from one Messenger to another and contained everything from recipes to the old myths and the histories of the Remnants after the Battle and Fall of Olympus. Some of her less valuable books, encyclopedia-like volumes on myths, she kept underneath the counter downstairs. She also had some volumes on mortal history and a smattering of fiction.

The books and parchments that described various Remnants and their descendants got the most use out of any in her collection. It was disconcerting how often she needed them to look up details as a crisis loomed over them. Since coming to the valley, the harpies had faced all manner of monsters. Like mortals, not all Remnants were good, and the harpies, while creatures of violence, did not tolerate harm and destruction wrought upon the places and people they considered their own.

Iris went upstairs to the wall of shelves in the main room. She ran her hand over the bindings, their familiarity a comforting thrill. She knew each of them, had pored over their words and gleaned their secrets. The urge to sit, read, and drink tea while the world outside continued washed over her. Iris stopped and tapped the binding of a dark grey book. The title was stitched in white and black and, though it was hundreds of years old, the binding was intact and well cared for. This was the one she would give to Henry. She pulled it off the shelf and ran her palm over the cover.

The morning was over before she knew it. Henry and Thomas arrived with Daniel Vine, Simon Kramer, and the two McKenzie boys.

After he had taken off his wet coat, Thomas said, "I hope it's all right that I invited everyone who was helping over."

"It's fine, of course. Go serve everyone something to drink." Iris was glad she had made two pans of crowdarounds.

Everyone was wet from the knee down, with cheeks and noses red. Iris sliced a wheel of James's cheese while her ears rang with the sound of conversations between friends over food. Iris could not think of a better way to spend a winter day.

Iris made sure everyone was served, then fixed a plate of her own and walked over to the back table where Henry, Daniel, and Simon sat. Thomas, Jonah, and Stephen sat at the other table, their heads together. Henry sat on the bench facing the door and moved over when he saw Iris approach. Iris thanked him before sitting.

The moment Iris sat, awareness of Henry flared. The bench was crowded enough that her side was flush with his. She took a breath and tried to get a hold of herself.

She cleared her throat and asked, "What are you gentleman discussing?"

Simon piped up. "Daniel has a new batch of wine he's saving for the next Aspen Jubilee, and he's been working with James and Petra to develop a cheese aged in wine. I'm trying to bargain with him to allow it to be sold in the mercantile. Sadly, he wants to auction most of it at the Jubilee to raise money for town improvements."

The Aspen Jubilee was the annual harvest festival in Turning Creek. Iris looked at Daniel, who met her gaze defensively. "That is a very considerate thing for you to do."

"I'm not a horrible person," Daniel mumbled.

Henry's deep voice washed over Iris. "Everyone makes mistakes. It's how you handle the consequences after that matter."

The flare of anger in Daniel's face vanished. "Thank you."

Iris knew the source of Daniel's antagonism. "Not everyone holds a grudge like Marina."

Simon waved half a roll at Iris. "I unpacked a shipment of pens and ink that Spuds brought in, if you'd like to see them, and I have some new paper I wanted to show you. If you send Thomas over, I can send some with him."

Simon paused for a minute and continued, his loquacious ways getting the better of him. "Thomas is such a good young man. I'm so glad you took him in. He's been a world of help to you and he's a wealth of information. Just the other day, he told me that Lily Hughes's sister is thinking of coming to live in Turning Creek come spring."

Iris spoke up while Simon took a breath. "I'm planning on doing the rounds in town tomorrow. I think Thomas will welcome a day off." Iris turned to Henry. "When he comes home after helping you shovel, he collapses by the fire like some overgrown puppy and only moves for dinner."

Henry turned towards her as she spoke. They were so close his face was inches from her own and she could see every line of blue cutting through the grey in his eyes. She felt heat rising to her cheeks and was unable to look away.

Henry's voice was soft and slid over her skin. "He works hard."

Iris felt her face heat even more with pleasure from the praise. With her fair skin, she thought she likely looked as red as an apple. Embarrassment followed, which made her blush worse.

"Are you feeling well, Iris? You look flushed," Simon said.

She turned away from Henry and concentrated hard on what remained of her midday meal. "I'm just hot. I must have put too much wood on the fire."

"If it snows any more tonight, we'll have to start shoveling off some of the roofs to prevent collapse," Daniel said.

Iris was thankful for the change in subject. The men at the table grunted in agreement. She felt her face slowly return to normal, though the rest of her was still thrumming with awareness.

Henry shifted next to her. "Speaking of work, it's time for me to be getting back to it, and I need to hang that board for you." He stood and went over to where the coats were hung. From the recesses of his coat he pulled out a hammer and a handful of long nails.

He turned to her. "Will you hold it where you want it, while I nail it in?"

Iris left the table and stood beside Henry with the board. Henry put six long nails into his mouth. Iris watched every detail of his movements. His hands were deft and sure. His motions with the hammer were strong and precise. She noted the path of the nail from his lips to the board. She shook her head and stared at the swirling pattern of the wood instead.

Henry drove the last nail home and stood back. "What do you think?"

Iris smiled at him. "Thank you, Henry."

"I almost forgot." Henry fished into his coat again. The hammer and nails disappeared and were replaced in his hands by a small wooden box and a piece of paper. He handed her the box. "This is full of tacks for the board." He handed her the paper. "And this is my posting for an assistant."

Iris tacked up Henry's post. "It's perfect."

"I'll be going."

"Wait." Iris stepped closer to him and her movement brought her closer than she would have preferred to the solid wall that was Henry's presence. If she were honest with herself, parts of her still preferred his proximity more than they should, despite her frequent intentions to the contrary.

"I have a book for you." She gestured towards the counter. Iris went behind the counter and removed the volume from the shelf. She grinned as she handed it over. "I thought you might appreciate the subject matter."

Henry took the book with reverence. He ran a work-worn finger over the title, stitched in bold letters: *The Lives and History of the Line Hephaestus.*

He did not say anything for some time. Iris twisted a handful of skirt in her fingers. "I thought you might like reading it. It includes copies of some journal entries, including forging methods. I have other things, if you'd prefer something different."

Henry was silent and Iris began to fear she had made a mistake. Some Remnants guarded their histories with a jealousy that bordered on obsession. Besides the rarity of the items of her collection, it was another reason she did not often lend her books out. It was better if not everyone knew all the secrets hidden away on her shelves.

Henry's hand on her arm stopped her thoughts. It was the first time he had touched her of his own volition. Iris felt his touch on her arm like a brand left in the forge too long. "I don't want something else. I was, I am, touched that you would lend this to me and that you have kept it at all. In my hesitation, I was searching for the right words of gratitude. Thank you. I promise to care for it well." He squeezed her arm before releasing it.

For hours afterwards, she continued to feel the ghost of that brand as she tidied up the depot. It seemed more snow was coming. Tomorrow would be a busy day.

Thoughts of Henry followed her through the evening. Iris felt slightly guilty as she sat to pen the next letter to her anonymous friend, like she was doing something untoward. She knew it was silly, but the feeling remained.

With a sigh, Iris pushed all other thoughts aside and composed her letter. She was careful to keep the information she shared general. If Jacob were the writer, he was a mortal, and Iris was not ready to tell him the truth. If it was not Jacob, she still felt caution was needed. Secrets always required caution, and she was the keeper of many.

Dearest Friend,

I have looked in vain to discover your comings and goings. I worry about you traveling in the dead of night in the snow for I surmise that is the only time you can do so undetected. Please do not put yourself at risk on my account as the sky looks heavy with more snow. I can endure a few days without a letter addressed to me in your hand, which I am coming to cherish. The snow has already begun to fall harder tonight again and so I worry, and not just for you. Some of the buildings are already showing the strain. We will have to begin removing snow from the roofs in the next couple of days if we do not find relief from the sky. It is dangerous, messy work and I worry for all the men involved.

Looking over that opening paragraph makes me realize I am caught up with worry tonight. How maudlin of me. Apologies.

Thank you for telling me about your childhood. Though I had many siblings, from the moment I was born, I was the favorite of my grand-mere. She was a great scholar herself and taught me everything she knew. She was a hard taskmaster and my studies left me little room for childhood pursuits. I was a loved, but often lonely, child.

After visiting a friend who lives alone, it has recently come to my attention that loneliness itself can be a great burden to some. I have decided to ease this loneliness in my friends whenever I am able. I hope you are well tonight and warm. I pray to the gods that, if you are alone, you are not lonely. I hope the knowledge that you have a friend in me will keep you warm during this cold night.

CHAPTER 11

The moment Iris's eyes opened, she launched out of bed, grabbed a quilt, threw it over her shoulders, and padded in stocking feet down the stairs. She unlatched the door and stepped into the frigid morning. Snow still fell in great, flakey clumps from a leaden sky. The town was once again pristine in the grey morning light. She flipped open the lid of the mailbox.

The paper bearing a familiar scrawl lay on the bottom. Iris did a jig on the boardwalk, then looked around to make sure no one had seen. She scooped up the letter and it sent fingers of heat over her hand. There were other emotions in this letter, but they all dimmed beneath the longing pouring from it. Iris's hand shook as she went inside and ran up the stairs. She went directly to the chair by the window, ignoring the low fire in the stove, and flopped in a pile on the couch by the window. She broke the seal with a tight ball of anticipation in her belly. Her emotions were too jumbled for her to sort which came from the letter and which came from her.

Dearest Iris,

Do not worry for me traveling in the recent snowstorms we have been having, though they are uncommonly frequent and heavy. I too am concerned for some of the town if the snow continues. No apology is needed. Your fears for your neighbors and for me are a sign of your compassion. I would never desire to disappoint you in any way, and so I will continue to write to you as often as I can and deliver the letters when I have completed them.

Thank you for sharing your childhood. I knew early what my work in life would be, continuing the family legacy, and it shaped my childhood. I think this early purpose can be both good and bad. It is good because there is never any wonder of your path, and bad because there is little room for deviation. I am content with where I am now and I hope you have found peace as well.

Your feelings towards your lonely friends do you justice. They reveal your deep and

It was unsigned. Iris reread the letter more times than she wished to admit, letting the emotions roll over her. She sat curled up in the chair watching the snowflakes dance in their journey to the ground and thought about what it meant to be pursued by someone. It was a heady feeling of power, anticipation, and uncertainty. While writing the letters was fun, Iris knew it would have to stop eventually. She would have to meet the man writing to her or they would have to cease to correspond. She had many questions. Would her growing ideas about her friend live up to reality? Would he be as gracious and honest in person?

Iris put these new musings behind the real worries for the town and Mrs. Stewart. Now that the snow was cleared again, it was time to turn her attention back to outfitting the rest of the valley. Doc did not want anyone going to the Stewart farm, but perhaps she could go and deliver some things to the family and leave them away from the house. With that plan in mind, Iris folded her letter and stood.

A door opened behind her and a bleary eyed Thomas emerged from his room.

"Good morning. Want me to make breakfast?" Iris asked.

Thomas mumbled what she thought was an affirmative answer. She went into her room, dressed, and braided her golden hair. The letter went into her pocket and she went to make breakfast.

***

"Can I go see Jonah today?" Thomas wound a scarf around his neck.

"Yes, but check in with Henry or Simon after lunch and see if there is shoveling to do. If there's a work detail out, they'll know about it, though I'm not sure what good it'll do since it hasn't stopped snowing for days. We still have plenty of deliveries to make from the bags Spuds brought in, but I'm hoping we can wait for the snow to go down before making most of them." Iris ran a finger down the row of slots and pulled out a fat envelope. "Take this to Mrs. McKenzie. Tell her I said hi and to come by later if she wants. I know with Reed and Marina gone, she might be missing some adult conversation." Claire McKenzie was a widow and Reed Brant's sister. She lived in a house on the edge of town with her two boys.

Thomas took the letter and ran out the door with a little burst of speed. Iris hoped he slowed to a mortal speed before running through the length of the town. Iris pulled the oil cloth bag she liked to use for deliveries from under the counter and began filling it with envelopes. If she was flying in the direction of Silvercliff, she could make some deliveries to the Eislers, who lived farther up the mountain than the Stewarts. She would also make some stops in town while she was out. She slung the bag over her coat and went out into the morning.

Iris walked to the clearing and launched herself into the air. The icy air burned as she flew south around town. Giving Turning Creek a wide berth every time she flew added time to her route. She did not begrudge the extra time in the sky, though her stamina was not what it could be. If there was no fear of mortals seeing her, she could have flown from her front porch. It would be a long time before that happened, if it happened at all.

There were some examples of Remnant communities who had tried to live side by side with mortals. Few had ended well. The Aello line of harpies, from which Dora hailed, had ruled off and on over an archipelago off the coast of Greece as royalty for generations. Dora's mother had ruled openly, but her tyrannical rule, like the rule of Zeus, had ended in violence and death.

Iris flew up Silvercliff and went to the Eislers' first. Caroline Eisler was the Remnant of Laelaps and George Eisler was something more benign. Exactly what he was escaped Iris's mind as she flew. She did not remember until she saw the smoke curling from the chimney of a small house. The smoke reminded her of spirits, which jogged her memory. George Eisler was a Remnant of one of the Theoi Meteoroi, a group of Remnants who could control the elements and weather, though she did not know which one. Some of the Theoi Meteoroi had been gods and goddesses. Others had been sprites of the air and weather. George Eisler had never elaborated on his parentage or his powers, if he had any, and Iris had never pushed.

Iris landed and did not bother pulling in her wings. She would not be here long enough and did not want to go through the process more often than she had to. She knocked on the door.

Caroline Eisler, lithe and tall, opened the door. "Welcome, Messenger," she said in her British accent. "Will you come in for some tea and get warm?"

"Thank you for the offer, but I can't stay long. I have to make other deliveries."

Caroline opened the door wider and admitted Iris into the house. The warmth of the small space hit her like a wall. Her face started aching as the heat and blood flowed back to her coldest parts. Her wings dripped on the dirt floor of the cabin, making small brown puddles. Iris gave Caroline a sheepish look.

Caroline took Iris's elbow and led her to the fire. A looming shadow rose from a bench by the fire and unfolded into a round man.

"Welcome to our home, Messenger," Mr. Eisler said.

"Don't worry about the water on the floor. It will dry in no time at all. Are you sure I can't get you some tea? Or do you drink coffee?" Caroline bustled around the tiny space, putting a kettle on the hook over the fire and pulling out a stool for Iris to sit on.

Iris sat and let her wings sag. She was colder and a bit more tired than she thought. She also knew that Dora and Marina were probably the only company the Eilsers had with any frequency. It would not be charitable for her to arrive and then leave without staying to visit.

Iris opened her bag and dug out a handful of letters. "Spuds made it through the pass before the snow started falling in earnest. These came for you."

Caroline's eyes lit up. "A letter from my mother, at last. I was beginning to worry. Do you like sugar or milk in your tea?"

"Black is fine." Iris accepted the tea and took a sip. It was weaker than she liked, but it was warm, and that was what she cared about the most in this moment.

"How are things in town?" Caroline asked.

"Fine, mostly. Everyone was happy to see Spuds. With the snow brewing, most people had given up on seeing him for a few weeks. It's been snowing so much since he arrived, he hasn't been able to leave." Iris's face was beginning to feel like a normal part of her body with the heat of the fire pounding it back into feeling.

"Been snowing steady for a few days now," Mr. Eisler commented.

"Yes. Henry Foster said the men will have to start clearing off the roofs of some of the buildings if we get another hard snow." Iris wondered what Henry was working on today. "Is everything all right here?"

George Eisler took his wife's hand. "We're right as rain here."

Looking at George with his wife, Iris could not imagine a reason why he would be the cause of the large amount of snow they'd been having. He was too at ease, too soft for such malice.

Caroline Eisler leaned forward. "Is there any other news?"

Iris sipped her tea, cradling the cup to get as much warmth as possible into her hands. "Margaret Myers just had a little girl and she's doing fine. Daniel Vine and James Lloyd are teaming up to make some wine-aged cheese."

Caroline patted her husband's arm. "My George loves the cheese from Lloyd's farm. That sounds wonderful."

"I'm not sure if Dora has been by lately, but the Stewarts have been ill. The middle daughter, Natalie, has died, along with Mr. Stewart, and most of the family is still sick. Doc says to give them a wide berth in case it is contagious."

"Poor Deborah. Her girls are her life." Caroline rubbed a hand across her middle. Iris noticed the gesture and thought it would not be long until the Eislers' family expanded.

Iris drank the last sip of her tea. "I know it's early in the season yet, but are there any supplies you need? I can send one of the harpies with supplies or an order from Simon's, if you tell me now."

Caroline's cheeks colored. "I do have a few things we need. Sugar, for one. I was glad you did not want any for your tea."

Iris reached over and patted Caroline's hand. "I am used to drinking my tea with whatever is on hand. I appreciate your hospitality. Do you want to make a list?"

"Make your list, Caro, and I will get the money to pay Simon." Mr. Eisler rose and went into the back room of the cabin.

"If you need any meat, include that. Dora's smokehouse is still half full, and I will let her know to bring you some." Iris stood and stretched her warm muscles. At least she did not have to go far. The Stewarts lived just around the ridge.

Caroline handed her a piece of paper with a handful of items. Mr. Eisler dropped some coins in her palm.

"Thank you for your service, Miss Iris," Mr. Eisler went back to sitting in his chair.

Caroline walked her to the door. "I'm so glad you stopped by."

Iris hesitated and then gave Caroline a hug. The woman returned her hug with more strength than Iris thought possible in her willowy frame. "It's my pleasure. One of the harpies, probably Dora, will be along in a few days or a week at most. Is anything on the list critical?"

Caroline looked back at her husband and warmth melted her eyes. "George likes sugar in his tea, but otherwise we are fine."

Iris laughed. "Never deny a man his tea the way he likes it."

Caroline opened the door and the frigid air hit Iris. She walked out onto the porch without flinching. She considered skipping the Stewarts. She was starting to loathe flying in the snow and cold. Iris covered as much of her face as she could and took off. She waved at Caroline, who had come out onto the porch to watch her fly away.

The warmth of the Eislers' home stayed with Iris as she approached the Stewart house. A pinch of apprehension gripped Iris as she dropped into the pristine snow fifty yards from the house. There were no footsteps in the yard. Nothing marred the smooth white expanse between the house and the barn. There were no marks in the snow from the porch to the pile of covered wood stacked along the south side of the house. The steady curl of smoke issuing from the chimney was the only indication of life. The pinch of apprehension twisted.

Iris cupped her hands around her mouth. "Hello, the house!"

Dora had asked her not to go into the house, and Iris did not intend to unless there was an emergency inside. Her intention was to leave the supplies she had brought a ways from the house for someone to retrieve. Iris shifted her weight. The cold seeped into her skin without the effort of flying to hold it at bay. She drew in a lungful of cold air and prepared to yell again. The door to the house opened. A small, freckled face poked through the crack of the open door. It was the youngest Stewart girl. Iris remembered her name was Nina, pronounced with a hard "I."

"Hello, Nina. I'm Miss Iris. Do you remember me?"

Brown eyes blinked at her. "Yes. You run the post office."

Iris smiled and nodded. "That's right. Are you doing all right?"

Nina's brown eyes widened. "Natalie and Papa went to sleep and won't wake up. Nancy is sick and Momma won't stop crying."

The need to walk forward and wrap the girl in a hug was overwhelming. Iris steadied herself with a breath. "Are you all right? Have you eaten today?"

Nina nodded. "I made corn cakes and ate some dried apples. I tried to give some to Momma but she didn't want any. There's nice beef broth on the stove, but Momma said it's for Nancy and Papa."

Iris opened her satchel with fingers that trembled and not from the cold. "I brought some cheese, oats, and some dried fruit. I can't come to the house because of the sickness, but I'm going to leave it here in the snow. Will you put on a coat and come get it after I leave?"

Nina nodded. "Can I make porridge from the oats? Momma showed me how to make it last month and it's one of my favorites. I put honey in it. Did you bring honey?"

The simple question made her want to cry with the need to hug Nina instead of standing useless in the snow. "I'm so sorry. I don't have any honey."

Nina shrugged. "Even without honey, I like it fine."

Iris pulled the packages out of her bag. "I'm going to leave these here." She put them down in the snow.

Iris hesitated. She should turn and fly away, but her feet were rooted to the ground. She could not bring herself to leave. Nina had opened the door wider, and Iris could see her twisting her small fingers in the skirt of her dress.

"Are your wings made of gold?"

"What?" Iris started then laughed weakly. "No, they just look like gold, they're not made of gold. Real gold would not make very good feathers. It's too heavy."

Iris could see the ideas processing in Nina's mind as she considered Iris's response. The girl tilted her head to one side. "We had a goose last year, but we killed him for the Winter Solstice dinner. His name was Goose. He had the softest feathers. Momma saved them and put them into a small pillow that she gave me. Are your feathers soft?"

Despite the cold and the pity she felt for the child, Iris found herself smiling. "They are soft." Iris spread her wings out and around, giving her access to run her hand along the length of the crest of the right wing. "I will leave you a feather, if you'd like one."

"Are your feathers magic?"

The question stopped Iris short. "I've never considered that. I don't know if they are. The truth is, I haven't had my wings very long, and I'm still learning how to use them. I'm going to leave you two feathers. If you discover any magical properties, will you let me know?"

The girl's eyes twinkled. "Yes. I'll tell you. I'll watch them all the time, but I promise never to show them to mortals. Momma said we must never ever tell anyone about our family, especially mortals. She said mortals don't like families like ours."

Not for the first time, Iris wished she knew what kind of Remnants the Stewarts were. "Your Momma gave you good advice. I appreciate your trust."

Iris grabbed one of the long primary feathers from the bottom of her right wing and yanked before she thought about it. The pain was sharp but faded to a dull ache quickly. Next she grabbed a shorter covert feather from the top and pulled. She flapped her wing to shake out the receding pain. Iris laid the two feathers, one long and wide, one half the size in length and width, on top of the parcels she had laid on the ground. They shone dully, a beacon in the grey day.

"Miss Dora will be here to check on you soon. Please let her know if you need anything. I will try to come back soon to see if you've discovered anything about my feathers."

Nina nodded earnestly. "I'll do my very best."

"Good girl. Now go inside and get a jacket and boots before wading out into this snow. Goodbye, Nina."

"Goodbye, Miss Iris." Nina closed the door.

Iris remained in place for a few seconds before pumping her wings and flying away. The image of Nina's large brown eyes followed her all the way back to the outskirts of Turning Creek. Iris landed in the clearing. With a deep breath, she pulled her wings back into her center. She could feel the essence that made her The Messenger tighten up and condense while the tingling and burning subsided.

It was past noon when Iris left the clearing to walk back into town. She went in the back door of the depot and continued through the room to her space behind the counter. Her hands and face were numb and her shoulders ached, but standing in front of the mail drowned everything else out.

Iris closed her eyes and forgot about everything – little girls without honey and endless days of snow – and focused on the pull of the letters. Without opening her eyes, she pulled a letter from the slot for Daniel Vine. Many of the other slots were empty, and some letters were waiting to be delivered to places farther out in the valley. For a moment, her concern over the Stewarts and the snow faded and the peace of the letters filled her. Iris smiled and opened her eyes.

Her first stop in town was the mercantile. Beth had her back to the door, straightening bolts of cloth, when she went in. She turned when Iris stepped inside the mercantile, shaking the snow from her shoulders.

Beth smiled in greeting, which transformed her face from mousy to pretty. "Good morning, Iris. What can I get for you today?"

"Simon said something about some new paper and pens."

Beth bustled over to the main counter. "He's out back shoveling some snow. He told me you might stop by." She disappeared behind a curtain and reappeared with a brown, flat parcel and a small box. Beth placed the items on the counter. "Here we go. There are two different pens. Let me know what you think of them. Decide how much of the paper you want, and I'll wrap it up for you."

Iris opened the box. In it were two gleaming fountain pens with different nibs. "These are beautiful. I can't accept these without paying you something."

Beth smiled. "They're already given. We appreciate you, and Simon wanted to give you something. I'll be by the cloth. Take your time. There's some ink there," Beth pointed to a bottle of indigo liquid, "if you want to try them out."

"Thank you." Iris picked up the first pen, made of marbled wood and silver. It was light and felt warm in her fingers.

The door to the mercantile opened and Lily Hughes walked in. Lily was the Remnant of Medusa and she could mesmerize people, but she almost never used her ability. Her brown hair was in its customary bun and her head was uncovered, making her large brown eyes her most prominent feature. Lily smiled at Iris. "Good morning, Iris. Beth."

Iris returned Lily's smile with a hug. "How are you this snowy day?"

Lily joined Iris at the counter. "I'm well, thank you. Those pens are exquisite." Lily ran a finger over the ebony and gold one.

Iris handed the pen to her. "I only need one."

"I don't need one at all. It's just beautiful."

Beth came up behind them. "Simon ordered them as a gift for The

Messenger. They are hers to do with as she likes."

Lily put the ebony pen back in the box. "I can't accept a gift meant for another."

Iris put the ebony pen in Lily's hand and closed her hand around it. "Take it. It will make me happy."

"Well, I could always just mesmerize you into giving it to me." Lily smiled and opened her eyes wide before laughing.

The three women laughed together, the joyful sound filling the room. Beth threw an arm over Lily's shoulders. "You wouldn't do that to a fly."

Lily's face turned serious and Iris knew she was thinking about the basement under the Nasso barn. Iris put one arm around Beth and one around Lily. "What's past is past, and you have kindness in you above all things."

"But maybe not forgiveness." Lily's voice was hard and Iris saw a flicker of Medusa's power in the woman's gaze.

"Don't hold on to that for too long. Bitterness is a hard root to pull," Beth said.

Lily sighed. "Sorry for turning a lovely day upside down."

Beth squeezed them both. "That's what friends are for. Now, take the pen Iris gave you and use it to write happy things."

Lily drew a ragged breath. "You have a good heart, Messenger, and you too, Beth."

Beth rubbed her hands over her apron. "Now, I know you came here for something. What can I do for you?"

Lily pulled a list from a pocket in her skirt. "I need to order some cloth for the spring and get some things for the girls. Paul is going to start teaching them how to do some basic tailoring, and he wanted me to order some smaller tools for them." Paul did most of the tailoring work while Lily added embellished embroidery to some of their higher-end items. They had seven-year-old twin girls.

"Can't get the girls to learn needlecraft?" Iris asked.

Lily's laugh was like silver bells. "They can barely be still long enough for one stitch. Paul is hoping cutting patterns and hemming will teach them some patience."

Iris took the package of paper and the wood and silver pen. "I'll take these. Put the paper on my account and thank Simon for the pen."

"Wait," Beth stopped her. "I have some letters for you." Beth pulled a stack of different-shaped envelopes from behind her counter. "Most of them are for families outside of town."

Iris tucked the letters in her bag. "If the snow lets up, I'll do a delivery soon. Some of the families need to be checked on once the snow settles."

Iris took her leave and walked back out onto Main Street. She hesitated in the gently falling snow. Her next stop on her list was the saloon. She had a packet for Daniel. Iris's gaze went from the saloon to the building on the other side of the boarding house. She could see the glow of the forge from where she stood, like a beacon in the afternoon. Iris walked up the boardwalk until she could see inside the open end of the blacksmith shop from across the way.

Henry's back was to her. She watched as he swung his hammer down in a rhythm she felt in her bones. Iris had no reason to go see Henry, but her feet took her there anyway. Iris clung to her conviction as she crossed Main Street, her heart beating with painful sharpness.

Henry looked up as she approached. Despite the crisp air, sweat ran down his face. His coat hung on a peg and he worked only in a shirt tied at his throat and a pair of trousers. There was something provocative about his lack of coat that Iris found unsettling in the most pleasant way.

"Good morning, Miss Iris. What brings you this way?" Henry put his hammer down and pulled off his gloves. He ran a hand through his hair, fluffing the curls up.

Iris cast about for a reason that was plausible. "I was wondering what your impression was of the book I lent you yesterday." She knew he had not even had it a full day. It was just as likely he had not looked at it at all.

Henry smiled at her and she felt as if he almost knew her question was a farce. She scolded herself. He could not read her mind. That was not one of his gifts. "Let me finish this hook, and then I can take a break and we can talk. Will you wait?" Henry motioned to a bench along the wall.

Iris nodded and sat down on the small bench near the door of the forge. As close as she was to the door, the heat from the fire battled with the cold of the snow, making the temperature comfortable except for small bursts of wind that beat back the heat. Henry pulled his gloves back on and picked up the hammer. He reached for a lever and the whooshing of the bellows filled the space. He turned back to his work and Iris was free to watch him.

Henry's movements were power and grace confined. The swing of the hammer, a turn of the hand, and the hook smoothed and curved under his tools. The sound of striking metal mesmerized her, and she ceased to be aware of anything else but what was before her. It was not unlike how she felt standing before the mail slots. The world in a pinpoint of existence. Iris found her mind rather enjoyed the freedom to watch Henry work in silence. Admiration for the man before her, both his form and skill, hit Iris like a blow. It was something to know he loved what he did with passion and looked beautiful while doing it. It took her breath to watch him.

The hiss of the metal as Henry dumped his work into the cooling vat shook her from her reverie. He limped over to the wall and hung his gloves and apron on pegs next to his coat. He sat down next to Iris with a sigh. Iris drew in a breath and found the air was filled with the smell of fire, metal, and male exertion. She resisted the urge to lean closer to him.

Henry leaned his head back until it rested on the wall, and closed his eyes. "The cold makes standing worse, though honestly, sitting down after standing in one place for so long is worse than the standing itself."

He was close and Iris drank in the sight of his face. "Do you ever wish you had been born with two normal feet?" She was asking him about more than just his deformity.

"Do you regret your wings?"

Iris thought of her golden birthmark and how the mark used to ache with a need to fly. "Never."

"The mark of our lines come with both burden and blessing, as do all things worth having. I accept what I've been given with thanksgiving, as you do, I think."

Iris laughed. "You know me too well. You forget, I know you as well. I think you enjoy playing the role of the honest sage."

Henry's eyes twinkled and Iris marveled that she had ever thought them to be plain grey. "You've figured me out. Don't know any other way to be." Henry shivered and stood to retrieve his coat. "I believe you came to ask me about the book you lent me." Henry put on his coat and sat down again, a smidgen closer than before.

Iris fidgeted in her seat and closed the gap between them on the bench in the process. Henry's warmth blazed against her hotter than the forge. She did not move away. "Yes. Did you get a chance to read any of it?"

"Some last night. Thank you again. I don't have words to tell you what it's like to read about the defeat of Zeus and the Fall of Olympus from the first of my name. Though he bore no love for the gods and he fought on the side of the resistance, it saddened him to have his home destroyed."

Iris relaxed into the bench and enjoyed the warmth radiating from the man beside her. "I don't think war is easy on either side. The resistance won, but they reaped generations of change and upheaval. Say what you want about Zeus and the gods, they did impart a certain kind of order with their despotism."

"I read far enough to get through some the entries chronicling those first few generations and their struggles to integrate into mortal society." Henry's voice warmed her as much as his body. "There were a couple references to the harpies."

Iris straightened away from the wall. "What did they say? I've just finished the account of Elpis, the fourth Messenger. Her writings are difficult to read and overly depressing." It had been years since she had skimmed over the volume she had lent Henry. She did not remember it mentioning anything of significance regarding the harpies.

"I have been thinking about your mother's theory and your own concerns about your harpies. It seems to me that there was a difference in the harpies after the Fall of Olympus. The generations that came after seemed," Henry paused and turned to Iris, "they seemed lost, and not just to each other, but in their own violence."

Iris knew her own harpies struggled to find a balance between their violent natures and the world around them. "That lines up with Elpis's account. I have a theory, but I've not shared it with them. I'd like to hear what you think, though I don't want you to share it with them yet."

Henry's eyes shone with secrets. "I can keep counsel well enough."

Iris blinked, shutting out the view of him so close before speaking. "You know the story, of the lost fourth harpy?" Henry nodded. "When Podarge died in the siege on Olympus without a daughter and someone to carry on her line, I think something broke in the remaining harpies. They were created in tandem; together, yet separate. I think the tie that tethered them together also tethered them to their humanity. I believe that when Podarge and her line was lost, the other three began losing their connection to each other and eventually to humanity. They became lost to the more violent side of their nature because there was nothing left to balance it."

Henry ran a hand over his beard. "Our harpies seem to be finding their link to humanity, not losing it."

Iris was pleased at his possessive use of the pronoun our. "I have an idea about that as well."

Henry tilted his head and searched her face. "You've been thinking of this often, I think."

Iris shrugged. "Recent events have required it." Events like two of her harpies taking mates for life. "The generations after the first harpies left Olympus scattered and had little to do with each other. The original three were each too lost in their own grief and violence to seek each other out again, and their daughters continued to live separately. I think our harpies are, for whatever reason, drawn to each other. This generation lives together and has claimed this valley as their own. Being together and defending Turning Creek has changed them. They live more like the first harpies did on Strophades. I'm proud of what they are becoming.

"I think the purpose they share here and the theory my mother has of their love changing them is working together. I think they're becoming more like the original four harpies. They are becoming what they were originally created to be."

Henry's lips quirked up. "It pleases me to see Petra and Marina finding themselves and their place. Dora doesn't spend time in the forge and I don't know her as well. She finds peace and counsel elsewhere, I think. She's still searching."

A knot of worry and grief tightened in her belly. "You're right. I think she is still looking for herself. She has not yet found the balance of what she is and what she can become."

Henry's hand covered her knee and Iris fought the tremor that ran up her leg. "You worry for her. She'll find her place as the other two have. Dora has her own timing." He paused, as if considering, and then continued. "With two birds settled, do you feel the need to settle in yourself?"

Iris had been asked a similar question in the letter she carried in her pocket. "It's my duty to watch over them and guide them. I'm not sure if that means I should wait until they have all had their own daughters or if I should seek my own partner in the meantime. I've my own line to continue, after all." Iris felt her face heat in a blush. *I blush entirely too much in this man's presence,* she thought, *like a young girl with no knowledge of the world.*

Henry's hand left her knee and she felt its loss. "As do we all. One day."

Iris stood and smoothed her hands over her skirt. "I should let you get back to work."

Henry stood, and the movement brought his body almost flush with hers. She had to crane her neck a bit to see his face. "I've something for you before you leave."

He walked around her and past the forge, his limp prominent then smoothing out as he moved to a long work bench in the back. Mallets, hammers, knives, awls, and all manner of tools hung in orderly rows on the wall above the bench. The wood of the work bench was scarred by fire and many hours of work. Iris followed Henry.

He lifted a small bundle of cream-colored wool wrapped with twine. Henry placed the soft bundle in her hand. His fingers brushed her palm and she felt the light touches in her core. "I've noticed you don't have a seal of your own. It seems to me The Messenger should have a mark for her letters."

Iris pulled the twine loose and folded back the wool. The seal was made of pewter and had a smooth handle that fit perfectly between her small fingers. She turned over the head to see the design. Her heart constricted. Two wings formed a circle around the word *charis*. Iris rolled the seal between two fingers. It was the most perfect gift she had ever been given.

Henry shifted his weight and ran a hand through his hair. "I can make something different if you want."

Iris raised her eyes from the seal and laid her hand on Henry's arm. "No." She squeezed the seal into her fist. "It's perfect. I'm touched that you would make this for me. Why the word *charis*, though?"

Iris thought of the letters in her pocket and the way they were signed. Charis was a common enough Greek word. There was no reason why it connected Henry to her letters. Given the nature of her last letter, Iris could not imagine Henry writing those words no matter how much she wanted to hear them from him.

Henry's eyes bore into hers and his voice was low. "Charis seemed the most fitting. Grace is one of the words I always think of when I think of you."

Iris could not have looked away or moved if she had wanted to. "What are the others? Words, I mean."

Henry did not answer, but a very bright red traveled up his neck. Iris noted its progress and the complete stillness of the man beside her. She tightened the hand holding the seal to keep it from moving up to touch his face.

"Well, this is a fine surprise." The voice cut through the moment.

Iris heard a puff of a sigh escape Henry. She wondered if it was from relief or frustration. It was a prick of frustration that niggled at her as she turned to greet Jacob.

"Afternoon to you, Jacob." Iris mustered a smile. She was normally pleased to see him, but his timing was inopportune today.

"I came by to see if some of the gears and hooks I asked for were ready."

Henry turned and walked back the bench and picked up a box with a thick rope as a handle. "I finished most of them. The large gear is not yet made, but these should get you started."

Jacob looked into the box and smiled. "These are well done. Thank you, Henry." He dug into his coat pocket and pulled out some round silver discs. "Here's the fee you requested. It includes the work for the large gear."

Henry took the payment. "I'll let you know when I'm done."

It was past time for her to be leaving. Iris put the seal in her pocket next to the letters there. "I have other letters to deliver. I'd best be leaving."

"Where're you headed?" Jacob asked.

"To Vine's. I have some letters for him."

"May I walk you there?"

Iris looked at Henry before answering. His face, which had been open before, was completely closed off. "Yes, that would be lovely." Iris put her hand on Henry's arm. "Thank you again for the seal and for thinking of me."

Henry's eyes moved from Jacob to her and his face softened. "I'll see you tomorrow, Miss Iris."

Jacob held out his arm for her, and Iris wrapped her hand through the crook in his arm and walked out of the forge. They left the warmth behind and the full wall of cold hit Iris. She shivered and Jacob pulled her closer to him. She was grateful for the warmth, though it did not match the heat she had felt with Henry.

The weight of the letters in her pocket was like lead. Iris felt her neck heat under her scarf as she thought of the bold words of her last letter. Henry, with his serious demeanor, seemed unlikely to be able to commit those kinds of words to paper. She could easily imagine the man currently beside her penning them. Jacob had no problem complimenting her to her face, which left her wondering why he was writing the letters at all. Perhaps he knew or suspected how much words meant to her.

"What happens tomorrow?" Jacob asked.

"What?" Iris had not been listening.

"Henry said he would see you tomorrow."

Iris had to think. All the days of snow ran together. "Tomorrow is Saturday. He has dinner with Thomas and me on Saturdays. He lives alone, and I don't want him to be lonely." Even to her ears it felt like she was qualifying her Saturdays with Henry. Remorse for her tone and words was swift.

A tingling in her spine alerted her the moment before the thought appeared in her head. Petra would be in town for dinner tomorrow. Her prophecy was mostly like that, soft urgings and thoughts. It was rarely the overpowering seeings, like she had experienced with Petra before the arrival of Zeus almost two years ago. It had been many, many weeks since Petra had joined her for a Saturday dinner. Jacob walked next to her, unaware of the power she possessed, and Iris felt the omission like a lie. She did not enjoy lying to her friends.

If she allowed this relationship to continue, she would have to tell him one day who and what she was. While she knew some Remnants who kept their true nature a secret from everyone, including their spouse, this was not a road she wanted to take. She wanted an equal partnership, free of lies and half-truths. Jacob seemed like an honest man. Iris did not know what she would be to him in the future, but felt he would want the same from his partner. She did not yet feel like she knew him well enough to predict his reaction to the truth of the world he inhabited.

"Would you like to join us?" Iris regretted the invitation the moment it was out and rushed to cover her own discomfort. "Petra Lloyd will be joining us. I don't think you've met her yet. She lives on the dairy farm with her husband, James, north of town."

There was no harm in asking Jacob to dinner if Petra was going to be there. Iris liked Jacob's company and she would not get to know him better if they did not spend more time together. The farther they walked, the more she looked forward to having a small crowd for dinner. It had been too long since she had entertained a full table.

"I couldn't say no to an invitation from such a lovely woman."

"We don't often expand our company. You'll be a welcome addition."

"I hope so. I've enjoyed being able to get to know you and spend time with you."

A warm feeling burgeoned within her, the power of being a woman and knowing yourself wanted. It was no less heady than the power of all the Messengers who had come before her. "I assure you the feeling is mutual."

Jacob pointed to a lopsided snowman on the boardwalk outside of the Hughes' shop. The snowman had started out with distinct body segments, but the snow, which was still falling, had turned the snowman into a pile of snow distinguishable as a snowman only by the arms and nose sticking out of the pile. "Have you ever made a snowman?"

Iris laughed at the absurdity of the question. "No, regretfully, I have not. I had many siblings, but I was not close to any of them, and it is not as fun to make a snowman by oneself."

Jacob's voice was grave. "Indeed, it is not. One must never set forth to make a snowman alone." They had reached Vine's and Jacob stopped and turned to face her. "I find it unacceptable that you've never made a proper snowman. May I come over tomorrow and make one with you?"

Iris smiled at his serious expression, though his eyes twinkled and gave him away. "Yes, I think I can find time tomorrow. After lunch?"

Jacob put down the box he was carrying. He slid her hand that was on his arm into his hands and bowed over it. "Until tomorrow, then." He straightened up, winked at her, and then continued on his way.
Iris watched him go, smiling. Jacob was an easy soul and he made her laugh. It was a simple thing to get caught up in his nature. She pivoted until the forge was in the corner of her eye. The real question she needed to answer was whether she wanted to.

CHAPTER 12

Saturday dawned as dusky as the day before. The snow fell unabated and lay in piles of white fluff around the depot. Iris went outside only long enough to haul in more wood for the stove. The air contained a menacing undertone. Iris was again struck by the idea that the snow was more than it appeared. There was something distinctly unnatural about the snow, both in its consistency and its duration.

When she had the fire in the stove roaring, Iris pulled three books off her shelves. Each was a kind of index of Remnants written by different Messengers from different eras. Her great-grand-mere had taught her to read Greek and Latin with these very volumes and she knew them by heart. She hoped against hope that something would jump out at her. Time lost meaning as she read the familiar pages.

Iris jumped as the bell clanged downstairs.

"Hello? Iris?" Jacob's voice called.

She had read through the late morning and lunch. "I'm up here. You can come on up." With a start, Iris looked at the books spread before her. She had to put them away before Jacob made his way upstairs. She looked at her bookshelf and knew there were not many explanations for the sheer number and content of the books she owned. She would have to make some kind of excuse for them eventually. It might as well be today.

She closed the books and stood. She was sliding the last book into place when Jacob stepped off the last stair. Iris turned to greet him. "I'm sorry. I completely lost track of time while I read. I'm not ready for snowman building yet."

"I'm in no rush." Jacob looked over her shoulder and his eyes widened when he took in the wall of shelves and books. "I've never seen so many books in one place."

"They're a family collection. They were given to me by my mother when

I left home." Iris put her hands behind her back and squeezed them together, waiting.

Jacob walked to the shelf closest to the kitchen area and farthest from her. The books there were quite old, though she kept the oldest ones in her room, and they represented a variety of languages. He reached out as if he were going to touch one, then dropped his hand to his side.

He cleared his throat. "Can you read these? All these?"

"Most of them with fluency, but all of them with reliable accuracy."

Jacob turned, a frown wrinkling his face, the first Iris had ever seen him make. "You're a surprising woman." The frown vanished and his usual smile appeared. "My mother always counseled me to find a woman smarter than myself. She said it would make my life interesting."

Iris stopped twisting her hands together and smoothed out her skirt. "I wouldn't say I am smarter than you."

Jacob waved at the shelves filled with her books. Books she knew like the back of her own hand. "Wouldn't you?"

Iris took a few steps closer to him. "Of course not. I know nothing of how to run a mill, let alone build one from scratch as you are doing. We all have different gifts and different purposes, all of which are important."

"Well said."

"I believe you are here to assist me in making a snowman."

"That was the agreement."

"Let me grab my coat and things."

Iris went into her room and looked at herself in the mirror. She smoothed her hair back and then frowned at herself when she remembered she would have a hat on. Iris fingered her skirt and considered changing into a pair of pants, but the skirt was more feminine. In the end, vanity won. She pulled her knitted hat on more forcefully than was needed and put on her coat. She emerged from her room to find Jacob standing at the large window overlooking Main Street.

"I'm ready." Iris wrapped her scarf around her neck and face.

Jacob moved away from the window. He looked down at her. "Your hat matches the blue of your eyes. It looks beautiful on you."

Iris was grateful for the scarf that covered the blush that warmed her neck and face. "Thank you." She led the way downstairs and out the back of the depot.

She gestured to the deep, unmarked snow. "I thought there would be plenty of snow here for our purposes."

Jacob put his hands on his hips and surveyed her small yard with a critical eye. "I think it'll do." He smiled, then laughed.

His mirth was contagious, and Iris joined his laughter with her own. "What's the first thing I need to do?"

Jacob knelt down in the snow. "First, make a ball of snow with your hands, like a snowball, but bigger."

Iris knelt in the snow. The cold and damp went through her skirt, which would be a sodden mess before they were through. Vanity was poor consolation when her legs were tangled in wet skirts and cold. There was no help for it now.

"Snowballs, I can do." Iris packed some snow together and held it up for inspection.

Jacob cocked his head. "Very nice. Now, put it on the ground and roll it around, like this."

Iris copied his movements and her medium-sized snowball grew until it was bigger than her head. She kept going, rolling the growing ball until it became too hard to push. "How's this?"

"Perfect. Now, roll it to wherever you want him to be."

"Her."

"What?"

"Her. My snowman is a lady. A snowlady." Iris maneuvered the ball until it was in the center of the area behind the depot.

"It's your creation, so she may be what you wish. A beautiful snowlady for a beautiful lady."

He handed out compliments as if they cost nothing. Iris did not blush this time. "Thank you. What do we do next?"

Jacob picked up the ball he had made. It was about half the size of Iris's, and he placed it with care on top of the body.

"One more ball, about half the size of mine," Jacob said.

Iris bent over, rolling the snow into another, smaller ball. Jacob scooped it up and set it in place. They stood back and surveyed their work.

"It's missing something," she said.

Jacob pulled off his right glove and plunged his hand into the front pocket of his coat. "I've come prepared." He pulled out two large metal disks and a stick the size of his thumb whittled down to a point on one side. "If you would like to do the honors."

Iris took the offered items. She ran her finger over the tip of the stick. Jacob had sat and made this for her, wanting to please her. Iris felt the complement of his time, but it brought no rush of pleasure to her. She thought of the letters she had left on her nightstand and imagined Jacob composing each word with the care and thought he had placed into making this snowlady with her. He was forward enough to write those kind of letters, but she was not sure she wanted him to be the author.

Iris thought of the pewter seal Henry had made for her, sitting beside her new pen. A smile came unbidden to her lips when she thought of Henry bent over the warm metal, shaping it with patience and skill. She bit back a frustrated sigh.

"I know most folks just find a stick for the nose, but my dad always used to whittle a nose for every snowman we made, and now I can't seem to make one any other way."

Iris focused her attention back on Jacob, embarrassed. She had forgotten he was there for a moment. She placed the disks and stick in the proper places on the top ball and walked back to Jacob to admire their handiwork.

"She certainly has character."

Iris agreed. "Yes, but I think the nose is a bit masculine on her face, poor thing. She must be one of those women who are said to be handsome rather than beautiful or pretty."

Jacob's laugh boomed into the quiet afternoon. "I think she'll do just fine."

The cold from her heavy, wet skirt seeped into her legs and Iris shivered.

Jacob turned serious. "It's a bit chilly out here. We should go in and get warm. I've never seen snow fall so steady for days before."

"Neither have I."

"It's uncanny."

It was, but Iris strongly suspected the reason behind it was not something she could share with Jacob. Iris walked around the snowlady. "I think she is passable for my first effort. Thankfully, I think there will be plenty more snow for me to try again tomorrow. Maybe I'll make her a snowman to keep her company."

"As long as he is a gentleman and doesn't mention her masculine nose."

"He'd never dare," Iris chuckled. "Would you like to come in for some cider or tea?" If he stayed, it would hardly be worth the effort for him to go home before it was time for dinner. Iris was glad she had started the soup for dinner after breakfast. She was beginning to be less glad she had invited Jacob. She liked him and he made her laugh, but she did not feel the desire to linger with him. Perhaps that would come in time.

The snow crunched in the trees beyond the yard. Footsteps and a muttered curse Iris recognized rang over the snow. Petra had arrived. The harpy, thankfully in her mortal form, waded through the knee-deep snow. Her salt and pepper curls were unbound and tangled from the wind. Her pants were wet from the thigh down and she had on a thick sweater but no jacket, hat, or scarf. It was obvious Petra had expected to be able to fly up to the back door of the depot. It was also obvious she was flaming mad about it.

Jacob stood open-mouthed while Petra made her appearance. Iris could not think of an excuse for Petra's sudden presence without proper attire or mode of transportation, so she made none.

Petra, olive skin flushed from flying and eyes snapping annoyance, stuck her hand out to Jacob. "I'm Petra Lloyd. You must be Jacob Wells, the miller with the wrong surname. I just came from seeing Paul Hughes. He's fixing a rip in my jacket. I figured I could walk to the depot without a coat."

Jacob did not point out that Petra had not come from the direction of the tailor shop. He shook Petra's hand. "Nice to meet you. I told my dad we should change our name and be done with it."

Harpies were hardy, but Iris did not want Petra standing around in the cold. "Come inside and have something hot to drink."

Petra waved to the snowlady as they walked to the back door. "He's nice."

"She." Jacob opened the door and held it open for them. "She's a snowlady."

Petra raised her eyebrows at Iris as she walked into the depot first. "Her it is then."

"Come upstairs and I will put on some tea. Jacob, you can hang your coat here." Iris took off her outside things and hung them up. "Petra, will you stay for dinner?" Iris already knew the answer. The three of them went upstairs.

"Yes, and I'll stay the night if you don't mind."

Iris ran a hand down Petra's arm. "You know I never do. I had a feeling you might be here this evening. I made up your bed this morning." Iris turned so Jacob could not see her face and she winked at Petra.

Petra rolled her eyes. "You know too much for your own good." She looked at Jacob. "And sometimes not nearly enough." Before Iris could ask her to clarify her last statement, Petra said, "Mr. Wells, tell me how you came to be a part of our lovely town."

"Please, call me Jacob. I wanted to go west, and this valley captured my heart."

He looked at Iris when he said it and Iris caught Petra rolling her eyes. She gave the harpy a stern look. Jacob was enthusiastic, but sincere.

"You can call me Petra."

"That's an unusual name," Jacob said.

Iris busied herself with the tea things. Petra leaned on the table with her elbows. "It is. My mother was a fan of Greek myths. She was a terrible mother, but she loved her history."

Jacobs's eyes flicked to the bookshelves. Iris felt her insides twist up. She did not like lying to Jacob. He was her friend, and he was not an idiot. If he were going to be around with any frequency, she might have to fill him in on the true origin of Petra's name and her own. Of course, she was not yet sure she wanted him around with greater frequency.

Iris laid teacups in front of Jacob and Petra and then poured tea. "Jacob, you should just stay here until dinner. There's no use in walking all the way home and then coming right back."

"He's staying for Saturday dinner?" Petra's teacup rattled as she set it down.

Iris raised an eyebrow. "Is that a problem?"

Petra gave Jacob another once over. "Just surprised. I thought Saturday dinners were sacred."

"Occasionally expanding the company does no harm. I invited you, didn't I?" Iris spooned honey into her cup with rather more force than needed.

"And look what fun I am." Petra toasted with her teacup and took a sip. "Don't tell James, but you make the best tea, Iris. His poor English heart would break."

Jacob watched all of this back and forth without comment. He took a sip of tea. "This is quite good. Thank you. I'll take you up on your offer to stay until dinner. I wasn't looking forward to trudging back to my house in the snow."

"Uncommon amount of snow we've been having," Petra commented with a pointed look at Iris.

Iris sighed. This would be an easier conversation if Jacob were not here. "It is, but some winters have more snow than others. Now that you two are settled, I'm going to change out of this wet skirt."

Iris heard Petra ask Jacob where he was from before she closed the door to her room. She hung her wet clothes up to dry and pulled on a clean skirt, a loose blouse, and a thick warm sweater the color of cream shot through with sky. The wool was soft from years of handling and washing, and Iris rubbed the sleeve absently.

She could hear Jacobs's low voice and then a bark of laughter. Petra joined in and Iris smiled. Jacob was an open man who made friends with everyone. He was mortal though, and for all his easy-going nature, a twinge of fear pricked her at the thought of telling him about Remnants. It was not a secret she had ever revealed on her own.

When Petra, Marina, and Dora had exposed their true nature to Reed, he had taken it in stride. He had accepted them and the help they offered him in keeping order and peace in Turning Creek. He had seen the loyal, fierce fighters under the gruff exterior of the harpies, and he cared about people more than he cared about what they turned into at night.

James had already fallen in love with Petra before he discovered her true nature. He had little room to judge at that point, since he was possessed by Zeus at the time.

Jacob's laughter boomed through the house again and Iris sighed. He did not need to know yet, if ever. If she continued to nurture his tender feelings towards her, she would tell him before things became serious. She did not know for certain if she wanted things to become serious, and she was afraid things had already progressed on his end. It was not a problem she needed to solve tonight, however. Iris rose from her bed and went back into the kitchen to join Petra and Jacob.

The back door slammed downstairs and a clomping up the stairs announced Thomas before he jumped up the last step. His coat and pants dripped water. His head was uncovered and his hair was wet with sweat or snow or both, Iris could not tell. His cheeks and nose were chapped and red, but his face was jubilant.

Iris took one look at his face and wanted to hug him. Instead, she said, "You're dripping everywhere. Go change and then you can tell me where you've been all day."

Thomas bounded to his room a smidge faster than he should have. Iris looked at Jacob, but he was smiling at Thomas as the boy closed the door to his room. Iris was relieved Jacob seemed not to notice anything out of the ordinary and a touch flustered that Jacob's visit had turned into so much more difficulty than she had bargained for. She was going to have to have a serious talk with Thomas about how and when he used his speed. His youthful exuberance over-powered his caution most days.

"Oh to be young and so full of life," Jacob chuckled.

There was a significant amount of banging and noise coming from Thomas's room. Iris took a step towards his door to check on him when the door burst open. Thomas had changed into dry pants and a thick flannel shirt. His hair was in even worse array than it had been a moment ago. Iris ran her hand over it and smoothed it down. Thomas immediately ran his hands back through it, causing it to stick up like a disgruntled porcupine.

Iris gave Thomas the hug she had withheld before. "Where were you all day?"

Thomas got a teacup down from the shelf. "The creek behind Stephen and Jonah's froze over. We were trying to smash holes in the ice."

"If the creek isn't frozen enough, it can be dangerous." Iris pushed the honey towards Thomas.

"We were careful. I'm quick enough to pull one of them back if they started to fall." Thomas put a generous amount of honey in his tea.

Jacob's face was serious. "Accidents happen quicker than anyone intends."

Petra and Iris both leveled warning looks at Thomas, who cleared his throat as if he were just now aware that Jacob was with them. "Biscuits?" he asked.

"Dinner will be soon."

"When?" he pushed.

"As soon as Henry is here, we can eat."

Thomas stood and pulled the jar from the shelf. "I promise I'll eat. Can I have a couple?"

Iris waved a hand at him. "Fine. Save some for after dinner for the rest of us."

Thomas shoved an entire biscuit in his mouth. "Yes, ma'am," he said around the crumbs.

Jacob chuckled. "Yours?" he asked, looking at Iris.

Thomas swallowed the mouthful of cookie and answered before Iris could. "My mother died two years ago when—" The boy stopped speaking abruptly.

"In an accident," Iris finished smoothly. She needed to have that talk with Thomas about more than just his speed.

Thomas continued. "I didn't have any other family, and Iris took me in."

"To answer your question, yes, he's mine." Iris looked at Thomas and a warm feeling settled in her heart.

Petra elbowed Thomas. "We all help keep him out of trouble." She ruffled his hair. "Can't be easy having the equivalent of four aunts flapping around you." Thomas smirked at her choice of words.

"Four?" Jacob asked.

Iris gave Petra a gentle nudge with her foot under the table. "Petra, Dora, Marina, and I have known each other our entire lives. Our families go way back." Further back than Jacob would ever know, further back than Jacob had been alive. The lie she had told so many times left a weight in her middle.

Petra took up the story they told most often. "We're like sisters. Iris orders us around as if she were the oldest. Which she's not, by a long shot." Petra muttered the last into her cup, and Iris had to resist the urge to kick her again.

There must have been a look of dismay or alarm on her face. Jacob waved his hands in the air. "I would never ask a lady how old she was and I'm sure if Iris was a bit bossy she was only doing it because she cares for you."

Iris nodded. "Exactly, right. I, what was the word you used, flap around you because I care."

Petra and Thomas laughed. Jacob laughed too even though he was only laughing at part of the joke.

"How are things on the farm?" Iris asked Petra.

Petra leaned back in her chair, a smile still tugging on her lips. "James and the boys are building a smoker for the cheese. They've taken over the back corner of the barn to frame it out. Once the snow settles and melts, they'll put it up behind the cheese house. Is Spuds still in town? I need to send some orders with him when he leaves. It'll be summer before we get anything, but I wanted to get them sent as soon as I was able."

Jacob rubbed a hand over his cheek. Unlike most of the other men in town, Jacob had not grown a beard for the winter months. "I was over by the boardinghouse this morning. Widow Finch makes an excellent breakfast. Spuds seems to have set up a permanent residence. He didn't look like he was leaving anytime soon."

"He's sweet on Widow Finch, but he loves his route and she loves her boardinghouse." Iris refreshed everyone's tea.

"I think they have an arrangement of sorts," Petra said.

Jacob cleared his throat. "In any case, he said his plan was to stay until this storm blew over. Hopefully, that will be soon."

Petra's dark eyes zoned in on Iris. "The snow is unusual."

Iris held her gaze. "I was thinking the same thing."

Jacob, oblivious to the looks the women were giving each other, said, "All storms must pass in time."

The bell rang downstairs. A surge of emotion sang through Iris. She tamped it down and her ears strained to listen as she imagined Henry unwinding his scarf and hanging up his coat. Her breath caught when his footsteps started up the stairs. She looked at his face first, so she saw the moment he realized there would be a crowd for dinner and his slight smile faltered. It was brief, and she was sure no one else noticed because he righted it quickly. Iris's heart twisted. She could make many excuses, but there was one main reason she could not seem to encourage Jacob in his attentions.

"Nice to see you again, Henry," Jacob said.

Iris looked away from Henry long enough to see Petra looking back and forth between the two men with a cunning look. She cocked an eyebrow in Iris's direction. Iris ignored her and walked over to where Henry stood, rooted on the landing of the stairs.

She stopped when there was the smallest bit of space between them. The smell of metal and wood smoke wrapped around her. Iris put her hand on Henry's arm and squeezed it briefly before letting go. "I'm glad you're here. Sit. Would you like some tea before dinner?"

Her touch put him in motion and he moved to an empty chair. "No, I'll do 'til dinner. After though'd be nice. Smells fine in here."

"Thank you." Iris sat back down.

Henry sat down and looked around the table. "Didn't know you'd have a crowd."

A pinch of regret that she'd asked Jacob touched Iris. "I knew Petra would stop by." Iris put special emphasis on the word knew.

Henry responded with an almost imperceptible nod. "Good to have company once in a while."

There was one empty chair. It was the one in between Jacob and Henry. *So this is how the evening will go*, Iris thought.

Petra leaned towards Henry. "I'm sorry I haven't been by the forge lately. James has been keeping a close eye on me. He thinks I'm delicate."

"He's just doing what all men feel the need to do, protect what's his." Henry's eyes went from Petra to Jacob, but they moved back so quickly Iris thought she imagined it. "He'll figure out soon enough that you are the furthest thing from delicate."

Jacob turned a dubious look in Petra's direction. Petra was tall, but lithe. Her feminine form was only camouflage for what was beneath. If Jacob had been a Remnant, he would have known instinctively that Petra was dangerous. He was not a Remnant. Jacob was a mortal, a trusting one at that, and all he knew of Petra was that she made cheese with her husband and wandered through the woods without a jacket or scarf in the snow.

"What did you work on today?" Petra asked Henry.

Henry ran a hand over his beard. "I worked on some of the larger gears for Jacob's mill. I'm almost done with those, I believe, and I worked on a smaller project that is coming along." He looked at Iris and graced her with one of his small smiles. She could not help but return it with a wide smile of her own.

"Do you think the mill will be running by the spring?" Petra asked Jacob.

Jacob nodded. "Should be. Should be. After Henry finishes with the larger gears, everything'll be close to running. I won't be able to test it out until the river thaws. I got the gears he gave me yesterday in place this morning, then I spent the afternoon doing something much better than working."

Iris felt her neck warm. "Jacob and I built a snowlady."

Thomas's brows drew down. "Don't you mean snowman?"

Iris and Jacob laughed. "She is mannish," she said, which made Jacob laugh harder. Iris giggled.

Henry, Thomas, and Petra watched them with different expressions. Petra and Thomas had various degrees of confusion on their faces. Henry's face was closed off. Iris's laughter faded at his expression. She stood and smoothed out her skirt.

"It's probably time to eat. Let me check everything." Iris went to the stove to stir the soup.

Henry got up from his chair. "Your wood box is empty. Jacob and I can bring up some wood now so you don't have to go back out in the snow tonight."

As if in answer, the wind rattled the windows. "Thank you." The men's booted footsteps clomped down the stairs. The back door opened and shut. Petra crossed her arms and lifted an eyebrow at Iris.

"What?"

"You know what."

Iris put the rolls into the stove to heat for a few minutes. She made a noncommittal noise in the back of her throat.

"Jacob?" Petra pushed.

"He's a nice man," Iris offered, hoping it would shut down Petra's line of questioning.

"And?"

Iris's shoulders slumped over the pot of soup. She stopped stirring it. "That's all, I think."

"Mr. Wells is sweet on Iris," Thomas added.

"Yes, I quite gathered that," Petra said dryly. "Do you still think he's the letter writer?"

"What letter?" Thomas asked.

"None of your business," Iris responded. To Petra she said, "Can't think of who else it would be."

"Can't you?"

Iris had considered Henry, but dismissed him early. The handwriting was not a match, and there was one other reason. "I don't think it's a Remnant."

"Why not?"

"Because the letter has never said anything that relates to me as The Messenger or anything else to do with Remnants."

"What else are you not telling me?" Petra moved until she was in Iris's face.

Iris clenched her mouth closed. She was saved from answering by the back door slamming shut. Jacob was telling a story. "Dad made me chop wood the entire day as punishment. I couldn't lift my arms above my waist for three days. I could barely feed myself. I never put anything in my sister's bed ever again." His laughter rang up the stairs.

Henry dropped his armful of wood in the box behind the stove. He pulled two pieces from the top and knelt in front of the door of the stove. "Snow is coming down harder. If the wind is not too bad tomorrow, we'll have to clear off some of the roofs." Henry coaxed the dwindling fire back to life.

Jacob unloaded the logs he had carried up and sat back down in his chair.

Iris and Thomas laid everything on the table: aged cheddar from James, small, crusty rolls, and soup made from potatoes and smoked beef. Everyone sat down and passed the bread and cheese around. Iris ladled soup into everyone's bowl. Once they were all served, Iris scooped up a spoon of soup and blew on it before eating it. She felt a moment of panic before the savory broth hit her taste buds. It was good.

Jacob took a few bites, then said, "It's nice to not have to cook tonight. It's hard to make this kind of meal for just myself."

"I'm glad you're here," Iris said, and she meant it. If he never became anything else to her, Jacob was a good friend and she cared about him.

"I'm glad to be here too, and to not have to cook, though I only have to cook every fourth day." Petra shoved the end of her roll into her bowl.

"Who cooks on the other days?" Jacob asked.

"James, Adam, Richard, and I take turns cooking. I'm not the best cook of the group, but I'm not the worst. We haven't starved to death yet." Petra took a bite of the soggy end of her roll.

"That's unconventional," Jacob commented.

You have no idea, Iris thought. "Before Thomas came, I only cooked every few days. The h—" Iris closed her mouth so fast she bit her tongue. "Ow." The mood around the table had been easy, and she had almost said harpies. "Sorry. I bit my tongue." Embarrassed, she looked down at her bowl and ran her tender tongue over the back of her teeth.

Petra saved her. "She only cooked big meals when Dora, Marina, or I were around, which was often. We all live outside of town, up in the mountains, so Iris keeps beds for us here."

"And I will continue to do so, because they still come home to roost often enough." And her birds needed a place to rest their heads.

Jacob chuckled. "You are like an older sister."

"Someone has to take care of us." Petra winked at Iris.

Iris made a rude noise but kept her retort to herself.

Jacob ladled more soup into his bowl. "I can help with the snow tomorrow."

"Good," Henry said. "You can organize the work on the north end, and I'll start at the south. We should do the houses first. Most of the buildings on Main Street are sturdy enough for deep snow. I worry more for the smaller houses."

"Once, when I was about ten, we had a white-out storm that lasted an entire day. In the morning, we woke up and had to dig our way out of the house. We made tunnels through the snow and built a castle from the drift we pushed off the roof." Jacob grinned. "That castle stayed up until April. It was a cold winter."

Iris could see the plans forming in Thomas's mind. She waved her spoon at him. "You can build a fort, but you must help Henry or Jacob first."

Thomas's shoulders slumped over his bowl. Jacob patted the boy on the back. "Work before play, but don't worry, with enough hands, the job won't be too bad. Plus, if you're on work detail, you'll get a say in where the extra snow goes."

Thomas straightened up. "That's brilliant. Iris, can I borrow the large wooden box downstairs and the sled tomorrow? After the work is done?"

Iris smiled. "Of course."

Petra polished off her roll and grabbed another. "Where do you think you'll build your fortress?"

Thomas rolled his spoon between his fingers. "Not too far, so we don't have to move the snow much. We could use the vacant lot in between Vine's and the boardinghouse. If we build it there, all the kids can use it."

"That is a fine and generous idea." Henry's voice was quiet but Iris heard every note of it. The sound traveled down her spine and settled in her core.

For the rest of the meal, Iris tried hard to ignore the fact that she was in tune to Henry in a way she could not replicate with Jacob, even if she'd wanted. Jacob doted on her and complemented her whenever he could, but it was Henry's contributions to the conversation that she strained to listen for, though they were general in nature and very rarely about her. She noted that as the meal continued, Henry spoke less and Jacob spoke more. Henry's quiet was louder in her ears than anything said around the table.

Jacob finished telling another story of snowy exploits undertaken by himself and his sisters. Iris turned to Henry before Jacob could launch into another tale. "Did you ever play in the snow when you were young?"

They had all finished eating and Henry stacked their bowls together. "I was an only child," he explained for Jacob's benefit, "and my parents were older. I tended towards seriousness as a child, and I spent most of my time in the forge with my father." He stood and carried the bowls to the counter.

His words were like a blanket on the conversation. Into the lull, Iris asked, "Mulled wine before the gentleman leave us?"

Petra yawned. "I think I'm going to pass. I'm worn out."

A blast of wind rattled the dark window again. A frown replaced Jacob's smile. "I have a long walk home in the dark. I want to stay and enjoy the excellent company," he said the words to everyone, but looked only at Iris, "but I think I'd better pass as well."

Jacob opened his mouth to say something else when Petra jumped up from her chair. "I'll walk you to the door."

A pained look crossed his face, but it was replaced with a polite smile. "That's very kind of you." The two went down the stairs, their conversation continuing in a friendly manner.

Thomas stood up. "Can I go read?"

"Of course," Iris said. Thomas dashed off before Iris had a chance to change her mind.

"Can I help you with the dishes?" Henry asked.

She knew protesting would get her nowhere. "Yes." Iris put what was left of the soup into a crock. She would put in the cold storage box on the back porch later.

Henry moved closer to her and she echoed his movement until there was very little space between them. "Thank you for not arguing. I can help when help is needed. Besides, it gives me an excuse to stay a bit longer."

A tight kernel of hope sprang to life within her. Perhaps Henry was not immune to her. Perhaps there was hope for the feeling stealing her breath. "I'd be a fool to say no to help with the dishes." Iris pointed to the water bucket. "Dump some of that in the basin. I'll wash this time if you dry."

Henry moved to do as asked and they fell into the routine of washing, drying, and putting away the bowls and spoons they had used at dinner.

"I like to cook and feed people," Iris said. "But I hate doing dishes and cleaning up."

Henry laid the spoon he was drying down in the small wooden box on the shelf above the counter. He angled his body towards hers. "You should've told me sooner. I would've been doing dishes every Saturday after dinner."

Iris put a hand on Henry's sleeve, realizing too late that her hand was wet. She jerked back. "Sorry. About the wet spot, not about doing the dishes. You are still a guest, Henry, and guests should not have to do dishes." She handed him the last spoon.

"Can I do them from now on?"

"Yes." Iris hesitated, considering how to say what she wanted to say without revealing too much. "It was different having more people here tonight. I hope it was all right."

"Sometimes different is good. It can put things into perspective."

"Jacob lives alone too."

"And I know how you hate for your friends to be alone." Henry smiled at her.

She wrung out the rag in her hands and started to lift the basin of water. Henry's hand covered her own. "Let me take this outside for you."

Iris nodded dumbly and took her hand reluctantly from underneath Henry's. His touch remained on her skin, familiar and burning, while she watched him disappear downstairs. He was so earnest. If he was the author of her letters, maybe that was the only way he could say those things to her. The thought gave her hope, even though she knew it to be a false, foolish one.

She was still standing in the same place when he came back upstairs. If he thought this was strange, he did not comment on it. He placed the basin back on the counter.

"I should head home too. The wind is picking up."

Iris followed him down the stairs. It was dark downstairs without the moon coming through the windows. She had not seen the moon since the snow had started. Henry pulled his coat off a peg and thrust his arms through the sleeves. While he buttoned his coat, she took his scarf and hat off the peg and squeezed them in tight fists. She wanted him to stay, but could not think of one reason why he should. The snow was not coming down hard or fast enough to give her an excuse to ask.

Henry did the last button under his throat. She threw the scarf over his neck and smiled at him. Only the outlines of his features were visible in the dim light, and she wanted desperately in that moment to see the blue in his eyes sparkle at her. Her hands rested on his chest for a moment, then she removed them. She took a step back from him, trying to get away from the pull he had on her and the overwhelming need to lean into his solid body.

Henry cleared his throat and held out his hand. Iris, feeling sheepish, put his hat into his palm without touching him again. She took a deep breath, but found her senses filled with Henry. It was what she imagined drowning to be like, and she was not sure she wanted to be rescued.

"Thank you for dinner. Saturday is always my favorite day of the week." Henry's voice was barely above a whisper. It could have been ten times louder. Iris felt it everywhere.

"I'm sorry about the extra company."

"Don't regret your kindness to others. Never that."

"Do you need a lamp for the walk home?" Iris looked out of the window. It was dark, and Iris worried. About him especially.

She caught a glance of a smile before he covered it up with his scarf. "I'll be fine. There's enough lights from the windows that I can stay on the boardwalk well enough. It's not snowing that bad."

"Goodnight, Henry."

He opened the door and paused before stepping outside. "Goodnight, Iris."

The door clicked closed behind him. Iris took two deep breaths before she ceased to breathe at all. She went to bed with the sound of her name in Henry's voice ringing in her ears.

CHAPTER 13

Iris dragged herself down the stairs the next morning to sort through what mail she had left and to decide when to deliver the letters she had waiting. She paused at the end of the counter, letting the tug of the letters and packages in the bird-holes pull on her mind. Their clamor was a comforting distraction. There was something else making noise, though.

Iris blocked out the noise from behind the counter and focused on the other thing tugging on her. She closed her eyes and followed the feeling to the front door. Iris went outside and stood in front of the mailbox. Unbelieving, she lifted the lid.

A single letter lay there, alone and dry, addressed to her. She picked it up. The first letters had brought her joy. Iris thought of how her name had sounded on Henry's lips and the letter in her hand felt like a weight. Reluctantly, she opened her mind to the letter and it felt like determination. She clutched it tightly and went inside.

Iris walked past the bird-hole slots and their contents calling for her attention. She walked back up the stairs and sat on the couch in front of the window. The paper was smooth in her hands and sealed again with a plain circle seal. She thought of her own seal and broke the wax.

Dearest Iris,

My heart is full tonight. People always say that snow is silent, but it whispers if one is quiet and listens to it. I have sat here listening to it for an hour now, wanting to write something to you, and hearing only the whisper of the snow and the occasional gust of the wind. Of all the words I would write, I believe I can sum them all up in a few simple words.

You have stolen my heart. You are precious and beautiful and I want to spend every day telling you these things. More than that, I want to be able to see your face and hold you close when I speak these words to you. I wonder if you will tremble the way I do when

Iris read it through multiple times. The letter had to be from Jacob. His manner was so easy in person, she suspected he hid his earnest nature in an effort to protect his feelings from being hurt. She tried to imagine Henry sitting down to write the letter, wished for it to be him, but could not imagine the fanciful words coming from him. But she could now admit to herself that Henry was what she wanted.

It was time for her to write a letter to her anonymous friend that was honest. She could no longer encourage this relationship if she was longing for one with someone else. She rested her chin on her hand and closed her eyes. She was going to have to pull back from Jacob as well. She wanted to be friends with him, but she should not encourage him. Iris wanted, above all else, to spare his feelings.

Thomas was already gone. He had gotten up early and headed out to help Jacob and Henry. Iris spent the morning putting off both organizing her letters and writing one of her own. She did the mending, which she hated, and made a list of things they were low on. Some items would have to wait, others, like meat and cheese, she could procure easily.

Iris sat on a stool, nibbling the end of her pen, when the door opened and Henry came into the depot.

"What are you doing here?" Iris winced at the harshness of her tone. "That sounded wrong. I thought you were working on the roofs."

Henry took off his scarf. "I did. We cleared the south end of town and I decided to stop in to see how your morning was going."

"What time is it?"

"Past noon. Everyone on my team took a break for lunch."

Past noon already. "My morning got away from me. Did you need something?"

Henry shifted his weight, his strong hands working and twisting his scarf. "I've been thinking about something you said about Jacob being alone, and I remembered you've often made the same observation about me. Being alone. It occurred to me that you're often alone." Henry stopped worrying his scarf with his hands and stepped into her space. "It occurred to me that perhaps you were concerned for your friends who are alone because you yourself don't care to be alone."

Iris stared at him open mouthed until something broke within her. He saw inside her so completely. She slapped her mouth shut and clenched her teeth together to keep from blurting out all of the emotions coursing through her.

A racket from up the street jerked Iris out of the moment. She pulled away from Henry and looked out the window. A small knot of men and a few women circled around something across the street in front of the saloon. Snow dusted their shoulders as they crowded and craned into the middle of the gathering.

Iris felt Henry come to stand behind her. "Wonder what the fuss is about," he said.

"They don't seem angry, just curious." An awareness of feeling hit Iris. Marina was back in town. A laugh rang out from the crowd, and Iris knew she was right.

Her face broke into a smile. "Marina's home early. Figures, she went straight for the saloon." She turned to Henry. "Want to come with me? I'm sure they have some stories to tell." In all honesty, she was not ready to part from the blacksmith yet.

Henry kept his eyes fixed on hers while he put his scarf back on. She smiled at him and watched as something blazed in his eyes. She grabbed her hat and coat and took the arm he offered for the walk to the saloon. Iris could feel the muscles of his arm under her hand. Every step made Iris more aware of the man beside her.

The crowd had moved inside, and laughter spilled onto the street from within. Henry opened the heavy wooden door of the saloon and a wall of voices, warmth, and the smell of ale and wine hit them. The knot from the street had moved to the bar. A tall, brown-haired woman with a riot of loose curls turned and saw them enter.

"Iris." Marina pulled away from the crowd and ran to her. Marina wrapped Iris in a rib-crunching hug and rested her chin on Iris's head. "Gods below, I missed you."

Iris returned the embrace. "Welcome home, my bird. I missed you, too. It's been a long time since any of you were gone for more than a few days. It's been quiet in town."

Marina released her and grinned wide. "Reed wanted to stay in Denver longer, but I wanted to be home. I told him I missed you, but really, I'd had enough of the city. I never liked cities, even though I grew up in one."

Iris ran a hand over Marina's unruly hair. "I'm sure he knows the real reason."

Marina leaned in close to Iris. "Don't tell him, though. If he thinks he has me all figured out, I'll never hear the end of it." Marina straightened. "I need a drink. Vine, you got any flip made up? I'm cold inside and out." Flip was one of Daniel's specialties in the winter. It was a mixture of eggs, molasses, warm ale, and rum stirred with a poker from the fire until it frothed into a creamy concoction sure to warm the soul.

Daniel waved a hot poker from the small stove he kept behind the bar. "I'm stirring one up now. Go sit and I'll bring you a round."

Marina reached into the knot of people at the bar and pulled the arm of a man, taller than her by a few inches, with a wide-brimmed hat pulled over his head. "Leave the sheriff alone, gentleman. He promised to have a drink with me before he went back to work."

Reed laughed and allowed himself to be pulled through the crowd by Marina. He shook hands with Henry and embraced Iris. "It's good to be home. I thought it was exhausting keeping Marina out of trouble in Turning Creek. She's even more trouble in Denver."

Marina led the way to one of the tables by the stone fireplace. Wood crackled and burned, giving off both warmth and cheer. "You loved it. Stop complaining."

"We weren't expecting you for another week, and with the snow we've been having, I was getting worried you'd be stuck and wouldn't get home before the spring thaw," Iris said.

Marina and Reed looked at each other and burst into laughter. Reed sat facing the door with his back to the fire and Marina joined him on his bench. Reed looked across the table at Iris. "Let's just say my wife was getting home regardless of the weather and she was very creative about how we got here."

Iris narrowed her eyes at Marina as she sat down across from her friend. "What did you do?"

Henry hesitated, then sat beside Iris. Her body hummed in awareness and she tried unsuccessfully to ignore it. Maybe it was time she stopped trying.

Marina grinned and flashed pointed teeth at her. "I wanted to get home, and I was not about to let a little snow blocking a mountain pass stop me."

Iris groaned. "Please tell me you didn't fly Reed over the pass. I can't imagine that would be a very comfortable flight for either of you."

Reed coughed. "It's wasn't, but thankfully she didn't insist we do that for very long. When she realized she couldn't carry me and our bags, she got creative."

Iris was about to press for more when Daniel came over with a tray of ceramic mugs. "I put a touch of extra molasses in them. Business has been slow without you here, Marina, so welcome home."

Marina took one of the glasses and saluted Daniel. "You may not be my favorite person, but I'll say this: I tried a lot of different drinks in Denver and nothing is as fine as your ale or your flip. You, sir, are a gift of the gods."

Daniel Vine straightened. "Dionysus *was* a god. He was not created by them." The original Dionysus had spent years wandering the earth forcing, sometimes through violence, mortals to worship him. In the war against

Olympus, he had remained neutral, waiting for the victor to emerge.

"Keep your hat on, Vine. I wasn't insulting you. I was trying to be nice." Marina took a sip from her mug. "If I ever really peeved you, you'd stop serving me this delicious stuff, and you're the only show in town."

Daniel relaxed, but his voice was stiff. "I think that was an apology, so I'll accept it."

"Take some advice from me," Reed said, "Harpies don't apologize often, and even then they do it badly." Marina elbowed him in the side. "Watch the drink, Sparrow. I've been cold for a long time and I need this." He looked back up at Daniel. "Accept the apology, Daniel, even one as ill given as that. Take what you can get." Reed winked at Marina, who made a show of rolling her eyes.

Iris laughed and felt herself relax. She had missed this banter. Relaxing brought her left side into closer contact with Henry. She did not shift away.

"Let me know if you need anything." Daniel took his empty tray and walked back to the bar.

"Marina, you could let up on him a bit," Iris said.

"I'm not ready to. Besides, he deserves it." Marina scowled into her drink.

Henry's voice was low and filled with censure. "You shouldn't define him by his actions on one day, but look at the whole." Marina dropped her eyes and sipped her drink in silence.

Iris sighed and was happy she was not the one to chastise Marina for once. "Just how did you two get back?" The closest railroad stop was a few valleys over, and they would have had a good amount of snow and passes to traverse.

"You've heard of those dog sleds they have in Alaska?" Reed asked. Everyone nodded. "I'm here to tell you that the best benefit of marrying a harpy is that in the wintertime you don't need a horse or a pack of dogs. All you need is a makeshift toboggan and a harpy ready to get back to her valley."

Marina grinned. Iris laughed at her. "You pulled Reed and your bags in a sled?"

Marina sipped her drink. "It was actually much easier than I thought it would be, and it's definitely easier than carrying this lump on the wing." She nudged Reed again, who responded by kissing her soundly.

When they broke apart, Marina said, "See why I keep him around?"

Iris could barely keep her smile contained. "I am glad you're both home. Things have been quiet, except for all the snow."

Reed rubbed the back of his neck. "I noticed the weather seemed to get worse the closer to the valley we got."

Henry shifted beside Iris and she moved to stay close to him. When she realized what she had done, she held herself still. Marina gave her an odd look and Iris shook her head.

"The snow has been falling steady for a few days. Two groups of men have been working today to clear off the roofs of the houses on Second Street. We'll take a look at the buildings on Main Street tomorrow," Henry said.

"We could check the buildings today and see if any of them need it more than others. That way, we can get started first thing in the morning." Reed swirled the contents of his cup. "If you've got the time." Reed's copper-colored eyes shifted between Henry and Iris.

"I've some time," Henry said.

Marina straightened in her seat. "Did you finish my swords?"

Henry shrugged. "I did finish a nice matched set for a lady I know. I'm not sure you're lady enough for them. They're very special swords."

Reed guffawed at the comment. Marina rubbed her hands together. "I'll be Hera herself if you let me get my hands on those blades."

Henry's lips quirked up. "They're ready for you. I don't like to talk myself up often, but they turned out beautiful, and I put some extras in them for you. I'll check the boardinghouse with the sheriff, and you can meet me thereafter. That'll give you some time to talk to Iris." Henry turned to face her. "Things have been quiet and I think she missed you."

Iris knew the smile on her face was huge, but he had said her name again and he was sitting a breath away from her. Everything in the room faded and pinpointed to the man next to her. It took all her willpower to turn back to Marina and Reed and pay attention to the conversation.

Marina and Reed told them stories about the celebrations marking Colorado's official entrance into the United States. "Just in time for a war," Marina quipped.

"Things are bad in Washington, but do you really think it will come to that?" Iris asked.

Reed scowled. "Possibly." He drained his mug. "Ready to go?" Henry finished his own drink, and the two stood.

The screech of lumber and breaking timbers stopped them before they could leave the table. Everyone put down their drinks and tumbled out of the door. A dart of fear ripped through Iris as she ran out into the snowy afternoon to greet the sound of a building being torn in two.

CHAPTER 14

At first Iris saw nothing amiss, but then she looked up. The third story of the boardinghouse had collapsed in on itself. Part of the wall was gone, and, even though their vantage was wrong to know for certain, the roof looked as if a giant had pressed down on the top of it and flattened it like a piece of bread. Boards stuck out at odd angles and still the snow fell as the building groaned.

Iris followed close on the heels of Marina, Reed, and Henry as they ran to the front of the damaged building. In the blank space between the saloon and the boardinghouse, Thomas, Stephen, Jonah, the Hughes twins, and a dozen other children stood open-mouthed on a pile of snow larger than they were. Iris ran to Thomas.

"Are you all right?"

"What? Yes, I'm fine, but the boardinghouse..." Thomas trailed off.

Iris hugged him hard and dragged him back to where Henry, Marina, and Reed stood with a growing number of people. The other work detail, led by Jacob, came running around the corner.

The door of the groaning building opened and Widow Finch and Spuds ran out, followed by a handful of people. Widow Finch's eyes were wide with shock.

Reed grabbed her arm as she walked by. "Was anyone staying on the third floor?"

Widow Finch nodded and ran a shaking hand over her face. "Margaret Ames. She has a daughter. A four year old."

Reed spoke calmly, though the sound of panic was starting to rise amongst the people gathered. "Is she the only one?" Widow Finch nodded. "Good. I need you to count everyone who came out and tell me who is missing. Can you do that?" The woman nodded. Her lip trembled, but she steeled herself and nodded again in confirmation.

"Good. Marina, get the people from the boardinghouse in a group so we can count them. Henry, come with me. We need to see if we can get upstairs and if anyone else is inside." Reed barked orders in a voice that no one dared to disobey.

Reed and Henry ran into the collapsed building. Iris's heart constricted as she watched them disappear into the ruined building. If the rest of the floors did not hold, much could be lost today.

Marina yelled and herded the people standing in the street with efficiency. Harpies had been created to lead and torment souls on their way to Tartarus. The Remnants of the harpies were able to use their voices to influence people to do things. Nothing far outside of their normal behavior, but Marina could calm a handful of people with ease. She also carried mortal authority as the deputy of Turing Creek. Both abilities helped her gather the people into groups for counting.

Iris rubbed her arms and scanned the crowd. She had left her coat in the saloon. She still had her hat tied around her neck, and she flipped it onto her head. Iris kept her eyes on the front door of the building. The wood continued to creak in an alarming fashion. *For Hera's sake*, she begged, *let them be safe.*

As the time ticked by, she thought of Henry trapped beneath the collapsed roof of the building. She could hear them calling for the girl and her mother, pausing to wait for a response. The worry in her gut clenched and she gave them another minute before she went in. The door opened and both Henry and Reed came out. Lines of worry traced their faces. Henry's eyes found Iris, and he made a beeline through the crowd to her.

He took his coat off and swung it around her shoulders before she could protest. Iris was enveloped in warmth and the smell of hot metal, wood smoke, and soap.

It took her a moment to find her voice. "Thank you."

Henry's face was somber. "You look frozen to the bone."

Iris could not tell him it was her worry for him that had chilled her more than the winter day.

Reed stalked over to them, Marina on his heels. "Mrs. Ames and her daughter are trapped on the top floor. We were able to talk to them, but not reach them. Mrs. Ames said there is some debris trapping them. The stairwell is completely destroyed. We've got to get on that roof from the outside."

"We can't put any more weight up there. If we walk around, we could risk crushing them if they are trapped beneath the boards or we could collapse more of the structure," Henry said. "It'll have to be someone small."

Reed rubbed his hands over his face. "There're no buildings close enough to jump onto the roof. A ladder might do the trick, but we'd still have to walk on the roof. I'm not sure there's a ladder tall enough to reach what's left of the top. I'm not sure we even have time to find one. The building could be fine after this initial collapse or it could implode completely. We have to get up there. Now. There's got to be another way."

Marina rubbed her hands together and her eyes gleamed. "There is."

Reed chopped the air with his hand. "No."

Marina stepped closer to the sheriff. "Yes. It's the only way, and you damn well know it."

Reed leaned into her face and hissed, "I won't have you expose yourself and the other Remnants like that."

Marina folded her arms across her chest. Something dangerous flashed through Marina's eyes, and Iris knew this was an argument Reed would not win.

Reed knew it too. "The Lord help me. If this gets you killed, I'll never forgive you. Or if we get driven out by an angry mob, I'll never forgive you. I like living here, and, for reasons I've yet to figure, I actually love your sorry hide." Marina preened a bit at his words. Reed continued, "Is Widow Finch a Remnant?" Marina nodded. He blew out a frustrated breath and called over the widow.

Iris could feel the power and excitement rolling off Marina in waves. She knew Marina was worried for the woman and her daughter, but the harpy's nature thrived on the unexpected. The moment Widow Finch came close to Marina, she took a step back and changed directions so that Henry stood between Marina and her.

Marina laughed. "I'm not going to hurt you. Gods, you're skittish."

Reed scowled at Marina. "You're not helping. Reel it in or I'm going to go stomping up on that roof myself."

Dread filled Iris. She knew what Marina wanted to do. She also knew Marina was right. There was no other way. What Marina proposed to do would impact more than just the harpies. It would affect them all, but there was a woman and a little girl whose lives were riding on this decision, and that outweighed everything else.

Iris felt the pulse of power radiating from Marina recede. She looked at Marina in astonishment. The harpy did not often behave when asked. Marina caught her eye and shrugged. "I obey when it suits me."

"I wish it suited you more often." Reed frowned as he spoke, but there was affection in his voice. He addressed Widow Finch. "Is Mrs. Ames a Remnant?"

"No. Why?"

Reed turned to Marina. "How many people on the street are regular folk?"

Marina closed her eyes, and Iris felt the push of power go over her again. Over half of the other people in the street turned towards Marina.

Some Remnant lines saw their power dilute over generations, but the harpies were still strong and still dangerous, and one took notice when a predator was in the hen house.

Marina opened her eyes. "A third, maybe two thirds, but some are weak."

"Too damn many regular folk. You're not flying up there." Reed pointed to the collapsed roof.

"Marina is right. You can't walk on the roof, and you can't leave Mrs. Ames and her daughter to die when we have the means to rescue them." Iris stepped away from Henry and went to stand beside Marina. "We have to fly up there and get them. Mortals will see, but I surmise many of them already know something is not quite right about this town. There'll be repercussions, but we have to do this. Even in the worst case scenario, this will only expose the two of us." Iris pointed between herself and Marina.

Iris looked over the crowd and her eyes found Jacob. He was trying to make his way towards her. This was not how she envisioned telling her friend her secret. She had resigned herself to not telling him at all.

"I don't need your help. I can carry the child and the woman free of the building without help." Marina crossed her arms over her chest.

Iris smiled. "I know, my bird, but what do you think a mortal woman will think when she sees you coming in your harpy form?"

Marina smiled and her teeth had gone pointy. "She'll think she's died and gone to the inner circle of hell to be tortured by monsters."

Iris sighed. "You enjoy being a monster too much." Marina shrugged. "I'll go with you and hopefully they'll see me first." With her golden wings, Iris would look much less threatening than Marina in full harpy form.

Marina wrapped an arm around Iris's shoulder. "This is going to be fun. I'm glad I got back in time for all the excitement." Marina spoke to Reed. "We'll have Mrs. Ames down before you can work up a decent list of all the reasons this is the worst plan ever. Look at the bright side: at least I'm not going alone."

"That's the tiniest bit of bright side you've ever given me."

Iris shrugged out of Henry's coat, leaving its warmth with a reluctance that was bigger than the loss of its shelter. Henry took the coat from her with his mouth pressed into a thin line.

She laid a hand on his arm. It was warm despite the fact that he was in his shirtsleeves and had been without a coat for a few minutes. "Do you disapprove of Marina's plan?"

Henry's large hand covered hers. Iris felt every inch of his calloused hand like a brand. "No. If we're to be exposed, best we do it performing a good work. It'll give people a reason to see the best first."

"Your words say you approve, but your face says otherwise," she observed.

Henry mouth twitched in that small smile Iris was beginning to look forward to. "I'm worried for your part in today's adventures. Nothing more."

Iris gave him a reassuring smile. "Thank you for your concern. It means a lot to me."

The crowd around them was growing restless with the need to do something to abate the tragedy unfolding before them. If they were going to act, it needed to be now.

Jacob finally made his way to her. "Are you all right?"

"Yes, but I need you to stand back for a minute."

"Why?"

"I wish I had time to explain, but there's not time."

"But, I don't—"

Marina, leaking power and her voice full of authority, said, "Stand back, Mr. Wells." Jacob stepped back meekly with a nervous glance at Marina.

Iris looked down at her shirt. It was one of her favorites, a warm cotton, softened with age. There was nothing she could do about it now.

She turned to Marina. "I assume you have at least one knife on your person."

Marina reached into her boot and pulled a long, sharp blade from a hidden sheath. She flipped it and caught the blade, offering it handle first to Iris. "You know better than to even ask."

Iris shook her head. "I need two slits in my shirt straight down from where the points of my shoulder blades are. I can't reach back there. I need you to do it. Just try not to ruin the shirt too much. I'll repair it if I can."

Marina nodded and made two parallel cuts down the back of Iris's shirt. The cold rushed into the openings and chilled her to the bone. Marina returned the knife to her boot.

"I think if we're going to cause the least amount of fear, I should go first," Iris said. Except for the first awful time, she had never changed forms in front of anyone except the other harpies. Despite the February air, she could feel her face heating in self-awareness.

Marina moved next to her and wrapped her in an embrace. In her ear, Marina whispered, "You're amazing and beautiful. It's time everyone else got to see them."

Iris nodded and moved back from Marina but kept her hands on Marina's forearms. Iris wanted the physical as well as the emotional support that touching Marina gave her. Iris looked to her left, away from the crowd, and met Henry's eyes. He nodded. She was ready.

Iris closed her eyes and reached for the curled power within her. She wound it around into a ball of energy and then imagined it filling the golden birthmark on her back. When she was young, she had done this a million times with no results besides an aching heart and sore muscles. Now, she felt the golden birthmark warm until it was like fire on her back. She marshaled herself for the last push and released her hold on her power. She felt her wings explode from her back and her soul sang with the release of the weight, even as the sharp pain of their emergence ripped through her.

Iris gripped Marina's arms hard and sought to keep her footing as the pain lanced down her back. She stretched her wings wide and the needles of pain receded as she stretched her muscles. She flapped her wings before tucking them in behind her. The top arches rose above her head and the tips touched the snow. A golden glow cut through the grey winter day.

The first person she saw when she opened her eyes was Henry. If she had the strength to let go of Marina, she would have reached out to touch him.

He swallowed visibly and took a step closer to her. "I never thought I'd stand this close to you when you did that. There are no words, Messenger, for the way you look that could come close to doing you justice."

Iris smiled and the glow from her wings increased. That was new. Her wings always glowed with some light, but it had never fluctuated before. She ruffled her feathers and grinned stupidly at Henry until she remembered the reason for her display.

Marina glanced around the crowd, which was staring with open mouths at the tight circle around Iris. "We'd best get this horrible plan of mine moving before they realize they're not having a mental fit."

Iris tore her gaze from the admiration raining down on her from Henry and saw that the reaction from the crowd was mixed. Jacob was still at the front of the crowd, but he would not meet her gaze. She could easily pick the mortals from the crowd. Most seemed curious; only two looked scared as far as she could tell. Yet. Marina still had to change.

"I'll be quick. Can you take off as soon as I'm airborne?" Each harpy had a unique power, and Marina's was speed.

"Yes." Iris could not match a fraction of Marina's speed, but she could get off the ground at a decent pace.

Henry's hand reached out to touch her shoulder, but realizing he would also touch her wing, he pulled back. "Be careful."

Iris ruffled her wing and brushed the hand he had pulled back. Henry's eyes lit with something that caused a warm curl of awareness to move through Iris. She flapped her wings again and their glow increased. Her face heated in response despite the cold air.

Reed's voice broke through Iris's thoughts. "Just find the woman and make all this mess worth it," Reed said in a harsh tone, but his eyes moved with anxious precision over the crowd. He planted a firm kiss on Marina's lips. "No theatrics. Just do the job and try not to scare anyone more than strictly necessary."

Marina nodded. Even though she was prepared for it, Iris blinked and

Marina was launching into the sky. In her harpy form, Marina had the tan and brown body of a bird of prey and the face of a woman. Her brown wings ended in claws and talons curled where her feet had been. She was also the size of a grizzly bear. Iris heard a few cries of alarm from the crowd. That was her cue. She gathered herself and launched into the air. She left the crowd and its reaction behind when her feet left the ground. They had a job to do, and every minute counted. As if to punctuate the moment, the wood of the boardinghouse creaked in the air that had suddenly gone quiet.

Marina was darting and diving over the remains of the third floor like a dragonfly over a pond in the summer. "Mrs. Ames? Can you hear me?" Her harpy voice was like the crunching of rocks and broken glass.

Iris gained altitude until she could fly around the boardinghouse in tight circles. "I'm not sure you yelling for her is a good idea either." Iris took over the job of calling to Mrs. Ames.

Marina cocked her head after one flyby. "I think I hear a child crying. Over here." Marina flew back over one area once and then twice more.

Iris flew as low as she dared. There was a flat patch of roof a few feet from where the crying was coming from. She landed as slowly as she could and held her breath as the boards settled under her weight. The wood creaked, but did not shift. Iris let out the breath she had been holding.

"Mrs. Ames. Can you hear me?"

"I'm over here. I can't see out. We're trapped in a pocket under the roof."

Thank the gods, Iris thought. "I'm going to tap on the section I think you're under. Let me know if we have the right place." Iris motioned to Marina, who darted over the spot and rapped it with the knuckles of her talons as she flew over.

"Yes. That's just where I am. Can you get us out?" The relief in the woman's voice was palpable.

Marina flew over the spot twice more, craning her neck for a better vantage. "There's a beam holding this section of the roof up enough to keep from crushing them. I think I can flip the beam and the boards it's supporting in one go. We'll have to lift it off quickly to keep anything else from falling in on them." She nodded to Iris. "If we are lucky, most of the debris will go over the backside of the building. Let me check and make sure there isn't anyone over there."

Marina darted over the back of the building. "All clear. Ready?"

Iris nodded. She took a deep breath and spoke to Mrs. Ames. "We can get you out, but I need to warn you about something."

"What?"

"You know how sometimes mothers tell stories about monsters to their children to scare them into good behavior?"

"Yes."

"You're about to find out that monsters are real, but we're not going to hurt you. We're here to help. Do you think you can remember that? No matter what you see, we're here to help." The wood under Iris shifted and she beat her wings to lift some of her weigh off the ruined structure.

"I think so," came the hesitant answer.

"We've met once, I think. I run the mail depot, and the deputy, Marina, is here with me and she is going to help me get the roof off you. Do you remember who we are?"

"Yes." The answer was strong and surer. Iris hoped she held onto that certainty.

Marina hovered as best she could near one part of the section under which Mrs. Ames was trapped. Marina looked at Iris. "I'll count to three and lift this as quickly as I can. If I'm able, I'm going to flip it clear and lift Mrs. Ames at the same time. You're easier on the eyes. You get the daughter. Ready?"

Iris licked her lips, and the effort was wasted as a wind gust blew snow in her eyes. "I suppose I am."

"One. Two. Three."

Marina's talons gripped a section of timber and flipped it. She pumped with her wings to maintain her altitude, sending loose snow and debris flying. With a shove, she flipped another small section of roof over the back of the building. The high, tight scream of a child cut through the air. Iris had a second to register the way the woman's clear brown eyes widened before Marina had gathered the woman up and away from the pocket of space she had been trapped in.

With Marina out of the way and her mother no longer shielding her, the little girl, tear tracks staining her face, could see Iris coming for her. Her scream stopped in a small hiccup as a pair of brown eyes loomed large in her baby face. Iris tried to swoop down, but she was not as agile in the air as the harpy and missed.

Iris clenched her teeth and flew a tight circle back to the girl. She was going to have to land on what was left of the building to rescue the child and pray the building held. Iris could hear the wind pushing through the feathers of her wings as she flapped them desperately to keep as much of her weight off the ruined wood.

It was not enough. The moment her feet touched down, the screech of breaking wood filled the air again. The board she was standing on shifted beneath her feet and Iris fell face forward. Her fall put her almost on top of the child, who had started to scream. She could hear Marina yelling at her to get up, but her focus was on the small, pale face in front of her.

The building shifted again and Iris sucked in a quick breath and held every part of herself still. When the movement stopped, she stood, pumping her wings to keep her balance. Her shoulders burned with the effort.

Iris reached out to the small hands grasping in her direction. Relief flooded her as she pulled and wrapped the little girl in her arms. The girl clung to Iris and reached over Iris's shoulder to try to touch her wings. Iris's wings were too tired to lift her completely into the air so she pushed off with her feet, causing the building to shift once again as her wings took over and they cleared the wreckage.

Iris's lungs burned as she took a deep breath and realized she had been holding her breath. She looked over her shoulder and saw Marina carrying a white-faced Mrs. Ames. The harpy's talons were twisted in the shirt and skirt that the woman was wearing. Not the best carrying method, but Marina only had to get the woman down to the ground without dropping her. Marina laid Mrs. Ames into a tidy heap at Reed's feet. Iris landed beside the woman and placed the toddler in her mother's arms. Widow Finch wrapped blankets around mother and daughter.

Marina drew her wings around Iris and squeezed. "You scared me to the inner circle of hell."

Iris drew a shaky breath. "I don't want to ever do that again."

The two drew apart to face the consequences of the rescue. No matter what happened now, they had done the right thing. Henry moved closer to Iris, putting himself between her and the crowd. Reed did the same for Marina.

"Pretty angel." The girl squirmed in her mother's arms, trying to reach Iris.

Mrs. Ames had not taken her eyes from Marina. Marina ruffled her feathers and changed back into her mortal form.

Mrs. Ames began to cry. She held a hand out to Marina. Marina hesitated, then took the woman's hand in her own human-shaped one. "You saved our lives. I'll never be able to thank you." Mrs. Ames threw her arms around Marina, squashing the little girl between them.

Marina patted her awkwardly on the back. "We don't need any thanks. We're just glad we were able to get to you and that you weren't hurt. It seems I came home exactly when I was needed."

Mrs. Ames, tears streaming down her pretty face, released Marina and hugged Iris. "You saved my daughter. Thank you."

A golden feather fell at Iris's feet and the small girl leapt from her mother's arms and grabbed at it. The feather lost some of its glow, but it still shone like gold. The child smiled and held it for her mother to see. The silence around them was like the pressure on her shoulder blades before her wings emerged, and Iris looked at the people watching them.

She tucked her wings as far back as they would go and took a step closer to Henry. The people looked stunned rather than afraid, but crowds could be unpredictable. Jacob had faded into the crowd and she could not find him.

Someone started clapping; Iris thought it was Simon and Beth Kramer, if she judged correctly. Others around the pair followed suit, and the sentiment spread like wildfire, though there were some who did not clap and stood silently. It was a long time before the crowd settled. Some were expressing gratitude now, but once they were home, alone in their beds, they would remember, and their memories might hold a hint of fear. People feared the unknown, and fear could be a dangerous thing.

Iris thought some explanation was needed before the mortals were left alone to their own ideas, and wanted this first explanation to come from her less-threatening-than-a-harpy mouth. "What you've seen today is a secret that has been guarded for generations. You know Marina. She has served you well as your deputy and fought to defend you often, though most of you didn't know it. She is a harpy, and while she does look like a monster," Iris could see Marina preening at the scrutiny, "remember that she fights for you and she uses her power to defend Turning Creek, our home."

"Are you an angel?" someone yelled from the back.

"No. I am called The Messenger, after the Greek goddess Iris, the first of my name." There was only so much Iris could reveal without exposing others. "If you have questions, you can come and ask them of me at the depot. Tomorrow." Laughter followed her last comment.

Daniel Vine stepped out of the crowd. He held up a hand. "Miss Iris might find more people in the depot than she can handle. You are all welcome at the saloon at noon. We can talk about what happened today, and what it means for our town."

Marina's face was full of shock at the announcement. Iris smiled inwardly. She knew Daniel was not the villain Marina thought him to be. Still, he was not exactly a hero either.

Iris caught sight of Thomas's face in the crowd and shook her head slightly, indicating for him to stay where he was. She did not want him getting caught in the fray if things turned ugly.

"Are there others?" Mrs. Ames asked.

Iris could feel the nervous energy of the Remnants around her. A trickle of power uncurled from Marina. The back and forth mood of the crowd was effecting the harpy. Anxiety welled within her, and she was afraid they had made a terrible mistake exposing themselves and other Remnants to the unknown mercy of a crowd, though there had not been much of a choice. Her breath hitched, then Henry grabbed her hand and squeezed it tight. She held on to his hand as if her life depended on it.

Reed stepped beside Marina and took her hand in his. "There are others, but that is their secret to share as they choose. They're normal folk like you and me, and want the same things we do – to live a good and peaceful life. Like anything, there are exceptions, but keep in mind, we have our very own monster keeping us safe at night."

That drew some nervous laughter and smiles from the crowd. Some individuals broke free from the crowd and walked away. Jacob's retreating form was among them, and Iris's heart sank. The sounds from the remaining people swelled into excited babbling. Iris could see some hesitation on the faces of the Remnants, but Turning Creek was a unique place. Perhaps it was time for Remnants to have a place they could live openly, without fear.

Marina pushed power into her words. The same power that had compelled souls along the way to Tartarus in the old myths, now compelled the people of Turning Creek to dispel in peace. "Go to your homes tonight. Be safe and warm and know that the people of this town and valley are under the protection of the harpies. It isn't an honor given lightly."

The shoulders of some of the Remnants in the crowd relaxed. Marina's words were both a comfort and a warning. Harpies defended their territory, once it was claimed, with violent intent. The wind picked up and the snow fell in hand-sized flakes. In moments, visibility had decreased and Iris was worried they would have a full-blown snowstorm on their hands. Reed began barking orders, getting people out of the gathering storm and headed for home. Those that had space to spare took in the people who had been rooming at the boarding house. Soon everyone had a place to stay for the night.

Mrs. Ames lingered and came to stand beside Iris. "May we stay with you? Sheriff Brant said you have a room, but he wanted me to ask."

A knife of wind went through her ruined shirt, and Iris shivered. "Yes, of course you can stay."

Iris clamped her jaw to keep her teeth from chattering. When she had been flying, she had not noticed the cold, but her cotton shirt was no protection from the bitter wind. A shiver ran from the top of her body and down her wings. She tried opening her wings enough to offer protection, but the wind was turning brutal.

Henry was before her in moments with his jacket open backwards to her. "Put your arms in the sleeves." Iris did it without question and the jacket covered her front, leaving her back and wings bare. "Let's get you inside. Home to the depot?"

"Home. The fire in the stove should still be going."

Marina scooped up the little girl and led Mrs. Ames towards the depot. Henry's arm went around Iris's waist as he guided her home. She was grateful for the support. All the effort of flying in controlled circles and the excitement of the afternoon had wrung her out. Iris forgot about the wind and snow and thought of nothing else but the heat of Henry walking beside her. She pulled on that strength and made her way home.

She had never been so grateful to cross the threshold of her own home before and so loathe to move away from Henry. She did both as she shucked out of his coat and handed it to him.

She called over her shoulder at Marina. "Bring them upstairs. There should be plenty of clean clothes in your room."

Iris went up the stairs and went straight to the black pot-bellied stove, shoving wood on top of the coals.

Henry placed a hand on her shoulder. "Allow me to do this so you can change into something warmer."

Iris handed him the iron poker with thanks and tried to ignore how close he was standing to her. She went to her room in a daze of exhaustion, hearing and feeling everything. Iris laid her hands flat against the door and used the quiet moment to focus, pulling her wings inside, winding her power back into herself. After everything, she needed the stillness and being alone to do it. *Gods, she was so tired.* Her wings disappeared and her shoulders ached. A dull throb was making its presence known at the base of her skull. Soon, she would have a full-blown headache.

Marina had a kettle of water on for tea when Iris emerged from her bedroom. Henry was shifting his feet uncomfortably by the window. He turned when she stepped into the room.

Marina moved to the stairs when she saw Iris. "I'm going to see if Reed needs any more help. The storm is getting worse."

Iris moved towards Marina, and rubbed her hands over Marina's hair and rested them on her shoulders. "You're a brave bird. Behave for the rest of the day. I know you're feeling awfully proud of yourself at the moment, but we need to keep things reeled in until we know how people will react. We can't have another witch hunt on our hands."

"I always behave." Marina winked at her.

"Liar," Iris said.

"I'll check back in if I have time." Marina started walking down the stairs.

"If the snow is bad, don't bother. Come tomorrow."

Marina stopped at the foot of the stairs. "Coming, Henry?"

"In a moment." He had moved to stand right behind Iris. She did not need to turn to know how close he was. Heat radiated off him. Marina looked at the two of them, smirked, and then turned and left.

Iris leaned against the table.

Henry shifted his weight. "You're all right then?"

"Yes, I'm fine." Iris wanted to tell him that his continued close presence was beginning to make her anything but fine. She held her tongue.

Henry ran a hand through his hair, fluffing his curls up. "I need to help Reed if there's something else that needs to be done. You'll ask for help if you need it? Send Thomas if you need anything."

Unable to resist, Iris reached out and put her hand on his arm. "I will. Thank you."

Henry gave her a curt nod, then turned and walked down the stairs. He turned the corner without looking back. A small part of her deflated. She had so wanted him to turn around one more time. Henry had been kind to her today, but as her friend, that was what she expected of him.

Jacob's shocked face loomed in her mind and Iris wondered if that relationship would be repaired. She was stuck with feelings for a man who did not return them and another man whose feelings may have soured completely now that he knew the truth. She was doing a very poor job of finding someone help her continue her line and start a family.

CHAPTER 15

Thomas came in about ten minutes after Henry left. Iris's relief at seeing him hit her in the chest. She wrapped him in a hug and lamented he was no longer short enough for her to kiss the top of his blonde head.

"Where have you been?" Iris hugged him again.

Thomas wriggled until she let him go. "I walked the McKenzies home, then ran here as fast as I could. I figured now I could run fast wherever I wanted."

Iris cupped his face in her hands. "You must still be very careful until this settles down. Some people will take this in stride, some will need time to get used to us, and some may not like us at all." She had never seen Jacob after the crowd had dispersed. Iris did not know which reaction he would ultimately display. She wanted to believe that the friendship and tender feelings he had displayed towards her would incline him towards understanding. She knew that life did not always deliver what one wanted.

"Promise me that you will not run through town, for a few days at least."

"I promise."

It was full dark by the time Iris plied Mrs. Ames and her daughter, Samantha, with tea and honeyed bread and tucked them both into warm beds. Iris's eyes were scratchy with sleep and she yawned wide enough to pop her jaw. Thomas went to bed with a book, and Iris was alone.

She took her boots into her room and changed into a nightgown and thick woolen socks. She swung a shawl around her shoulders and retrieved the letters from her friend and the seal Henry had given her. There was one more task she had to complete before collapsing into her own bed. She wanted to write one more letter. She was almost certain it would be the last, given Jacob's reaction today.

The stove downstairs was banked for the night, so Iris gathered what she needed and laid it out on the kitchen table upstairs where the fire was still flickering and warm. She made a cup of tea and sat down to her task. She only got as far as the salutation when she heard the door of the depot open downstairs.

A trickle of fear prickled her. She had never locked her door before. There was no guarantee that everyone in town had taken the sight of her in stride, and the trickle of fear turned into a full bloom of trepidation. Her eyes went to her door. She had two guns. One was downstairs behind the counter and one was in her bedroom. The first was on the other side of whomever was downstairs and the second was close, but maybe not close enough. Iris stood and crept as noiselessly as possible to her room.

She had one foot across the threshold when Marina's riot of curls came into view on the stairs.

Relief flowed over her like water. Iris sagged with exhaustion. "Thank the gods it's just you. You scared me half to death." Iris walked back to the table.

Marina chuckled quietly. "A bit jumpy tonight, are we? Were you going into your room for the gun I'm always telling you to keep closer by than you do?"

"Maybe," Iris grumbled.

"If I'd meant you harm, it would've done you no good in there. Good thing I'm friendly." Marina lifted the lid of the teapot and wrinkled her nose with a sigh.

"Sorry. No coffee tonight, though I do have some bread and honey." Iris sat back in her chair and pushed the pile of letters under the almost empty page she had been writing on. Marina was getting down the honey pot and had her back turned to Iris. "What brings you here? Is everything all right?"

Marina sat and spread a generous amount of honey on a slice of bread. "Everything's fine. Reed wanted me to come check on Mrs. Ames and on you." She took a large bite and chewed.

"They're asleep, as I will be soon. You don't look tired at all." It was an accusation. Iris crossed her arms over her chest. Marina not only did not look tired, she was radiating energy, which irritated her.

Marina took another bite. "I'm not that easy to wear out."

"Are you saying I'm delicate?" Iris huffed.

Marina put her bread down, and her face lost all hints of teasing. "You're more delicate than we are. You've been flying for only a year now. You don't have the stamina I have, and we did some fancy maneuvers today. You don't have to be a big bad monster, Iris. That's my job."

Iris relaxed. "A job you are wonderful at, my bird."

Marina polished off the bread and rubbed her hands together. "Now, the real reason I came. I need to talk to you."

Iris did not like the glint in Marina's eyes. "About what? Are you planning something that will get you in trouble?"

Marina laughed, and Iris shushed her before she woke the whole street. "Sadly, no. I'm planning no trouble. Yet. I need to ask you a question."

"You can ask me anything. You know that," Iris said.

Marina pulled a flask from her boot. "First, a drink." She took a sip then passed the flask to Iris, who took a very small sip, afraid that any more than that would put her directly in bed. She was exhausted. Marina waved a hand at her. "More than that. You need it."

"Fine." Iris complied. "Ask your question."

"What's going on between you and Henry?"

Iris had an answer for almost any question except that one. Iris felt her face heat and she pursed her lips in frustration. "Nothing."

Marina snorted. "You look about as innocent as a maid caught in Zeus's bed."

Iris moved her half full cup of tea around in a circle and watched her hands as she spoke. "I've recently noticed Henry is a very handsome man. That's all."

Marina laughed quietly, but the effort made her entire body shake. "Oh, hells, Iris. The man can make magic swords. What's more attractive than that?"

Iris waved a hand. "Most women, including me, do not count sword-making as an attribute. Only you care about that."

"I don't know. Some women care a great deal about a man's sword." Marina leaned in and waggled her eyebrows at Iris.

Iris pushed Marina away and blushed harder. "That's not what I meant. Henry is a good man. Kind. Thoughtful." Iris smiled. "And he has the loveliest eyes. He made something for me." Iris picked up the seal from the table and handed it to Marina.

Marina's jovial expression sobered. "You admire him and I think it's mutual. You've been thinking about this a lot."

Iris had hardly thought of little else the past few days. "Do you disapprove?" Iris asked.

Marina chuckled. "It wouldn't be my place to do so, not that it would stop me if I wanted to make an objection." Marina sighed. "Look, you're family. I would do anything for you. Henry is one of my few true friends. I'd do anything for him. I think the two of you would suit each other, and he didn't seem to object to being close to you earlier, so that's a plus."

Iris twirled her cup again. "It's complicated, though."

Marina's eyes bored into hers. "Complicated how?"

Iris removed the letters she had hidden under the blank paper. "I've been receiving these letters from a man who'd asked to court me. I think they're from Jacob Wells. He's been spending time with me. He's very attentive."

Marina opened one of the letters and began scanning the contents. She looked up a few times, then kept reading. "These are sweet and beautiful."

Iris wrapped her hands around her now-cool tea cup. "I feel torn between a man who has declared his intentions, and Henry, who has declared nothing, and yet makes me feel like I'm on fire whenever he walks into a room." Iris hid her face in her hands. "Jacob has left little doubt that he is interested. Until recently, I would've told you Henry was not at all interested, but the past two days he has been different."

Marina whistled at her. "You're in a bad way."

"The worst part is, when I write to my friend, who I think is Jacob, I've started to feel like I'm betraying Henry. When I'm with Henry, I feel like I'm betraying my friend. I'm not honest with anyone. No matter what, I feel like I'm losing. I think I need to talk to them both. Tonight, Jacob took one look at me with my wings and melted away into the crowd. I think I might have lost my friend. I'm also afraid I'm misreading Henry and seeing things that aren't there. Everything's a mess." Iris's insides were tight. She felt her fears and anxieties leaking out as tears, and she did not stop them.

Marina pulled Iris's hands from her face. "I'm not good with tears, so please don't cry on me." Marina brushed her cheeks. "I think you're reading the signals just fine. Henry is not a brash man and moves at his own pace. Just give him some time. I saw him with you today. Despite what you think, he does not look at you the way he looks at everyone else. Sometimes things have a way of working themselves out. I don't know about Wells, but I would like to wring his neck."

"Don't hurt Jacob. He's had quite a shock today. When did you become a sage?"

"Marriage, it seems, has been a good influence on me." Marina grinned and flashed her pointy teeth at Iris, same as ever.

"In that case, thank the gods you found the one man on earth who will put up with you," Iris said.

"I'm thankful every damn day." Marina stood and walked over to Iris and hugged her. "Now, I have to go home to that man who probably thinks I'm out terrorizing the town and peeking in people's windows trying to frighten them."

Iris twisted in her chair to look at Marina. "You wouldn't do that. Would you?"

Marina shrugged. "It would be wildly entertaining, but I think no. I'll go home to my long-suffering husband. I've missed my own bed. Write your letter. I'll see you tomorrow."

Marina left and Iris settled down to write.

Iris paused, her pen poised. She could feel Henry's arm around her waist and the smell of his coat around her body. Her palm prickled with the memory, and heat uncurled in her belly. Her pen dripped onto the parchment and she cursed. If she told her friend the truth, that she was falling for another man, would he continue to write to her? Would he work harder to win her affections? Did she want him to?

A selfish part of her wanted to keep both. She wanted the seduction of being lured by beautiful words on letters meant only for her and she wanted to see what heat lay behind the careful attention of a thoughtful and sincere blacksmith. Iris knew to keep both was a deception and she could not continue it. The time for half-truths and falsehoods was past. She sighed and dipped her pen in the black ink and continued writing.

CHAPTER 16

The snow swirled and piled against the windows all night. When Iris woke and looked out of the second-story window, the flakes were so thick she could not make out Vine's saloon across the street. A small knot of worry tightened inside her at the thought of the weight of all that snow building up overnight. While she wished the snow would keep the curious from coming to the saloon today, she knew, despite the snow, many would take her up on her offer to ask their questions of her. Turning Creek was a small place, and she had just given them the most exciting thing to do in months, perhaps years.

Iris flopped the covers back over her head and pulled her knees up to her chest. She let the warmth of her cocoon seduce her into staying in bed for a few more minutes. If she stayed wrapped in her blankets, no one could bother her with questions, and she would not have to think about the relentless snow.

The snow concerned her, and not just because it was piling up in dangerous amounts. If she opened her senses, the snow felt like sorrow. Perhaps sorrow was the wrong word for the complexity of the feeling the snow invoked. It was despair, inevitability, and grief tangled into a mess of uncontrolled power. Of one thing Iris was certain, there was something unnatural about the storm that had been plaguing the valley. The power of it had been building, and she was now absolutely certain this was no natural storm. Iris wanted to make a list of possible causes, and for that she needed to get up and start going through her books.

Iris flipped the covers off and got out of bed. Halfway through straightening the quilts, she remembered the letter she had left, fastened with her new seal, in the box downstairs. Anticipation roared through her. She grabbed her shawl from the peg on the wall and raced down the stairs in her stocking feet.

Even under the covering of the porch in front of the depot, snow had drifted against the door, and Iris had to kick through a foot of it to reach the mailbox. Iris flipped open the lid. The empty bottom of the box mocked her haste and her hope. The snow had already begun to melt through her wool socks, but she stood staring at the bottom of the box. She closed the lid and opened it again. With a disgusted noise, she dropped the lid with a satisfying bang.

By the time she went back upstairs, her anger had morphed into hurt. Jacob had been her friend. Her heart ached with the betrayal.

The morning was advancing, and soon, despite the snow and wind, Iris was certain there would be people in the saloon looking for answers. Besides fielding questions from some townspeople, she needed to do some reading to try to see if there was a Remnant who could be responsible for the snow.

Iris got dressed and worked on stowing away her emotions to complete the task ahead. When it was time to slide the letters into her skirt pocket, she hesitated. She had been keeping them close since she started receiving them. Today, they felt like lead in her hands and ashes in her mouth.

She placed them underneath the book on her nightstand, *A Retelling of the Myths of Old*, by Archibald Summers. It had been the book her mother read to her at bedtime, and she kept it close out of habit. She rarely read it anymore. She had most of the stories memorized. The seal Henry had given her was next to the book, and she slipped that into her pocket instead. Its weight reminded her there were people who knew who and what she was and loved her because of, not in spite of, it.

Iris went about making tea and coffee. She placed cups and mugs on a dented metal serving tray. The dent had been left in its smooth surface when Petra had used the tray as a blunt object to hit Marina over the head during an argument. The tray had sustained more damage than the stubborn harpy's head. Iris had long forgotten the cause of the fight that had ended with the two harpies laughing and rolling around on the floor. A tiny smile quirked at her mouth and peace slid into the cracks in her heart.

Iris had a purpose and she had a family, even if it was an unconventional one. She knew Dora, Marina, and Petra would fly to the moon and back for her. They loved her as much as she loved them, and gratitude for what she did have washed over her. She had more than many, and she should not forget it.

Now that she knew for certain that her feelings for Henry were serious, she would have to win him over. She knew he already liked her company. They were friends, after all, and friends could always become more given enough time and encouragement. Marina thought it was possible. Iris could be patient and persistent. The best things often required some time.

The door to the extra room opened. Mrs. Ames poked her head out and her eyes searched the room. Her hair was already tidied back into a bun. Samantha peeked around her mother's skirt and, upon seeing Iris, dashed towards her. Iris scooped her up and was surrounded by the smell of soft, half-awake toddler.

Samantha put both hands, one on each side, on Iris's face. "Where're your wings, Angel Lady?"

Iris laughed. "I don't keep them out all the time. They're big and get in the way."

"Oh. Can I see them?" A small finger tapped Iris's cheek as the child spoke.

"Maybe later," Iris replied.

"Now."

Mrs. Ames took the child from Iris. "I'm sure Miss Iris has other things to do, Samantha."

Iris motioned to Mrs. Ames's dress. "I see you found the dresses in the chest. It looks like it may be a bit short." Mrs. Ames was a couple of inches taller than Iris. Most people were. "Lily Hughes, the tailor's wife, do you know her?" Mrs. Ames nodded. "She's going to bring you some dresses she has ready made for you to wear until we can get your things from the boardinghouse."

Iris went to the kitchen and pulled out the last of her eggs and bread. Mrs. Ames put a hand on her arm and Iris stopped her movements.

"Please, Miss Iris. I need to tell you something."

"Mrs. Ames, please call me Iris."

"Only if you will return the favor and call me Margaret." Iris nodded and Margaret continued, "Thank you again for what you and Mrs. Brant did for us. I lay awake last night and couldn't stop thinking about what it cost you to rescue us. The way you risked yourself for us, almost strangers to you."

Margaret took Iris's hand. "I hope that you will accept my gratitude and my friendship. I'll tell everyone who asks that regardless of appearances, you and Mrs. Brant will always be angels of mercy to me."

Iris embraced Margaret. "Thank you for that. It was never really a choice for us. We could help, and so we did."

"I know, and that is what makes the act so extraordinary."

"You should know that Marina generally goes by Deputy Marina rather than Mrs. Brant. It's a quirk she has."

"I'll remember that." Margaret waved towards the plates. "Can I help?"

Iris and Margaret ate a late breakfast and cleaned up.

"Should we go to the saloon early?" Margaret asked.

Iris was about to say yes, but then knew with a tingle of awareness they needed to stay at the depot. "We need to wait for Reed and Marina, then we can all walk over together."

Margaret tilted her head to the side. "Did you arrange that last night?"

"Not exactly." The time for secrets was past. "I possess the unpredictable gift of prophecy. Sometimes, I get glimpses of important things, but mostly I get a feeling like I should wait or that someone is coming to see me. I'd better make some coffee. Reed and Marina prefer it over tea. Nothing is worse than a grumpy harpy in the morning."

Margaret's eyes were wide. "That's amazing."

While they waited, Iris made a list of Remnants that could control snow while they waited for the others. They did not wait too long. The bell on the front door rang as Marina and Reed rushed in amidst a gust of wind, snow, and ice. They lived above the sheriff's office, only a few doors down, but they were already covered in snow. Iris tucked her list and books away. There would be time tomorrow to solve the problem of the snow. Today, they would find out if their town would survive the truth.

Reed stood by the door and stomped snow from his boots. "Morning, ladies. I'd advise staying in today. Isn't fit for civilized folk out there."

Marina began loosen her scarf. "You went out in it."

Reed revealed a wolfish grin when he removed his own scarf. "That's because the most uncivilized lady I know told me to get moving because we had to get to the depot first and then to the saloon before the rest of the town."

"Oh, I'm a lady now, am I?" Marina's eyebrows went up towards her hairline.

"Get here first for what?" Iris asked.

The door opened again to admit Dora and Petra, whose clothes lacked a layer of snow and ice, which meant they had flown to the front door in their harpy forms before changing. Iris supposed they figured if the secret was out that there was no point in changing outside of town and trudging down Main Street in the snow.

Petra saw Marina and stomped her foot. "Styx, you beat me here."

"Told you she would." Dora walked over to Iris and hugged her. "Good morning."

Iris laid a hand on Dora's cheek. Her eyes were red rimmed and smudged with lack of sleep. "Are you all right?"

"I have some news, but it'll hold until this business is over," Dora said. Iris let it drop.

Marina flashed her teeth at the other two harpies. "I win. I rescue ladies and am the first to arrive, ready to face the angry mob."

Iris wagged a finger at Marina. "Don't look so hopeful about the mob. I think people took it rather well." Petra chuckled. Iris moved her finger in that direction. "And you, I knew you'd all be here in plenty of time. I've never had any doubt about where your loyalties lie. My birds, stop being ridiculous. It's going to be a long day as it is, and I'm not sure I can take your antics all day."

Iris made introductions where they were needed. Margaret sidled up to Marina, and they talked in low tones. The others went back to the stove to get coffee.

Reed brought his cup of coffee over to Iris. "The weather is the worst I've ever seen it. I'm not sure how many people we'll have at Vine's."

"Word will spread fast enough, and there will be enough willing to come despite the weather." Iris drummed her fingers on the countertop. "It was nice of Daniel to offer to have everyone there."

"And expose himself in the process," Reed said.

"Exactly."

Petra joined them with a steaming cup of tea in her hands. She peered into the sheriff's cup and wrinkled her nose. "I don't know how you drink that swill. It's uncivilized."

Marina waved a bottle of whiskey in the air. "Add some of this and it'll taste better than your tea. I promise."

Petra grabbed the bottle and opened the front door. She pretended to throw it out.

Marina grabbed for it. "You wouldn't dare."

"I might, just to see you cry." Petra opened the bottle and poured some of it into Marina's coffee. She handed the cup and the bottle back to Marina. "Best way to start what should turn out to be an interesting day."

Marina laughed. "By the gods, yes it is."

"Did you come armed?" Petra asked.

Marina gave her a disgusted look and pulled two long throwing knives from her boots. "Reed made me leave my new swords at home. He said they're too intimidating and would only incite people to violence, but they're gorgeous. You'll have to come see them later."

"The word I used was frightening, not intimidating," Reed said.

"Same thing," Marina shrugged.

Reed turned to Dora. "Can't you do something about these two?"

Dora just shrugged. "Why would I? Their bad behavior means most of my faults are forgiven in contrast."

Reed turned to Iris, imploring, and she shrugged and said, "You knew what you were getting into."

Reed looked at Marina and his face lit with contentment and what Iris could only describe as love, though the word paled against that smile. "A decision I'll never regret." He paused and winked at Marina. "Probably." Marina winked back and the two started laughing.

When Petra stopped laughing at Marina, her face turned serious. "James and the boys wanted to come, but they never would've made it through the snow. James wanted me to tell you that he'll support you no matter what happens, of course, and he told me to keep Marina from getting into any fisticuffs."

"Did he actually say fisticuffs?" Iris asked.

Petra's lips quirked in a grin. "You know how stuffy he can be sometimes. He told me I was under no circumstances to let Marina get into a fight because then I would be obligated to help out and then he would be obligated to be annoyed at both of us for acting like ruffians." Petra and Marina grinned at each other until they both cackled.

The contentment Iris had felt earlier increased. There were many people here who cared about her and, no matter where this conversation with the town went, she had their love and loyalty. Henry was a loyal friend; she just needed to win his love as well.

They finished their drinks, put on their coats, and walked through the snow to the saloon. Daniel greeted them and then put them to work serving tea and coffee. Marina complained until Daniel let her stir and serve the pot of flip he had made instead.

People arrived in twos and threes over the course of the next hour. Many more residents of Turning Creek were willing to brave getting lost in the snow to hear what Iris and Marina had to say than Iris had anticipated. The Remnants who came, and there were many, mingled with the other townspeople. Iris wondered how many of them would keep their identity a secret, even after this. She wagered many would. Old habits were hard to break when the security of your life and family were at stake.

Each time the door opened, Iris's body tensed in anticipation then released when she saw who it was, or rather who it was not. Neither Henry nor Jacob had made an appearance. The room filled and every chair and bench was taken. It was a storm of icy cold outside, but Vine's was warm and packed with the humanity of Turning Creek.

Iris had ceased to watch the door when Jacob arrived. He caught her eyes, then he ducked and pushed his way through the crowd to walk away from her. Iris had prepared herself for rejection, but tears still pricked at her eyes.

Marina was next to her in a flash. "Want me to go bite him?"

"No."

"Just a little bite? A 'you're treating my friend like dirt' bite. One that will heal eventually but will scar up just a bit?"

Iris laughed. "No, but thank you for making me laugh."

Marina shrugged. "I still want to bite him."

Iris shoved her away, still smiling. That was when Henry arrived. Even though the room was filled with people talking, Iris heard none of it as she stilled and waited. Henry's eyes found her and he walked straight towards her without deviation. Her crushed feelings burgeoned like a sail in the wind, and her world righted again.

She was standing behind the wooden bar, but Iris felt his presence like a physical pressure. She laid her palms flat on the counter and leaned forward to hear him in the noise. He had forgotten his scarf and his beard was dotted with snow. He laid gloved hands over hers on the counter.

"I'm sorry I'm late. I was finishing a new project, and I lost track of time." Henry's hands did not move from hers.

She leaned farther over the counter and Henry mirrored her movement until his face was inches from hers. "Don't worry. I had no doubts you'd be here."

"Did I miss anything?" he asked.

Iris wished the room full of people would disappear for a few minutes or hours so she could keep looking at the flecks of sky in Henry's grey eyes. "I was waiting for you."

Henry's face lit with a smile so bright Iris blinked to adjust to its shine. Iris noted the gleam in his eyes and reconsidered her firm notion that there was no way Henry could have written her letters. Perhaps winning him over would not be so hard after all. He leaned back from her and waved across the counter. "I'm here now. Would you like to get started?"

Iris walked around the counter to Henry and held out her hand. "Would you mind giving me a boost to the top of the counter?"

Iris had thought Henry would steady her with his hand as she climbed up a stool and onto the counter. Instead, Henry wrapped his hands around her waist. The heat of his grip turned her insides to butter. He lifted her high enough to place her feet on the top of one of the stools, then held out his hand and guided her to take the last step to the counter. It took a moment for her legs to regain their balance after his touch.

From this vantage point, Iris could see everyone. She saw the faces of many of her Remnant friends. Simon and Beth Kramer. Daniel Vine. Lee Williams. Widow Finch. Paul and Lily Hughes. L.A. and Johnny had come as well, and their wives sat next to them. There were others, like Grant Korman, that she knew, but not well. She was too high up. She wanted this to be a friendly conversation, not a lecture or a show of power.

She gathered her skirts again and lowered herself until she sat on the top of the counter, allowing her legs to swing free. She tucked her skirts around them. Sitting on the counter meant that Henry's face was level with hers. He shifted position to stand to her right. The three harpies, their mortal forms a range of complexions, but all beautiful in her eyes, stood to her left. Reed leaned nonchalantly against the door. He looked relaxed, but Iris was certain there was no detail in the room he had not already noticed.

"Please, everyone find a seat or a place to be comfortable." The room shifted and settled and Iris got started. "I'm glad so many of you have come today. I know you have a lot of questions, but I must lay down two rules before we begin.

"First, you must know that the things I'm going to tell you today have been a closely guarded secret for generations. I ask, for the safety of the people in this town, people who are your friends and neighbors, that you keep this secret close. Turning Creek has become a refuge for people like me, and I want it to stay that way. We call ourselves Remnants, and this is our home too.

"Second, I will only answer questions as they pertain to me. There may be others who wish to answer questions with me, but that is their choice. I will not tell you who is who or who is what. Those are secrets to be told by the individuals themselves. I will not allow this to turn into anything other than a pleasant conversation." Iris tensed and waited. The heads in front of her nodded in agreement and some even smiled encouragement. Some of the faces in the back row lacked smiles but were not outright hostile, and Iris hoped this would sway them her way. Jacob stood as far from her as it was possible to be.

Henry's eyes followed her gaze, and his mouth thinned into a hard line. He slid his hand in hers. Iris jerked hers in surprise, then squeezed his hand in thanks. Regardless of whether Henry had written her letters or not, he was paying attention to her now and standing by her side when she needed him most. She relaxed and began.

"The basics are this. All those Greek myths you've read about or heard about when you were young are real. When Mount Olympus fell, the characters in the myths dispersed into the world, intermarried with mortals, had children, and lived mostly peaceful lives. We are called Remnants, because a piece of the old myths reside in us. Some of us have powers that we can use for the good of others. Most of us live longer than a normal mortal life, though I would still advise you not to ask a lady what her true age is." That got a chuckle.

"I am Iris, The Messenger of the gods, and named for the first of my line. I'm a postmistress because that is my special purpose, to deliver letters." Iris left out the prophecy and sensing emotions from letters part. No need to dive head first into the entire lake on this size of stage. One small puddle would do.

Iris turned to the three harpies. "I have these ladies' permission to tell you about the harpies who have guarded you. Marina you saw yesterday. Dora and Petra are also harpies. They are fierce and loyal and I trust them with my life and the well-being of this town, as you have countless times over the past couple years, whether you have known it or not. As you saw yesterday, they are fearsome in their harpy forms, but I want you to remember they fight to defend you even if they look like monsters.

"There are many other things I could tell you, but I think it might be easier to just have you ask questions." Iris waited.

Art Turner, a short man in stature and wisdom, spoke first. "So there are more of you Remnants then just you four. Should we be worried for our safety?"

Marina sighed heavily next to her, and Iris resisted the urge to roll her eyes. She answered before Marina had a chance to open her mouth. "There are as many different kinds of Remnants as there are people. Some are good and some are not. You should only fear a Remnant as much as you fear any other person you know.

"The world has not always been a safe place for Remnants, but Turning Creek is our home and a different kind of place, a place where people can be safe, no matter where they come from, a place we're all proud to live. For years now, some of us have defended you, without your knowledge, and kept this a safe place for everyone. I hope that earns us some measure of goodwill."

Aidy Lowell stood in the back. Her red scarf stood in bright contrast against her grey dress. Her husband tried to pull her back down. She waved him off. "Those words sound fine, but you're asking us to trust you about other people or things over which you've got no control. How can we trust that our children are safe if we don't know what's out there prowling around? I want to know who the Remnants are." There was some murmuring of agreement.

Simon Kramer stood and his wife, Beth, followed him. She twined her fingers with his, a fierce look of determination on her plain face. Simon spoke. "Dora and Petra rescued me last year from being kidnapped. I'm not a Remnant, but Beth is. Turning Creek is a better place because of the kind of people who live here." They remained standing.

Lily Hughes gave her husband a look before she stood. He followed her and put an arm around her shoulders. Iris's heart clenched at the way Lily breathed deep before speaking. Lily's voice was strong but quiet. The room stilled to listen.

"Many of you know that I was taken last year. It was Dora, Petra, and Sheriff Brant who found me and brought me back to my family. They gave me my life back and gifted me their friendship after they rescued me. I'm also a Remnant, and I'm here to beg you for a sliver of the loyalty these people have shown us in the past year.

"Our families live in fear of people finding out what we are. For the first time, Remnants have a place we can live and raise our families without fear. Before yesterday, that peace was because, for the first time in memory, the harpies have come together to protect us. There are dangerous Remnants out there, but the harpies are fierce creatures who take defending their territory seriously."

Marina and Petra preened under the praise. Dora's expression remained solemn.

Lily continued, "Again and again the Remnants of Turning Creek have stood in the gap for all of the people here, mortals and Remnants alike.

Now, we need you to stand in the gap for us."

A man stood next to the Hughes. Mark Farlan was older, a widower who had come to live in Turning Creek in July. "I hear what you're saying, and I understand that some of you people are honorable, but what about the ones that aren't? You all talk about danger averted and kidnappings solved but didn't all those things happen because we have monsters in our valley? I think every trustworthy Remnant should have to make themselves known."

Agreements echoed from some areas of the room. Someone in the back yelled, "We want a list."

Iris's heart was in her throat. This was what she hadn't wanted, this distrust and anger and fear. People did things they regretted, things that hurt others, when they were afraid of the unknown. Iris knew this because she was afraid right now, afraid she had made a terrible mistake in exposing herself and it would cost them all dearly if the intentions of the crowd were not swayed.

Iris's eyes swept the room and two pairs of brown eyes captured hers. Margaret and Samantha Ames held each other on the side of the room. *It had been worth it*, she thought. *There is no doubt.* She had saved two lives yesterday and they had a right to live more than she had a right to keep her secret. Her fear whirled into tight, hot anger.

"Help me stand up on the bar."

Henry did not question her request. He held out his hand and gave her a boost up. Iris had spent her whole life wrangling unruly harpies, true monsters who could rip things to shreds for the joy of it. She could handle a room full of mortals.

"We are not making a list." The room did not settle, so Iris repeated herself, putting all of the painful anger in her heart into her words. "We are not making a list. There'll be no lists. No registrations. No public outings of neighbors. History has shown that witch hunts never end well for the witches or the zealots. This is a refuge and a place of peace, but it will be a place of war if you make it so, and I promise you, you will not win."

"'Bout time our Iris showed up," Marina muttered, only loud enough for those directly around her to hear. The harpy was grinning with an unpleasant smile.

Iris felt bolstered by the show of force. "I may deliver letters, but my ancestors were warriors. You will harm people, Remnant or mortal, in this valley, over my dead body, and I swear on the River Styx that I will take some of you wrongdoers down with me."

There was a steady pulse of power coming from the harpies, and Iris was not the only one who noticed. The people standing near them had inched away from the wall of violence. Marina was rubbing her hands together, soaking in the feeling in the room. Dora and Petra were standing still, looking menacing.

For once, Iris felt the wild violence in her heart that she had seen in the harpies, and she did not disguise it in her tone. "We will not harm you or others, but we will defend what is ours. Turning Creek and its people are ours." She let the threat linger in the air.

Henry took a step closer to her. His voice was firm, but it managed to be soft at the same time, and it carried to the back of the room. "We all want the same things you do, to live honorable lives. We only ask that you allow us that freedom. I hope that our actions up to this juncture have earned us your trust."

The room was filled with a heavy silence. Iris felt her own heart swell, and not just from pride at Henry's words. To have this man stand beside her in irrefutable solidarity was priceless. She had the feeling that as long as he went with her, she could do anything.

Reed spoke next. "I know some of you need some time. Please know that any of the people who have spoken today are willing to answer your questions honestly. Some of you may decide this is not the town for you." Reed paused. "I add my request to Iris's: if you leave, we ask that for the safety of the families in Turning Creek that you keep our secrets. I hope that in time you will come to see the Remnants are not so different than me or you. I think we all need some time to think over the events of the last couple days."

There were murmurs of agreement from the crowd, but not everyone was happy with the result of the meeting. Most people stood from their seats to mill around, talking in small groups. The noise level in the room rose until Iris could not hear the conversation going on between Marina and one of the Hughes's twins. She could never tell those girls apart.

Iris leaned over to Henry and yelled in his ear. "I need to go talk to someone."

He did not reply, but instead lifted her off the counter. His hands lingered on her waist. She smiled at him then wove her way to the back of the room. Jacob was standing alone in the corner. His face was shuttered.

"Can we talk?"

He hesitated for so long Iris thought he was going to refuse when he nodded. It was too loud for what she wanted to say, so she led him out the back door to the garden. The snow was coming down hard. This was going to have to be quick.

The door closed behind them and the roar of the saloon was replaced with the howling of the wind. They stood in what was the bier garden in the summer. The benches were hidden under piles of snow, and the vines on their trellises were withered and brown.

"I'm sorry I lied to you. I hope we can still be friends."

Jacob's jovial face of the past few days was gone, replaced by something

Iris had a hard time identifying. "I liked you, Iris. I thought I might care for you, but this…" He waved his arms over her shoulders where her wings would be. "This is more than I want to handle."

Regret stabbed at her. "Can we start over? I would like to be friends with you even if I can't return any of the more tender feelings you may have had towards me."

"You're some kind of monster. How can I be friends with you? You're not even a human being."

His words were a blow. Iris staggered back into the door. She had never been on the receiving end of such a look and it hurt more than she thought it would have. She finally recognized the expression on his face. It was disgust. "How can you say that?"

"How could I not speak the truth? Don't talk to me again." Jacob turned and stomped off into the swirling snow.

He had played the part of a friend, but he could not accept her the way she was. Iris slumped against the back door of the building. This was the reason why Remnants did not share their secrets. Mortals could be hateful when faced with the truth. She would not have thought before today that Jacob was a small-minded person. The tears leaking from her eyes turned to ice on her cheeks.

The door she was leaning against moved, and Iris stepped away from it while wiping off the tears on her face.

Dora poked her head out of the door. "Iris, it's freezing, get back in here." She grabbed Iris's arm and yanked her back inside. Dora leaned close to her face. "Have you been crying? What did that louse say to you?"

Marina and Petra moved through the crowd with a speed Iris would not have thought possible given the sheer number of bodies in the room.

"Why has Iris been crying?" Petra asked as soon as she stood beside them.

"Jacob Wells is an idiot. I saw the way he was looking at you while you were talking. Like something was stuck on his shoe. I'm going to kill him." Marina shoved past Petra to get to the door.

Petra took hold of Marina's arm. "You'll have to wait in line. Henry's coming this way and he looks angry. I've never seen that expression on his face before, and I'd like to see where it leads."

The three harpies and Iris watched Henry's progress across the room. He could not get through the crowd as quickly as the harpies.

Henry put his hands on her shoulders. "Did he hurt you?"

Iris shook her head, but her eyes welled up against her will. Henry's hands tightened on her shoulders, then he wrapped his arms around her. She returned his embrace with all her strength. She had lost a friend today, but she had other people that loved her exactly the way she was. Henry released her before she was ready. She could have stayed in his arms all night, but they were in a room full of people, and it was the most physical affection Henry had ever shown anyone, public or private.

"Nothing is hurt but my misplaced feelings of friendship."

Henry's hands remained on her shoulders. "You shouldn't waste your tears on him if he can't see you for who you are."

Reed opened the front door, took one look outside, and slammed it shut in a swirl of snow and cold.

"Folks, I hate to break up this party, but the snow's getting worse. Everyone needs to head home in groups of two of more. Stick to the boardwalk, with your hands on the buildings when you can. Don't let go of your partner. I don't want to go looking for anyone in this mess," Reed said.

Everyone scrambled to pair up. It took a while before the room had cleared. Despite the danger, no one wanted to leave. Iris saw Marina sharing her flask with everyone who came up to her to shake hands. L.A, Johnny, and their wives were some of the last ones to leave.

Reed stopped L.A. with a hand on his shoulder. "Do you want Marina to go with you? Wasn't exaggerating about the danger of going out alone, and I know you live a ways out."

Marina spoke up. "I can go with them and fly back all right, even in this storm."

Reed and Marina exchanged a glance before he stepped into her space. "Be careful, Sparrow. I've come to appreciate having you around."

Marina grinned. "I'd hate to disappoint you." She left with the two older couples.

Reed watched them until the door closed then went to pour another cup of coffee. He sat next to Thomas and the two of them talked in low tones.

Margaret scooped up Samantha, who was nodding off in a chair. "I'm going to take her back to the depot. I can make it there alone. It's just across the street." She left.

Dora and Petra were talking in the corner by the stove. They made a beautiful picture of contrasts. Petra's dark face crowned with curly salt and pepper hair was bent in concentration towards Dora's pale, freckled complexion. They looked up, as if sensing her regard, and motioned her over.

Henry stopped her with a hand on her arm. "Iris, I need to get back. I've got to finish that project I'm working on."

"The snow is dangerous. You shouldn't go alone," she said.

"I'll follow the boardwalk down so I won't get lost in the snow. If Mrs. Ames can cross the street, I can follow the wooden boardwalk."

Iris stepped closer to him; she could not help the movement even if she had wanted to. Once she got close enough, it was as though she was propelled with a magnetic pull, and she was done resisting. His hand still rested on her arm and she placed hers over it. His hand curled towards hers until she was able to grasp his hand. The contact stole the breath from her.

"Henry."

"Yes?" His voice dropped, and Iris felt something shift between them.

"Be careful."

Henry nodded. "Good night, Iris."

One word and yet it held power over her. She had heard her name thousands of times, but on his lips with his face so intent on hers, it felt more like a benediction. Someone coughed behind her and Henry took a step back. Iris felt her face heat to a bright red.

Henry turned and said goodbye to the others. He dipped his head to Iris before he left and then he walked out into the snow.

Petra whistled once the door was shut. "For Hera's sake, Iris. Just kiss that man already."

Dora snickered.

Iris's face burned hotter, which she had not thought possible. "What is it you two wanted with me?" Iris sat next to Petra and smoothed her skirts out, ignoring the giggling harpies. Dora stopped laughing. Petra poured a shot of whiskey into Dora and Iris's cups. Petra swirled the tea left in her cup and drained it. "If you want my advice, you should just kiss him. He's never going to make a move otherwise."

Iris sipped her whiskey. "Funny, I don't recall asking for your advice."

"You need it, regardless," Petra said.

Iris ignored Petra and looked at Dora instead. Despite the smile on her face, Dora's eyes hid exhaustion. Iris felt her own exhaustion catching up to her. "What is it you wanted to tell me?"

"Petra's right, about Henry, but that's not what I need to tell you." Dora finished her drink and placed the cup gently onto the saucer. "The oldest Stewart girl died. Mrs. Stewart is crazy with grief. She was already in a bad place after Natalie and her husband died, but I think losing Nancy has pushed her over the edge. Her youngest daughter, Nina, is only three. I'm worried Mrs. Stewart is too caught in her grief to care for her remaining child."

Dora paused, drawing breath to continue. "I checked on them before I came, but she was still sitting in the same place I'd left her the night before. Nina had managed all right, but she can't stay there forever if her mother won't care for her."

"I was there a couple days ago, and Nina was the one who came to the door," Iris said.

Something rattled in Iris's mind. "Daniel, thank you for having us, but we need to leave. Right now."

Daniel looked annoyed, but he kept picking up cups and things from the tables. "You're welcome for the space."

"Daniel, it is deeply appreciated, but I just remembered something I think is important. Thank you." Iris hurried out of the saloon.

Petra followed Iris out the door. The snow whipped their faced like tiny knives. "What is it?" Petra asked.

"I forgot something." Iris ran the rest of the way to the depot despite the thick snow pulling on her ankles.

She had something for Mrs. Stewart. Something that might break her grief and help her to turn to her younger child. Iris rushed through the door and rounded the counter. She stopped in front of the pigeon-holes. One of the letters was pulling on her. This close, it was an audible yell in her mind. This letter had waited some time to be delivered. When it was given to her, its time had not yet come.

Iris pulled a faded envelope from the top left corner, nearest the wall. It was simply addressed to "Mother" in a precise but juvenile hand. Iris did not have to close her eyes to feel the words the letter contained. It wrapped around her like a blanket on a cold winter night. It felt like the embrace of love and encouragement.

Iris tapped the letter. "How old was Nancy, the Stewart's oldest daughter?"

Dora thought a moment. "Sixteen, I think. Why?"

Iris laid the letter flat on the counter. Dora and Petra leaned over and read the anonymous address of the letter.

"Sometimes, I'm given a letter before it is ready to be delivered. Sometimes, it's a letter that should never have been written. Sometimes, it's not the right time for those words. Nancy Stewart gave me that letter three years ago. I knew when she handed it to me that it was not the right time for that letter. She knew it as well, and she asked me to hold it and only deliver it only under two conditions. One, if she married and moved away from Turning Creek." Iris paused and licked her lips.

"And the other?" Dora asked.

"If she died," Iris whispered.

Petra's eyebrows went up. "She knew something was going to happen."

Dora rubbed her hands on her arms. "And she knew her mother would not take it well."

"Mrs. Stewart is a Remnant, but do we know of what line she is descended?" Iris asked.

Dora and Petra both shook their heads. Iris handed the letter to Dora, who put it in the pocket of her blue skirt. "I was going to stop by there tonight on my way home. I'll take this with me."

"If Nancy knew her mother so well, hopefully she has written the words her mother needs to hear to break her grief." Iris hoped she was right.

"I should get going too. James will be worried." Petra went to the door.

Iris looked out the front window. "Are you sure flying is safe on a night like this? I worry about you, you know."

Petra hugged her and rested her chin on Iris's head. "We know you do. It's one of the reasons we love you. Someone has to worry over us, and now we all know how very scary you can be when you want. I'm very proud of you."

Dora chuckled. "Poor mortals all thought we were the scariest thing in the room tonight when it was little Iris the entire time. I'm glad you're our Iris."

Iris squeezed her back, harder than she normally did. "Oh, bird. I love you so much." Iris leaned back so she could see Dora too. "I love all of you. You're more important to me than anything else in the world."

Petra and Dora exchanged a glance. Dora tucked a strand of hair behind Iris's ear. "Why so serious? You look sad."

Iris shrugged, unable to say where the sudden melancholy came from. "Maybe it's the letter to Mrs. Stewart," Iris paused. "Jacob's refusal to accept us hurt more than I thought it would. It has made me think, and I'm thankful to have all of you here, alive and safe."

Petra shared another glance with Dora, then replied, "We aren't that easy to get rid of. Styx, with all the scrapes Marina gets into, she should've been dead ten times over, and we're still stuck with her. I think you'll have us to fuss over for years to come." Petra ran a hand through her greying hair. "Even if we have a little less lifespan to live than normal. For us."

Iris kissed them both on the cheek. "Go on then. Be safe. Come back tomorrow if you can, and we'll see if we can make sense of the list I started today. There's something off about the snow."

Iris opened the door and a swirl of darkness and snow barged into the room. The harpies linked arms, ducked their heads, and went out into the night. Iris closed the door and rested her head against the wood. Exhaustion settled on her like a mantle. With half open eyes and her brain in a fog, she went through the steps of closing up the depot.

She peeked in to check on Margaret and Samantha. Mother and daughter were curled around each other in sleep. Iris envied them their warm bed. She knew hers would be cold when she crawled in, and there was no one to help her warm it. Henry popped into her mind, but she waved that thought away. She was too tired. Iris looked in on Thomas. The lump in his bed rose with his breathing. He always slept completely covered in the winter, like a bear in a den.

Finally, blissfully, she collapsed into her own bed. The frigid sheets jolted her awake enough for her to notice the stack of letters wedged under her book on the nightstand. She felt her brain start to wake up. The bed warmed and Iris thought better of thinking about anything. She closed her eyes and instead slipped into sleep.

CHAPTER 17

Iris wiped the snow from the lid and peered inside the empty mailbox the next morning. She did not even know why she looked. Jacob had been clear about his feelings. Her last hope that he would change his mind about their friendship after a night of sleep dissolved. The snow still fell. While it was not quite a blizzard, it was close enough that Iris was now positive about her earlier suspicions. This was not a natural blizzard.

Marina was the first to arrive. She held a steaming cup of coffee in her hand and set it on the counter while she took off her coat and scarf. "I brought my own drink because I know it'll be tea all day here."

"I'll make a pot of coffee for you if you ask nice," Iris said.

"Not worth it. Besides, I bet you that Reed comes traipsing in here in less than two hours with another cup for me." Marina smiled with an air of self-assurance.

Iris laughed. "It'll be cold by the time he walks down here. He's not going to drag a cup of coffee from your office to the depot just to please you."

"He might."

Iris wanted to know how Marina would win this bet. "What will you bet for it?"

"No research for me after he shows up. I get to do something else."

Iris knew Marina hated doing research. It involved too much sitting and not enough shenanigans. "Deal. You'll be flipping through books all day, though."

"We'll see."

Iris pulled a book from under the counter. "Start with this. I marked where I left off."

They both sat and got to work. After an hour, Iris looked over the list they had compiled and made some notes. They had everything on the list from nymphs who could control the weather to any one of the Theo Meteoroi, the group of sky and weather gods. The first Iris had been a member of the Theo Meteoroi, but those powers had since faded from her line. The possibilities were so diverse, ranging from ultra-powerful to almost null, that it felt like they were grasping at straws. Petra came in while Iris was trying to organize the list into categories, and Iris put her to work too. Dora made it into the depot about mid-morning. By the look on her face, Iris knew she did not have good news.

Iris poured Dora a cup of tea. "What did Mrs. Stewart say when she read the letter?"

Dora took the steaming cup. "Nothing. She said nothing. I tried to talk to her about it, but she just kept reading and rereading the letter. I fed Nina and came here. I think we need to bring them somewhere until Mrs. Stewart can care for herself and her daughter again. The problem is getting them somewhere, anywhere, in this snow."

Petra tapped her fingers idly on the book open in front of her. "You could stay with her until the snow lets up, and then we can help them move somewhere in town until Mrs. Stewart gets her feet underneath her."

"I could do that," Dora agreed.

Iris nodded. "That solves some of our problems. How did town seem to you today?"

Dora shrugged. "The same."

"I got a couple side-eyed looks," Marina said as she flipped a page in the book she held.

"You get those anyway," Dora said.

Marina chuckled. "True."

Iris looked out the window. "It may take weeks or months to know the full outcome of yesterday's revelations."

"Don't worry. Turning Creek will weather this. If we can handle a reincarnation of Zeus and a family of monsters, we can wrangle a few disgruntled mortals," Dora said.

"For once, I'm the one lacking patience. You're right, of course. Now we need to figure out the snow." She handed Dora a set of parchments. "Some of these are in a Norwegian dialect. Can you read them?"

Dora took them and got to work.

Marina looked at the list again. "Isn't George Eisler a Theo Meteoroi?"

"I considered him; it just seems so unlikely. Mark him on the list anyway," Iris said.

It was quiet as they read and another hour ticked by. The door opened and Iris rubbed her tired eyes to see who was bringing in all the cold air. Reed slammed the door behind him and shook snow from his jacket, careful not to spill the steaming cup he held.

Marina stood and curtsied to Iris. "I win. No more research for me."

"It's been longer than two hours." Iris pointed out.

Reed handed her the cup. "Here's the coffee you wanted. Did you win something good?"

Marina planted a loud kiss on his lips. "Gods, yes. No more research for me. You arrived just in time. I was about to turn to stone with boredom, and my cup's been empty for an hour."

Iris sputtered. "You told him to come? That's cheating."

Marina laughed. "I never said I didn't ask him to come. I just said he would."

"Because you asked." Iris put her hands on her hips and gave Marina a stern look. It was ruined by her smile. The dupe had been clever.

"I still win." Marina took a sip of the coffee. "Perfect."

Iris threw up her hands in mock anger. "Cheater. I'm leaving."

There was a plate of molasses and butter biscuits on the counter. Iris piled them into a cloth and tied it with a knot. It would be nice to get outside, even if the snow was terrible. She needed to air out her head. The list was starting to make her eyes cross. If she stayed on the boardwalk, she could make it to Henry's with no problem.

Iris went upstairs to get her coat. She stopped in front of the mirror and smoothed down her hair. She knew the wind would have its way with it as soon as she stepped out of the door, but she wanted to make an effort.

Marina watched her come down and noted her coat. "Iris, I was just teasing. Don't leave."

Iris patted Marina's arm. "I know, my bird. I need some air. I'm going to walk down to Henry's and pick his brain. He might see something we've missed. You three stay here and keep working."

The three harpies all stared at her with the same knowing expression. Marina snickered. "What?" Iris asked.

"So you've chosen Henry over your admirer and Jacob?" Dora asked.

"Of course she has, Dora. Keep up." Marina laughed.

Iris frowned, but she was not mad. Going to see Henry gave her spirit a lightness that no amount of teasing could reduce.

Petra smiled at her. "He's a gentle but loyal soul. If you win his affection, it will be yours until the day he dies."

Reed followed the conversation with growing understanding. By the end he was grinning like a boy. "Best of luck to you, Iris. Though I don't think you'll need it."

Iris paused with her hand on the door. "I won't?"

"Trust me." Reed's grin spread even wider.

"Take our advice from yesterday," Marina called after her as she left.

Iris hoped Reed was right and tried not to think about the harpies' advice. The wind was strong and the snow whipped around like angry pieces of fire. It stung her cheeks and burned her lungs. She could only see a few feet in front of her through the white storm. It took more effort than she had thought possible to keep the buildings on her left and the wooden boardwalk under her feet. With the snow falling so quickly, the men had not bothered to shovel it from the walkway today, and Iris found herself trudging through drifts up to her knees in some places.

Walking between the depot and the sheriff's office should have been easier since Reed and Marina had come that way recently, but the snow had already wiped away their path. After the sheriff's office, the drifts were worse, almost up to her thighs, and Iris questioned the intelligence of going out at all. She crossed the street once she was past Reed's office. The snow in the middle of Main Street was worse than on the boardwalk. If she were being rational and intelligent, she would have stayed in the depot where it was warm. There was no real reason why she needed to go see Henry, except one.

She *wanted* to see him. Henry had been a fixture in her life for years, ever since she had settled in Turning Creek. He was always there, always dependable. His quiet steadiness had caused her to overlook him many times, she admitted to herself. It was easier to focus on the people who caused turmoil and disruptions in her day-to-day life. There had been a fair share of both the past couple of years. The harpies seemed to attract the kinds of problems that required the bulk of her energy.

That was unfair, Iris thought. It was not their fault. There was something about this town that attracted both the best and worst of people. For better or for worse, the concentration of Remnants here meant that when a problem arose it was often of mythical proportions, literally. There was not a doubt in Iris's mind that it was no accident the harpies were here, that she had followed them, and that Remnants were drawn here in turn.

The mortals of Turning Creek knew about them now. It could be a second renaissance for the Remnants, a time when they could again live openly and in peace as they had during the first Olympus…only without the tyranny of the gods raining down upon them. The future of Turning Creek should prove to be interesting indeed, and Iris wanted to be a part of that. She wanted to find out what that future would look like, and she wanted to do that with Henry by her side.

Iris had been looking at her feet and concentrating to keep them on a straight path. Her musings had brought her to the forge. Iris could barely make it out in the storm. The fire of the forge glowed, even in the cold and without Henry to tend it. She walked through the area where Henry so often worked, through the back door of his work area, and into the small, orderly yard behind the shop.

A cottage with snow-filled flower boxes at the windows sat in the middle of the yard. Cords of firewood were piled as high as the south wall of the house. Light from gas lamps shone from the windows, and Iris could see Henry bent over a book by the fireplace. The snow was undisturbed in the yard, and Iris had to wade and push her way to the front door. She knocked on the door with gloved hands and prayed Henry would hear the muted sound over the noise of the wind. She did not want to take off her gloves.

Henry opened the door and pulled her inside in one swift movement. He shut the door, blocking out the wind as a pile of snow and water fell at her feet.

"Iris, it's not exactly a lovely day for a stroll." Henry brushed the snow from her shoulders. Even annoyed, no one else said her name the way he did. She smiled.

The warmth of the room was beginning to make all the smaller bits of her body tingle with renewed blood flow. "I needed some fresh air."

Henry's deep laugh washed away her remaining chill. "It might've been easier to just stick your head out of a window for a minute."

Iris laughed and unwound her scarf from around her neck. "True, but I have two other purposes for my visit."

Henry took her scarf from her and put it on a peg by the door. "Let's get you by the fire and warmed up, then you can tell me whatever it is that drove you out into the snow."

Iris did not tell him that standing in this room alone with him was warming her up nicely. She removed her woolen hat and tried to smooth her hair. She vainly hoped she did not look too frightful. Henry motioned for her to sit in a chair by the fire, and he poured her a cup of tea.

Iris popped up from the chair almost as soon as she sat down. "I almost forgot my first reason for coming." She went over to where her coat hung and pulled the parcel of molasses and butter biscuits from the pocket. "I brought you these."

Henry took them from her and placed them on the hearth were they would get warm from the heat of the fire. "I know that was not the most important reason you came here. If you keep feeding me biscuits every day, I'll be too fat and lazy to work the bellows on the forge, let alone swing my hammer."

Only inappropriate remarks sprung unwarranted into her mind. Iris felt her cheeks flame up. She looked around the room and hoped Henry would think her red cheeks were the result of her walk.

She had never been inside his house before. The small space was orderly and cozy. The main room was a kitchen and living area combined. A small shelf of books sat against one wall with a writing desk. Another wall held a workbench, a smaller version of the one Henry had in the forge outside. Whatever his current project was, it was covered by a canvas cloth. There was a doorway without a door, which Iris assumed led to his bedroom. Iris put her focus firmly back onto her tea. Her face heated again at the thought of what was beyond that open doorway.

Henry moved a chair from the table and placed it near the fire and Iris. She felt the heat of his closeness as much as she felt the fire.

"You did a fine job with the townspeople yesterday," Henry said.

Iris raised her eyes then and met Henry's steady regard. Pleasure at his praise slipped through her. "I didn't do it alone. I couldn't have done it without the harpies or you beside me. It meant more than you'll know that you were willing to stand up with me from the beginning."

"I'll always be here when you need me. No matter what."

Iris reached out and put her hand over Henry's. She ran her thumb over his knuckles and watched his eyes as the grey melted into shards of blue and his breath stilled. She moved her thumb again and smiled with the simple power she had over him. The thrill was doubled because she knew he had the same power over her if he wanted to exert it.

Her voice was steady, despite the emotions coursing through her. "Thank you. I admit I have become quite used to having you around in a crisis, and even on the days when there's not one brewing. I hope the trend continues." Iris squeezed his hand. "Not the crises, though. Those I could do without."

Henry's mouth quirked into something Iris had never seen on his face. He smirked at her. "I would never want to disappoint you, so I suppose that means you'll have to endure my company as often as you can stand it."

Henry was flirting with her. Iris felt her face break into a loony smile, which Henry returned. They remained that way, hands entwined, for the span of a few breaths.

"You said there were two reasons you came. You brought biscuits. What was the other reason?" Henry did not let go of her hand. He leaned closer to her.

Iris thought Henry's curly dark hair shone like raven's wings in the firelight. "What?" She had missed what he asked. He was too close for her to pay attention to anything but his solid presence.

"The other reason for you being here, Iris. What is it?" Henry asked, smiling wider.

She leaned away from him and pulled her hand back, hoping the space would give her clarity. "There's something unnatural about the storm we've been having. The snow is filled with a wildness, a sadness."

"It's been too continuous without stop to be natural. I agree," Henry said.

"Good. The harpies and I've been compiling a list of possible causes of the storm and so far nothing sticks out. I was hoping you might see something we haven't noticed before." Iris pulled the list out of her pocket and handed it to Henry.

He scanned the list and looked up at her. "This is a fairly thorough list, though some of the things here seem far-fetched. Pandora's Box? We'd have more trouble on our hands than snow if that was the culprit."

"I know, but Marina thought of it and she was particularly proud of her deduction. I had to include it. Did you know that some versions of the old myth describe Pandora's Box as a jar?" Iris reached for her tea cup to give her hands something to do.

Henry tapped the paper. "I didn't know that."

"There's one other thing I wanted to tell you while I was here. The two oldest Stewart girls, Nancy and Natalie, and their father, Mr. Stewart, have died over the past few days. Dora has been keeping an eye on Mrs. Stewart. She's not been handling the news well."

Henry had straightened up while she talked, and he had ceased to look at the paper on his lap.

"What is it?" she asked.

Henry rubbed his beard. "Maybe nothing. Go ahead."

"I remembered last night that Nancy Stewart had left me a letter for her mother a couple years ago. She asked me not to deliver it until she was married or dead. She must have known something was going to happen and that her mother would need a word from her."

Henry stopped her from continuing by placing his hand on her arm. "Where's the letter now?"

"I gave it to Dora, who gave it to Mrs. Stewart this morning. We had hoped it would break her grief enough so that she would begin to care for her youngest daughter, but Dora said there's been no change. Why? What're you thinking?"

Henry's hand squeezed her arm. "You left a possibility off your list. Demeter."

Demeter was the goddess of corn and of the harvest. She had been one of the few goddesses with a sense of justice and a tender heart for the mortals because of her tie to the earth. When her daughter, Persephone, was captured by Hades and taken to the underworld, she had gone insane with grief. The world had been plunged into eternal winter until Hades had agreed to let Persephone visit her mother every spring. Thus, according to the old myths, the seasons were born.

Demeter would have been at the top of Iris's list except for one thing. "Demeter's Remnants died out only generations after the Fall of Olympus. No Remnants of the major gods lasted past a few generations."

Henry raised an eyebrow at her. "Didn't they? You and I are here, after all, as proof that's not the case."

"But Hephaestus was not like the other gods, always seeking and needing worship and approval. His line weathered the Fall because he was unlike the other gods, and the Messengers survived because their fate is tied to the harpies."

"I would argue that Demeter, with her understanding of mortals, also might have survived the Fall and been able to hide her status as a Remnant. Does anyone know from whom Mrs. Stewart is descended? Doesn't the pattern fit Demeter? Lost daughter. Inconsolable grief. A daughter who knows the heartache her absence would create. It fits better than anything else on your list, and there are many reasons the knowledge of a Remnant line could be lost or purposefully hidden."

Iris considered Henry's theory. If he were right, everything made sense. The gradual building of the snow and how it had gotten worse after Dora had brought the news of the Natalie's death. The way it snowed without ceasing for days on end in the worst blizzard Iris had ever seen. Mrs. Stewart's uncanny knowledge about the snow. The longer she thought about it, the more she realized that Henry was right.

Iris stood. She had to go get the others and then go find Dora. "You're right. How could I not even have considered it?" Iris stepped closer to him and her skirt brushed his knees. "You beautiful, blessed man. I knew you would have the answer."

She leaned down into him, as if she had done so a thousand other times, and kissed him on the lips. Her hand rose of its accord and cupped his bearded cheek against her palm. Time slowed around her and she felt him still and then tremble before she straightened up. Henry's blush hit his face the instant hers went numb from her lips out.

An apology started forming in her mind, but before she could utter it or move away, Henry's arm went around her waist and pulled her closer. His other hand went to her neck and brought her head back down to his. Iris felt herself smiling at the rightness of his hands on her, then her lips met Henry's again, and she forgot everything but the sweet fire of his touch.

Henry pulled her into the circle of his legs as he deepened the kiss, and Iris ran one hand through the silky black curls on his head that had been taunting her for days. She moved the rest of the way into the V of Henry's legs and sat on his lap. The hand on her waist dug into her hip with possessiveness. With his other hand, Henry loosened the binding of her hair until it fell in waves down her back. He lifted the curtain of it and kissed the side of her neck. It was a soft kiss, but a jolt of desire slammed into her and escaped with whatever air had still been in her lungs.

Henry lifted his head and his face was a breath from hers. He gathered the golden mass of her hair and settled it over one of her shoulders.

"I did not mean to do that." His voice rumbled with desire and Iris canted towards him, unable to resist the draw of him.

"I hope you don't regret it, though. I don't." Iris ran a palm down his cheek, feeling the roughness of his beard again.

Henry's hand, still on her waist jerked. "Good." He hesitated and Iris saw a trickle of uncertainty enter his eyes. "When you get back from seeing

Mrs. Stewart, I'd like to speak with you again, alone."

"How do you know I'm not going to just send the harpies and stay here?" She should get up from his lap, but she made no move to do so. Her fingers curled into his beard. She so wanted to stay. She wanted many things, very desperately now.

Henry leaned into her touch. "I know you. Will you speak with me when you get back?"

Iris cupped his face with both hands. "I will. On one condition."

"Name it."

Being in his arms made her feel bold. "Kiss me again when I get back."

The radiance of his smile would have burned her if she were not already in flames. "I believe that can be arranged."

Iris stood with great reluctance. Henry's hand did not move from her waist. She leaned down and touched her lips to his once more. It was brief, but there was a promise of more to come in his touch, and she knew Henry always kept his promises. Iris stepped outside of the circle of his body and moved towards the door.

"The snow's still bad. Come home safe." His voice followed her to the door.

"I will. I promise." Iris put on her coat and wound her scarf around her head while watching Henry. He returned her regard with a face full of unhidden desire. Her skin felt as though he still touched her. She wanted this errand to be over quickly so she could pick up this conversation exactly where they had left off, but without the talking bits.

Iris's feet led her back to the depot. The rest of her still thought of Henry. When she stepped through the depot door, Marina took one look at her face and held a hand out to Petra. The other harpy grumbled with a smile on her face and handed over some coins.

Petra plunked the last coin into Marina's outstretched hand. "Iris, you look like a woppy-jawed idiot, and you lost me a dollar. Now fess up. Who kissed who first?"

Iris turned her back to them to take off her coat. "I took your advice."

Petra howled. "I knew Henry would never make the first move. Give me some of that money back, you scoundrel."

Marina cackled. "Gladly. I'd pay more if it meant those two moved it along."

Iris turned around and put her hands on her hips. She tried to scowl, but a smile kept breaking over her face and ruining the effect. "He asked to talk to me after we go see Mrs. Stewart. I said I would if he promised to kiss me again." Iris laughed.

Marina rubbed her hands together. "That's our girl."

Reed, always the one to zero in on the particulars, asked, "Why do we need to go see Mrs. Stewart?"

Iris explained the possibility of Mrs. Stewart being a Remnant of Demeter. The harpies wasted no time and were ready to go before Iris had finished her explanation.

"I'll stay here and wait for you to return," Reed said.

Iris turned to Margaret. "You're welcome to stay here as long as you want. Take or use whatever you need. We shouldn't be gone long." Iris turned to Thomas. "Take care of things while I'm gone." Iris pulled the lanky teen into a hug.

"Be safe," he said in her ear.

"Are you sure you three don't need backup?" Reed asked. Worry laced his voice.

Marina flashed her pointed teeth at him. "Are you suggesting that three terrifying monsters and Iris can't handle one sad woman?"

Reed took a step closer to Marina. "I'm not suggesting. I'm asking. You tend to run into situations without looking. I'm just asking you to look ahead and come home in one piece that does not require Doc's intervention. Understand?"

Marina planted a kiss on Reed's lips. "Perfectly. See you in a few hours."

CHAPTER 18

They flew northwest towards the base of Silvercliff. Iris knew that was where they were going but in the white haze of snow, she was hard pressed to know which way was up. Marina and Petra flanked her and Dora flew point. They were dark blots in the whiteness of the storm, and though Iris had been flying for only a year, she felt safe surrounded by the harpies.

In the air, they were in their element. Their mortal forms were mere reflections of their true essence. In their harpy form, they radiated power, violence, and self-assurance. She was one of the few who knew what a facade the self-assurance was. Each of them struggled with their violent nature. Each of them had chosen a different path, and each struggled in her own way. They were the first harpies in generations, perhaps the first since the original four, to come to peace with their world and find good places in it. Iris was unendingly proud of how her harpies had chosen to live.

The wind howled around them, and Iris lost feeling in her nose and ears. Her head ached with the cold, and her eyes streamed tears from the wind. The harpies made flying look effortless, even in this weather. Iris felt the muscles in her shoulders start to burn. When they started their descent to the ground, Iris wanted to weep in relief, but she knew the tears would freeze on her face.

Iris could not make out the shape of a cabin until she was a few feet from the ground. They landed in the yard, and the three harpies changed back into their mortal forms. Iris kept her wings. She wanted to save her energy for the flight back. If they were correct about Mrs. Stewart and all went well, they would not have to fly back in snow, but they would have to fly back regardless.

Dora knocked loudly on the door. "Mrs. Stewart, it's Dora. I've brought some friends," she yelled over the storm. When no answer came, she said, "We're coming in."

Dora led the way through the door. The light was dim in the cabin. Only the fire was going in the hearth. Its low flame provided minimal warmth and the inside of the cabin was frigid. No candles or lamps had been lit, though Iris saw both. Deborah Stewart sat in a chair by the fire, staring at nothing. Her hair was unbound and tangled. In her hand she held the letter Dora had delivered earlier that day. A small girl, Nina, with brown hair and eyes the color of mountain columbines, sat near the fire and fed it small sticks from a pile by her feet.

Dora shook her head. "She was like this when I left this morning. It's been the same the last couple days. She occasionally moves, but not much."

Mrs. Stewart did not even acknowledge their arrival in any way. She just sat and stared into whatever secrets the ineffectual fire had to impart.

Marina went to the girl and sat down next to her on the rock hearth. "My name is Marina. Is it all right if I sit by you?" The girl nodded and put another twig in the fire. "The storm outside is awful, and I'm worn out from flying."

Nina looked at Iris, then craned her neck to look at Marina's back. "Where're your wings?"

Marina leaned towards the child. "Mine are too big to fit inside. I put them away to come see you. What's your name?"

Nina smiled at the harpy. "Nina. I don't have wings, but I can make flowers grow. Momma says when I'm older, she'll show me how to make it rain on the fields to bring crops and snow when the harvest is over."

They all shared a look. Henry had been right. Mrs. Stewart held dominion over the seasons like the goddess Demeter. Iris had not thought it possible. During the long flight, she had held out hope that it would be something easier, simpler. Mrs. Stewart had still not moved.

Iris went over to her and knelt in front of the woman. "Mrs. Stewart, I need to talk to you. Do you think you can come back to us enough to just talk?" There was no movement. Not even a blink.

Petra sighed, walked over to Mrs. Stewart, and slapped her on the face. The woman started and looked up, startled. Iris whipped around and glared at Petra.

The harpy shrugged. "What? If she won't snap out of it for her kid, she's not going to just because you asked real nice."

Marina chuckled. "You saved me the trouble of doing it."

Iris admitted Petra was right. She turned back to Mrs. Stewart. "Do you know who I am?"

Mrs. Stewart nodded. "The Messenger. Do you have another message from Nancy? I was not pleased with the contents of her last letter." Mrs. Stewart's eyes shifted and she seemed to see Marina for the first time, sitting by Nina as she kept the fire going.

A flash of fear, followed by rage, traveled over Mrs. Stewart's face. She flung her arm wide, shoving Iris off balance. Iris tumbled to floor, and Mrs. Stewart lunged past her, her hands in claws as she dove for Marina.

"Get away from her, Harpy. Are you here to take her to Tartarus with the rest of them? I won't let you have her! You can't have her. Take me. I wish to go. Keep your filthy hands off her."

Marina grabbed Mrs. Stewart's wrists and held them away from her face. The woman continued to writhe and shout.

Petra came up behind Mrs. Stewart and wrapped her arms around her, pinning her arms to her sides. "Hush now. We're not here to hurt you or your daughter."

Mrs. Stewart stopped struggling. Marina released the woman's wrists. Mrs. Stewart's lip trembled, and tears spilled over down her face. "My daughters are dead."

Anger flashed across Marina's face. She wrapped an arm around Nina's shoulder and drew the child close. "You have a daughter, right here, and she needs you to get a handle on yourself. Don't allow your grief to rob you of what you still possess."

Mrs. Stewart continued to sob. Iris stood and brushed off her pants. She laid a tentative hand on Mrs. Stewart's shoulder.

"Are you the Remnant of Demeter?" The woman looked up at Iris with eyes full of fear. After the Fall of Olympus, the gods and goddesses had fled, fearing to share Zeus's fate for the harshness of their rule. Demeter's line had probably survived because they had perfected the keeping of secrets.

Iris kept her voice low and soft. "We're not here to hurt you. We just want to know if you are the one making it snow. If you are, we need you to stop. This much snow is dangerous for everyone, especially the mortals who live here, and they are under our protection. Please, are you of Demeter's line?"

Mrs. Stewart stopped crying and squared her shoulders. "I am Deborah, Remnant of the goddess Demeter, the giver of spring and the harvest and the one who can bring the eternal winter."

"Pardon me for pointing out the obvious, but the first eternal winter thing didn't go over so well either." Petra relaxed her hold on the woman but stayed close.

Mrs. Stewart looked out the window. "How long has it been snowing?"

Iris let her hand remain on Mrs. Stewart, as though she could anchor her to sanity. "It's been days. I'm not sure when the natural storm stopped and yours began. Did you know it was happening?"

"No, but it is right. The snow is needed to mark the passing of my family," Mrs. Stewart said.

"Not all of your family is dead." Marina's voice had dropped an octave, and it was laced with anger.

Iris could see the impatience in the set of Marina's face and knew if she did not get this moved along, Marina would be less than gentle in her handling of the situation. She took the well-being of children very seriously. "Mrs. Stewart, I know you've lost much, more than I'll ever know, but please, we're begging you. Stop the snow and care for the daughter you have left."

Dora stepped into Mrs. Stewart's line of vision. A tremor ran through the woman, and Iris suspected she had not even known the third harpy was there. Dora held the other woman's gaze and spoke in a soothing tone. "Remnant of Demeter, your grief is harming those around you, and endangering your daughter with neglect. By our claim, this is our territory, and we've vowed to protect the people here. If you do not stop the snow, we will be forced to act to carry out this vow. We'd rather you choose to do the right thing instead and not deprive Nina of a mother."

"No." Mrs. Stewart's answer came without hesitation. "I will not stop the snow while I still live."

Iris heard Marina hiss behind her. Petra put a hand on Mrs. Stewart's shoulder. Dora reached out and wrapped the woman's wrist in a vice-like grip. "Then we will make sure your life is not long," Dora said.

"No." Mrs. Stewart said again. "I will decide my own fate. You say I need to stay alive for this child, but she is of my line. She has the seasons in her blood, and she will understand when she is older that I did what I had to do." She placed a hand over Dora's on her wrist. "You will not have to kill me, Harpy. I see the reluctance in your eyes to do so. I will be the orchestrator of my own demise. Allow me to walk out into the snow, alone, and I promise you the storm will be gone by morning."

The storm would be gone because Mrs. Stewart would be dead, frozen in a sea of white. "You don't have to do this," Iris pleaded.

"I do. I must follow my eldest into the underworld, as the first of my line followed hers. It is the way."

"You don't have to blindly follow the old ways," Marina said. "You can choose a new path." The grey hair running through Marina's deep brown curls was proof that her words were true.

Mrs. Stewart removed Dora's hand and Petra's grip on her shoulder. "This is my choice. This is my path." She stepped around Dora and stopped in front of Marina. "You have a heart for children. I can see it in your anger and indignation for my actions. Will you watch over my daughter and teach her of her history?"

Marina nodded. "If you are bent on this path, then yes. I swear by the River Styx, I'll guard your daughter as if she were my own. I'll teach her the history of her line, but I will do more. I'll teach her the value of her line and make sure that if she is ever presented with this choice, she'll choose life and the lives of others over useless tradition." Marina had given the vow on the river of the underworld. It was a binding promise.

Mrs. Stewart nodded in agreement. "By the River Styx, I accept your vow."

Mrs. Stewart moved her gaze to Iris, and Iris felt the weight of the vows in the room. "Messenger, I know you will hold her to it."

Iris nodded. A sense of unreality trickled through her. A part of her wanted to rant, to try harder to make Mrs. Stewart change her mind. "I swear by the River Styx that I will also be bound by the Harpy's vow."

Satisfied, Mrs. Stewart knelt in front of her daughter. "Please know I love you, but I can't stay here with my grief. I pray to the gods you never know the loss of your own firstborn daughter. It's an unbearable weight. The snow will cleanse me of it and mark our family's passing. Don't forget me. The harpies and The Messenger will keep their vow and you'll grow to be strong. I pray you'll be stronger than I was able to be. Choose your path well, Remnant of Demeter." She embraced her daughter.

Nina did not say anything, but she kissed her mother's cheek. The child twined her small fingers with Marina's and held on tight as her mother rose from her kneeling position on the floor. Mrs. Stewart cupped her daughter's face then turned and walked out of the door, leaving behind the memory of her grief and her small, round-eyed daughter.

Mrs. Stewart did not shut the door and the snow surged around her. She was engulfed in a tornado of white as she walked. Iris stood and walked to the open door, watching with a sense of horror as Mrs. Stewart disappeared into the snow. Iris wrapped her arms around her middle to keep in the urge to run into the storm and drag the woman back. A keening sound rose from the wind outside and it rang in their ears. She turned and shut the door on the howl of the storm. The wind picked up and rattled the windows.

"I think we need to leave," Dora said.

"I'm not sure leaving is the best idea." As if to add emphasis to the point, a gust of wind ripped one of the shutters off one of the front windows. Another gust of wind came and the walls of the cabin shuddered. Iris felt the storm shift. The snow was no longer laced with sorrow alone. It was filled with anger and vengeance.

"I've a feeling Mrs. Stewart isn't going to leave much of this house standing in a few hours." Petra looked around. "Nina, where do you sleep?" The girl pointed to the loft as another gust of wind ravaged the house. "Good. I'll go pack up whatever I can find for the girl."

Iris suspected there were other things that should be saved. "I'll go see if Mrs. Stewart had any heirlooms or books she'd want Nina to have."

"There's a chest in her room there," Dora pointed.

Iris knelt in front of the girl. "Nina, go get the pillow your mother made you from Goose's feathers." Dora and Marina gave her a weird look. "It's a story we don't have time for at the moment," Iris said.

Iris found the chest and rummaged around in it. She found some old parchments, a journal, and a handkerchief with an odd pattern. Iris held the faded cloth up to the light and saw the pattern was some kind of map. She threw it, the books, and the parchments on the bed. Iris went through some shelves in the corner and found an oiled leather bag and a necklace. She shoved the things she had found into the bag and went back into the main room.

The wind had succeeded in removing some of the wooden shingles and the snow was now falling from a small hole in the roof.

Iris handed the bag to Marina. "You carry the bag. I'll carry Nina."

Marina hesitated. "Are you sure you're strong enough? We could rig some kind of sling and I could carry her in my talons. She weighs almost nothing."

Iris watched the snow fall into the room. "The girl will be cold."

"She'll be cold no matter what, but I'm a stronger flyer than you, and I can bear the weight better," Marina persisted.

In the end, Iris had to agree. She had seen the harpies carry a deer for miles without tiring. Even with the storm, Marina would be able to fly back to town with Nina. Iris was worried about getting herself back. Marina bundled up the girl while Dora and Petra fashioned a sling Nina could curl up in from the quilt taken from Mrs. Stewart's bed.

Petra tied one last knot in the red and gold quilt. "Do you think you three can make it to town on your own? I want to get home before James gets worried enough to do something stupid."

"Actually, I think I'm going to head up the mountain." Dora said. "My cabin is only a couple miles up."

A trickle of unease went through Iris. "I'm not sure we should split up."

Marina spoke up. "We'll be fine. We don't need them to get back to town."

Marina's self-assurance did not allay Iris's reluctance to split up, but she agreed to the plan. She hugged both Petra and Dora. "Be safe, birds. Come and see me when the snow has stopped. I'll want to know all is well with you." They both agreed, then left.

Iris helped Nina crawl into the sling. "Are you comfortable enough?"

"Yes. I've never been flying, but birds in the sky like it. This will be an adventure." Tears rolled down her cheeks and ruined her brave words.

Iris wrapped her arms around the small frame of the girl. "I'm so sorry, my dear. I promise that we'll take very good care of you. Marina here is extraordinarily stubborn, and she is not going to give you up. Not for anything."

Marina embraced both Nina and Iris. "That's right, sunshine. You're stuck with me. Flying is fun, and I promise once the weather is better, I'll take you flying again and show you the sights. Deal?"

Iris felt the girl nod against her chest. "Deal," came the muffled reply.

"All right then. I'm going to change into a big, scary bird, but I'll still be me. Understand?" Marina asked. Nina nodded. "Good girl."

The howl of the wind went up in volume. "We'd better get going," Iris said.

The flight back was worse than Iris imagined. The snow and cold burned her wings and exposed skin like sand. More than once she was pushed almost out of eyesight from Marina as they flew. Iris did see the harpy bank a few times, but her wing beats were always sure. The sight of Marina flying steadied Iris when fear threatened to overwhelm her.

Iris thought of all the people who steadied her: Marina, Petra, Dora, Thomas, and Henry. No matter what happened, if even one of them was left, she would choose to survive to be with them, to love them, and to stand with them whatever came their way. It was what you did when you loved someone.

In his quiet way, Henry had always stood with her, and he had always been in her heart. She just had not realized how much until recently. When she got back, she would not waste any more time.

It was impossible to know which direction they were going. The moon was not visible, and Iris had to fight to keep Marina within sight through the snow. As they continued, Iris realized how much her thoughts were becoming a liability. Marina kept flying without hesitation, so Iris tried to relax and trust they were headed in the right direction. After what seemed like hours, they began to descend. Turning Creek must be close, but Iris could only see white.

Marina turned her head to yell something to Iris, but Iris never heard it. A gust of wind went between them and pushed them apart. Iris tumbled through the air. Everything was white, and though she blinked and tried to wipe the snow from her face, the view and color did not change. Iris's muscles seized with fear as she began to fall, head over heels, buffeted like a dandelion fluff in the wind.

Her downward motion gave her an idea about which way was down. She had no idea how close the ground was and, with the way the snow was blowing, she would slam into it before she saw it. Iris pumped her wings and fought to right herself.

Iris tried calling for Marina. The wind stole her voice before it passed her lips. She quelled the panic growing within her and kept flying. Turning Creek had to be close. If she flew low enough, she should be able to find a building or landmark and find her way from there. Iris dropped a few feet in the air, but nothing looked different. Everything was an endless desert of white. Frustration fed her panic. The air burned her lungs, and a tight band of helplessness pinched her chest. At this rate, she would run herself to ground before she found her way home, or fall from exhaustion and freeze.

The next gust of wind rammed her from behind. Her wings were forced back into an unnatural angle. Pain lanced up from her shoulder blades and burned through her torso. By the time Iris saw the wall of the building, it was too late. She heard the crack of her own head over the screaming of the snow, and then, Iris heard nothing at all.

CHAPTER 19

Everything was dark and the sound of the storm was gone. Iris was warm, and her body felt heavy and bruised. She opened her eyes and a weak light streamed in through a window in a room she did not recognize. She lay on her stomach. Iris stretched and she felt her wings unfurl. A tremor of pain rippled over her back. Before she could think of a reason why she was in bed with her wings still out, the pounding in her head intervened over all other concerns. With one hand, she felt the tender area on the side of her swollen head.

If she was in pain, she was not dead, and everything hurt. With a steadying breath, she looked around. She blinked a few times until what she was seeing stopped swimming and jumping. A lamp burned on a wooden table next to the bed she lay in. Iris took another deep breath and stilled. She was surrounded by the smell of warm metal and wood smoke. Iris's head snapped around and surveyed the rest of the room. There was no one with her, and her head pounded in protest at the sudden movement. She laid her cheek back on the pillow and waited for the throbbing to pass.

Something silver on the table by the bed caught her eye. Iris propped herself up on her elbows, ignoring her head's protests over the change in elevation, to take a closer look. She reached a hand out from underneath the quilt and pulled a silver chain with a pendant into her palm. It was cold.

The silver chain was fine and strong, each link made with care. The pendant was a pair of wings stretched into a circle, a mirror of the seal Henry had made for her. Her heart pounded in her ears. Each feather on the wings were carved and etched with precision. Iris turned it so it caught the light of the lamp. They looked almost real. She flipped over the pendant and all the air in her body went out.

Written up the back of one wing was the word *charis*. On the other wing was the word *agapeo*. A letter sat on the table. Her name was scrawled in a familiar hand. Black spots danced in front of her eyes, and Iris laid her head back on the pillow. She closed her fingers over the necklace and told herself to breathe. She pulled her power into herself and hissed at the burning sensation on her back as her wings disappeared.

The anticipation within her flared until she tasted it on her tongue. Iris grabbed the letter. She closed her eyes and reached for the emotions of the words. Exhilaration. Hope. Love. The last slammed into her with a force that made her breath catch and her heart stutter. She opened her eyes to read the words behind the emotions. The letter was not sealed.

Dearest Iris,

After your last letter, I realized you thought these letters were from someone else, someone who did not deserve your loyalty or your regard. I apologize for not being honest with you sooner.

I have a confession to make, and it is encapsulated in one word. No matter what happens to me during the course of my life, I place my heart in your care. It has been yours since the day we met, and now I gift it to you completely. I cannot imagine another over whom I could ever speak this word.

Agapeo. I love the way you smile when you hand someone a letter addressed to them. I love the generous way you welcome each person as they come into your domain. I love the way you shepherd and challenge the harpies to be better than the paths they were given. I love your strength as you have endured the loneliness of your own calling. This strength and hope is why I never stood a chance of not loving you. My heart was always meant to be yours, and so you have it.

Regardless of your feelings in return, I do not regret my heart, so freely given.

Agapeo,

Your friend, Henry

Agapeo, sacrificial love. Iris traced a finger over the curves of the word and felt her heart crack. Agapeo. It was the most beautiful word written in the most perfect way possible. A dream she had never dared to dream for herself. This was a gift she had never thought to be offered.

She flipped over on the bed and tried to sit up. She needed to find Henry. The room swam in front of her eyes and she eased herself back down. She must have made a sound, because Henry rushed into the room.

He stopped short in the doorway and called over his shoulder, "She's awake." He looked disheveled. His curly hair was more unruly than normal, as though he had spent the last day running his hands through it.

Marina was inside the room in seconds. "Had enough beauty rest then, have you?" Worry pinched the corners of her eyes.

Henry sat down in a chair that Iris had not noticed by the bed. "We were worried about you." He made no move to touch her but his eyes did not leave hers.

Iris licked her lips. Marina took a cup from a dresser against the wall. She sat on the bed and slipped an arm around Iris's shoulders to help her drink the water.

The water restored some clarity to Iris. "How did I get here?"

Marina put the cup down. "When I got home, I realized you were no longer behind me. I left Nina with Reed –I think I might have a competitor for his affections, by the way – and went looking for you. Henry found me first. He heard something slam into his house in the storm. It was you. He'd already brought you in here when I ran into him. I went to get Doc, and he came back here to look after you. You weigh a ton with those wings, you know."

Henry's eyes left hers and flicked to the empty bedside table. He looked back at Iris with trepidation in his face. Iris gave him a small smile of encouragement.

Iris shifted her focus to Marina. "What did Doc say?"

"You'll live, but your head will ache something fierce for a few days. He said you were not to be moved until you can walk without passing out or dizziness." Marina ran a hand down Iris's arm. "You scared me. I'm the one who's supposed to get hurt, not you."

"I'll be fine." Iris grinned. "Marina, go home."

"What?"

"Go home."

Marina raised her eyebrows at Iris. "I can stay with you. Reed can care for one small child alone for a few more hours."

"I'm in no danger of dying, my bird. Come see me in the morning. I have some things I need to discuss with Henry." Iris winked at the harpy.

Marina snorted and looked at Henry. She slapped him on the shoulder as she left the room. "Good luck to you then. She's probably a terrible patient."

Iris waited until she heard the front door close before speaking. "I suppose it's no longer snowing."

Henry pulled the chair closer to the bed and put his hands on his knees. "It stopped early this morning." Henry hesitated, then moved one of his hands to cover hers. "You found the necklace."

"I did." Iris turned her hand in his and opened her fist, exposing the pendant with the words that had slain her heart. "And the letter."

"You know what it means." Henry twined his fingers with hers, covering the necklace between their palms.

"I do." Iris squeezed his hand.

"In the last letter you wrote, you said there was someone else," Henry said. Iris felt the hesitation and fear radiating from him, but she saw the hope burning in his eyes.

"There is someone else. Someone I saw every day, but took for granted until recently. Did you know, I never noticed until two weeks ago that your eyes are not truly grey? They are shot through with the most amazing shades of blue I've ever seen." Iris grinned at him. "I have a question."

Henry smiled. "Of course."

Iris pulled the letter from under the pillow. "This is not your handwriting. I've seen your handwriting, recently, and this is not it, yet here is your name."

"I knew if I wrote you a letter you'd know right away it was me. You've seen my correspondence. I didn't think I had a chance to win you. I needed time. I'm ambidextrous. I can write, though not as well, with my left hand. I hoped it would be enough to fool you."

"How come I did not hear from you after the boardinghouse collapsed? I thought Jacob had written the letters and stopped."

"I realized after your last letter you thought the letters were from him." Henry's face hardened. "I also knew I had wasted too much time." He blushed. "I wanted to finish the necklace before writing the last letter and you wrote that you wanted another letter if I still wished to be friends. I do not want to be your friend, Iris."

Henry covered both their hands with his. "Iris, agapeo. No matter what happens to me during the course of my life, I place my heart in your care. It has been yours since the day we met, and I gift it to you completely and without reservation. I love all that you are. My heart is yours. By the River Styx, I give agapeo to you and swear it as a life oath."

Iris felt her heart unfurl at his words. Pure joy ran in her blood and the pain of her head vanished under the power of that emotion. "I'm not sure what I did to make you turn your head my way, but I'm thankful you did. I never stood a chance against you once you employed words against my heart. I'll admit to you, if you'd kissed me sooner, I wouldn't have stood much of a chance that way either. It seems I was going to fall in love with you no matter what." Henry's smile broke over his face and continued to widen as she talked.

Iris cleared her throat and said, "I accept your vow on two conditions."

"Anything you want. All you have to do is ask."

The events of the past month raced through her mind. Iris smiled and squeezed his hands. "First, I wish to make the same vow to you, Henry. Agapeo. No matter what happens to me during the course of my life, I place my heart in your care. I gift it to you completely and without reservation. I love you more than life, more than grief, more than flying. By the River Styx, I give agapeo to you and swear it as a life oath."

Henry's hands trembled around hers. "And the second thing?"

"Kiss me."

THANK YOU

Thank you for reading the first book in the Turning Creek series.

Would you like to know when the next book is available? You can sign up for my newsletter at www.wanderingeyre.com. On my blog, you will find all kinds of fun information and general shenanigans. Follow me on Twitter @wanderingeyre, or like me on Facebook at https://www.facebook.com/MichelleBouleAuthor.

I appreciate all reviews. They help readers find books and mean the world to authors.

Turning Creek Reading Order
Lightning in the Dark
Storm in the Mountains
Letters in the Snow
Plagues of the Heart
Journey of the Lost

MYTHOLOGY CODEX

This is a list of mythology characters and mythological locations mentioned in the Turning Creek series and a brief description of each. The information in this codex is for the mythology as it relates to this fictional series. As an author, I have taken some liberty with the original myths.

***

Achilles - The original Achilles was fatally wounded by a shot to his heel because this was the source of his power, speed, and strength. Thomas, the Remnant of Achilles, has the gift of speed and delivers mail in Turning Creek.

Aegis - The aegis is the name for the four warriors who make up the Shield of Zeus which is the title for his bodyguards and henchmen. They are Ioke, Alke, Eris, and Phobos.

Alke - Alke is the personification of strength. He is part of the Shield of Zeus and his main weapon is a sword.

Aphrodite - The Greek goddess of love.

Asclepius - A Greek physician who was granted the power over life and death by the gods. Lee Williams is a Remnant of Asclepius and the doctor in Turning Creek.

Atlanta - Atlanta was a famous huntress who made an oath of virginity to the goddess Artemis, but was later tricked into marriage by Aphrodite. Atlanta, named for the first of her name, travels with her companion and partner, Cyrene, in a quest for the next adventure and hunt. (also known as Atalanta in the Greek myths)

Bellerophon - Bellerophon was one of the hundreds of bastard sons of Zeus who spent his life trying to attain acknowledgement and vindication from the gods.

Charon - Charon is the ferryman who took souls across the River Styx on their way to the god Hades in the underworld, sometimes also referred to as Tartarus.

Cerberus - A three headed dog, the son of Echidna and Typhon, who guarded the door to the underworld for Hades.

Chimera - A monster, sired by Echidna and Typhon, whose front and torso is that of a lion and whose bottom half is that of a snake.

Cyrene - Cyrene was a princess and huntress who once wrestled a lion with her bare hands. The current Remnant of Cyrene travels the world with Atlanta in search of the next greatest hunt.

Demeter - Goddess of the harvest and agriculture. She was one of the few gods who had close ties with humanity because of her purview.

Dionysus - Dionysus, god of the vine, stayed neutral during the battle and Fall of Olympus, making him unpopular with those on both sides. The Remnant of Dionysus, Daniel Vine, owns the saloon in Turning Creek.

Dryad - Similar to a nymph, a dryad is a spirit of the forest, the trees, or other natural phenomenon. This affinity to nature can give them the power to communicate with nature or similar abilities.

Echidna - The original Echidna was called the Mother of All Monsters in the time of the old myths because her children became the nightmares of the Greek era.

Eris - Eris is the personification of strife. He is part of the Shield of Zeus.

Hades - The god and ruler of the underworld.

Harpy - A harpy has the body of a bird of prey and the head of a woman, though their face is more angular in this natural form. They have the ability many Remnants have of taking the form of a mortal when needed. There were four harpies who stood against Zeus in the uprising; Aello, Celaeno, Ocypete, and Podarge. The Remnants of the three surviving harpies lived in isolation from each other, and most of the world, until the current generation.

Hephaestus - Blacksmith to gods, he had the ability to craft weapons of magic and power in his forge, lit by the fires of Olympus. The Remnants of Hephaestus carry some of this original power and are marked with a clubfoot. Henry Foster of Turning Creek is a Remnant of Hephaestus.

Hera - Hera was the wife and queen of Zeus. By the time of the uprising, she had became angry and bitter over Zeus's many affairs and bastard children. She turned a blind eye to the work of the harpies and fled before Olympus fell.

Ioke - Ioke is the personification of onslaught and pursuit. She is part of the Shield of Zeus and her main weapon is the crossbow.

Iris - The original Iris has golden wings, delivered the messages of the gods, and had the gift of prophecy. She shared parentage with the harpies and argued on their behalf often, softening their punishment when Zeus's anger turned against them. The Remnant of Iris, also called The Messenger, is marked with a birthmark of golden wings. The Messenger chronicles the history of the Remnants and the harpies in particular.

Ladon - The Ladon is the serpentine monster child of Typhon and Echidna. Also known as a dragon or a drakon.

Laelaps - A mythical hound, created by Zeus, who never failed to catch its prey

Lernean Hydra - The hydra is another serpentine-like child of Typhon and Echidna. It is a nine headed serpent who occupies bodies of water and spits acidic venom on its victims.

Medea - A powerful and vengeful witch who helped Jason of the Argonauts in many battles and later became his wife, bearing him six children.

Maenads - Maenads are women controlled by Dionysus who turn into raving, mad women. They have been known to tear apart men with their bare hands in their rage.

Manticore - This creature has the head of a woman, the body of a lion, and the tail of a scorpion. It was a meliai, a kind of nymph from the island of Melos.

Medusa - Medusa, in the old myths, was a creature with snakes for hair and eyes who could hypnotize a man. Lily Hughes, the Remnant of Medusa, has the power of persuasion if you look into her eyes.

Mount Olympus - The mountain that was the seat of Zeus and the center of his kingdom during the time of the old myths.

Nemean Lion - The Nemean Lion can only be killed by strangulation. It is one of the monster children of Typhon and Echidna.

Nymph - A nymph is a fairy-like creature with an affinity for nature.

Orthus - Orthus is a two-headed hound and the son of Typhon and Echidna.

Phobos - Phobos is the personification of fear. She is part of the Shield of Zeus.

Satyr - A creature with the lower body of a goat and the upper body of a man. They were creatures of Dionysus and known to harass and sometimes rape women during festivals.

Scylla - Scylla was a sea goddess with a woman's head and torso and the body of a serpent.

Sphinx - The Sphinx had the body of a lion and the head of a woman. It was the offspring of Typhon and Echidna and was known for asking riddles of men and then eating them when they answered incorrectly. The Remnant of the Sphinx is Pearl Nasso.

Styx, River - The River Styx is the body of water that separates the underworld from the living. To swear on the River Styx is to give a binding oath.

Tartarus - Another name for the underworld where souls go to be punished for their bad life choices.

Theoi Meteoroi - The gods and goddesses who controlled the sky and weather. Their abilities and powers varied greatly. They were under the control and power of Zeus and Hera.

Typhon - Typhon was monstrous being. He had one hundred dragon heads sprouting from his neck, a human torso, and a snake body. He is called the Father of Monsters because he sired the worst of the Greek monsters with his wife, Echidna.

Zeus - The Father of the Gods, Zeus was the tyrannical ruler of Olympus. While heralded as an innovator of culture, he ruled with violence and vengeance and held his kingdom together with blood and war. He was notorious for his hundreds of bastard children. Zeus was unseated in the Fall of Olympus which occurred during the uprising led by the harpies.

ABOUT THE AUTHOR

Michelle Boule has been, at various times, a librarian, a bookstore clerk, an administrative assistant, a wife, a mother, a writer, and a dreamer trying to change the world. She is married to a rocket scientist and has two small boys. She brews her own beer, will read almost anything in book form, loves to cook, bake, go camping, and believes Joss Whedon is a genius. She dislikes steamed zucchini, snow skiing, and running. Unless there are zombies. She would run if there were zombies.